Ruth Thomas was born in Wellington, Somerset, in 1927 and educated at various schools in the county. She received a B.A. Hons English and a Diploma in Education from Bristol University and taught at a number of primary schools in the East End of London. After taking time off to look after her young son, she returned to teaching in the London Borough of Brent – the source and inspiration for all her writing.

Ruth began writing soon after she retired in 1985. Her first novel, *The Runaways,* won the Guardian Children's Fiction Award, and has been translated into several languages. This was followed by four further critically acclaimed novels, including *The Secret,* which was dramatised by Thames Television. A documentary about her life and work, 'Ruth Thomas Writes' appeared on Channel 4. Ruth received a further accolade when Henwick School in south-east London named one of its Year Six classes after her. She now lives in Kensal Green, in north London.

Also available in Red Fox by Ruth Thomas

The Runaways
The Class That Went Wild
The New Boy
The Secret
Guilty!

HIDEAWAY

Ruth Thomas

RED FOX

My thanks go to my niece Rachel for medical information, and to my nephew Peter for information on police activities in the Dartmoor area.

A Red Fox Book

Published by Random House Children's Books
20 Vauxhall Bridge Road, London SW1V 2SA

A division of Random House UK Ltd
London Melbourne Sydney Auckland
Johannesburg and agencies throughout the world

3 5 7 9 10 8 6 4 2

First published by Hutchinson Children's Books 1994

Red Fox Edition 1995

Printed and bound in Great Britain by
Cox & Wyman Ltd, Reading, Berks

Random House UK Limited Reg. No. 954009

ISBN 0 09 938551 1

To my son Justin, with gratitude for his indispensable help

1

Asking for trouble

Leah knew she was doing wrong. She was doing something *very* wrong, not for the first time; and she couldn't get rid of the guilt, however hard she tried. The guilt was like something alive, like a little mouse with sharp teeth, gnawing away inside Leah's chest – reminding her every moment that she was supposed to be at home looking after Darren and Joel, not larking about the streets with Jack and Charlie.

And today there was something extra to feel guilty about. Today the three of them weren't just larking, they were planning to steal! Only chocolate bars from the shops, but that was still wrong, and Leah would never have done it by herself, she wouldn't have thought of such a thing. Charlie wouldn't have thought of it by himself either. It was Jack who had put them up to it – Jack, who had this way of looking at you with eager eyes, and smiling, and sweeping you along with him by the sheer power of his will.

'Let's make it into a competition,' said Jack. 'Let's take it in turns, eh? See who can score the highest!' His smile was innocent, disarming; he might have been suggesting a game of hopscotch.

'Me first, OK? OK, Jack? OK?' Charlie was ten, and small for his age, and Leah didn't like him very much. He was pushy, and cocky, always showing off how brave he was, to impress Jack.

'All right, Leah?' said Jack.

Leah stood mute outside the corner shop, her dark skin prickling uncomfortably.

'I think she's chicken,' said Charlie, delighted with his own superior performance.

'Shut up, you!' Leah's voice sounded oddly high in her own ears, squeaky and forced. I don't want to do it really, she thought, but I can't seem to make myself say so.

'I'll give you an easy job to start,' said Jack, kindly. 'You stay outside and watch for police. . . . All right, Leah?'

Leah nodded, her head with its bunches of black hair bobbing up and down. She would do this one, and then she would go home. Just this one.

Inside the shop, Jack asked the man behind the counter for cigarettes. He didn't want cigarettes, of course, he just wanted to hold Mr Malik's attention. Mr Malik politely explained that Jack couldn't be sold cigarettes because he was too young. Jack said he was seventeen really, he only *looked* eleven. Mr Malik said he was sure Jack didn't seriously expect him to believe that! Jack said the cigarettes were for his father, actually. Mr Malik said it didn't matter if they were for the Prime Minister. Jack said he hoped the robbers would come soon, to burn Mr Malik's shop down. Mr Malik said this conversation was getting nowhere, and would Jack like to go and bother someone else, now.

Jack smiled forgivingly at Mr Malik. He could see, out of the corner of his eye, that Charlie had finished helping himself. 'Four!' said Charlie proudly, outside. He sneezed over the chocolate bars, as he shared them round.

Leah rubbed Charlie's sneeze off the wrapper of

her chocolate bar before she opened it. Charlie sneezed again. 'Do you mind? That went right in my face! Haven't you got a tissue?' Leah spoke with difficulty, because her mouth was dry, and the chocolate she had crammed into it was sticking all round the sides.

Charlie felt hopefully in his pockets, and shook his head. 'There's some in my school bag.' He sneezed for a third time. 'But my school bag's in my house.'

'Well, look the other way, can't you? Me and Jack don't want all your germs! We don't, do we, Jack?'

Jack was indifferent to Charlie's germs. His grey-green eyes travelled, restlessly, up and down the sunny London street. 'Let's get on with it now, eh?'

This was where Leah meant to say, 'Excuse me, but I have to go home now.' What she actually said was, 'Whose turn is it?'

Jack smiled at her. 'Don't worry, it's not your turn, it's mine. I'm doing the Greek shop, and I'm doing it all by myself.'

'Don't you want me to chat them up for you?' said Charlie, disappointed.

'I said I'll do it by myself. More fun.'

While he's inside, Leah thought. I'll go while Jack's inside, so he can't smile at me, and make me stay. But she dithered on the pavement, and then it was too late because Jack was coming out already.

'Easy peasy,' he said, scornfully. 'Easy *peasy*.' The light brown hair, which needed cutting, flopped over his face. Jack flicked it back, impatiently.

'How many did you get, then?'

'Six. I could get another six if I wanted to. . . . I could get twenty if I wanted to. . . . I could get a *hundred* if I wanted to.' He seemed annoyed, almost disappointed.

'Can I have my turn in there, then?' said Leah. 'If it was so easy.'

'It's not worth it,' said Jack. 'It's no fun.'

'I don't mind if it's no fun,' said Leah.

'You're just chicken!' Charlie jeered.

'Shut up, you!'

'. . . I got it!' said Jack. 'I know what, let's do old Mother Burton's!'

Leah's heart began to pound. 'You said *not* that one.'

'I changed my mind.'

'You said it's risky, though.'

'Good. More fun.'

He's going to make me, Leah thought. He's going to make me do my turn in horrible old Miss Burton's. The one who sees everything you do without even looking. I'm going to get caught, I'm going to get caught!

Her face showed her fear. 'It's all right,' said Jack. 'Trust me!'

She must run home now, Leah thought. She needn't say anything; she could just run off, and go in her house, and shut the door. She could leave these stupid boys to their stupid wrong games, and not come out with them again, ever. However powerfully Jack enticed! However fed up she was with minding her little brothers – day after day, hour after hour; minding her little brothers for Mum, till Mum came home from work. . . .

'Trust me,' said Jack, again.

Leah opened her mouth to say 'No, I'm going home now,' and found herself saying 'All right, then,' instead. She felt the way a fly must feel, caught in a spider's web. She didn't want to do this thing, but she *was* doing it. She was doing it *now.* She was actually walking into Miss Burton's shop with the intention of taking chocolate bars and not paying for them!

'Packet of twenty,' she heard Jack say.

'Twenty what?' The voice suspicious, unwelcoming. Miss Burton detested children on principle; she would rather no customers at all, than children. 'Come on, twenty what? I can't read your mind, and I haven't got all day.'

Leah stood by the confectionery stand and trembled. She put out her hand, and jerked it back again empty. 'Fags of course,' said Jack. 'I want a packet of twenty.'

'Don't be ridiculous!'

'Pardon?'

'Get out!'

'Who, *me?*'

'You heard!'

'Yes, I did *hear.* I heard, but I thought I made a mistake. I thought a nice lady like you couldn't have said any such a rude thing.'

'Don't give me that lip!'

Leah put out her hand again. 'Mind your head out the way!' said Miss Burton sharply to Jack.

'Do you know something?' said Jack, with a pleasant smile. 'I think you should just take your ugly old donkey face and stuff it in the dustbin.'

Leah grabbed two Milky Ways, and made for the door. She heard Miss Burton's shout: 'Put them sweets back, you thieving little cow!'

'Somebody nicking *sweets?*' said Jack, shocked.

'Police!' hissed Charlie, from the doorway.

'THIEVES!' screamed Miss Burton. She was furious at the trick, beside herself with rage.

Charlie was already scuttling down the road, away from the patrolling policeman. Terrified, Leah blundered after him, the Milky Ways still in her hand. Jack, trying to get out of the shop, collided with a young mum and a pushchair, just coming in. 'Do you mind?' said the young mum, indignantly.

'Got a bus to catch,' said Jack, enjoying himself.

'You wanna get after this one!' the young mum's friend called to the policeman.

Jack streaked away, on long graceful legs. The policeman began to give chase. Jack passed the others, and led them around a corner. By the time the policeman reached the turning, the children had disappeared from sight.

2

Trouble indeed!

They had disappeared, in fact, into an abandoned car at the roadside. The car had a smashed bonnet, and various bits missing, but there was room on the floor for Jack and Leah and Charlie. 'Good, innit!' said Jack. 'Good fun, this!'

Charlie's breath was coming in noisy gasps. 'I'm scared,' said Leah. The car smelled of hot leather, and dust.

'Trust me!' said Jack.

'That's what you said before, and then we got caught.'

'No, we didn't, we escaped.'

'We got chased, then.'

'Did I say we wouldn't get chased? Did I say that?'

'. . . No.'

'I said we would have fun, and we did. We had fun being chased.'

'. . . Did we?'

'And now we're having fun hiding here. Didn't I find us a good place, then?'

Leah lay in Jack's good place, and worried. It was a clever idea, but what if the police thought of it too? If the police should look inside the car, they would all three be done for, trapped. 'Suppose the police look in the windows?' said Leah.

'They won't.'

'How do you know?'

‘Trust me!’

‘Anyway, I don’t like it here,’ said Leah. ‘This floor is very dirty. And too much germs.’

‘All right, we been here long enough most likely. I’ll just have a peep and see if that copper is coming.’

‘No, don’t, don’t! Don’t show your head, he might see you!’

‘. . . It’s all right, he’s gone.’

‘Are you sure?’

‘I said so, didn’t I? He’s gone, he’s give up.’

‘He might be tricking us, though,’ said Leah, fearfully. ‘I changed my mind; I rather stay here. And Charlie is still out of breath.’

‘I’m *not!*’ said Charlie.

‘Follow me,’ said Jack.

They all ran. Jack sprinted ahead, and the others followed blindly, through street after street. Look at this mess I got in now, Leah thought. We’re going further and further from our road. And I want to go home, I want to go home!

Charlie stopped and bent over, clutching his middle, his breath coming in noisy gasps again. ‘Jack!’ Leah shouted, but Jack was round the next corner, and didn’t hear her. Leah stumbled on, alone now, with Charlie at a halt behind her, and Jack out of sight. She felt terrible – and more so when she discovered she was still clutching the incriminating Milky Ways, squashed into a sticky mess from the heat of her hand. Leah threw the Milky Ways over the nearest hedge, and thought she would never fancy chocolate again, ever. The very idea of it would make her remember this day, and want to be sick.

Her legs were numb. She sat on someone’s wall,

and thought about how to get home. Not back the way they had come, not that way for certain! Not back where the policeman was, and Miss Burton standing in her doorway, probably, watching out for the girl who stole two chocolate bars out of her shop.

A long way back, Leah could see Charlie, forlornly hesitant on the pavement. Where was Jack, where *was* he? It looked like he just went off and left them. Never mind about her and Charlie, oh no! Jack used their company when it suited him – that was to say, Leah suspected, when no one else was available. He could even be kind, when it suited him to be. But he didn't care about anyone else but himself really, did he?

Slowly, Leah began to walk back towards Charlie.

There was a scowl on his small, sharp face, his straw-coloured curls limp, and soaked with sweat.

'Let's go home,' said Leah.

'I don't usually get out of breath like this, you know.'

'Don't you? Anyway, let's go home.'

'I'm a very good runner, actually.'

'Let's go home, though.'

Charlie pulled a face. 'I rather find Jack, and have some more fun!'

'All right, you do that. I don't want no more of this kind of fun. I don't want to get caught by the police, and I don't want my mum to find out I been doing wrong things.'

'I don't know why Jack bothered to ask you in the first place!' said Charlie. 'You're just chicken!'

'All right, I'm chicken. I don't care if you say I'm chicken, I *am*. I don't want to get had up in court, I don't want no beating off of my mum, and I certainly don't want one off my dad! And besides, it's wrong what we done, and I don't like that neither. I don't see the fun in it.'

'Chicken!' Charlie was always jeering at people for being less brave than himself; he seemed to take a special pleasure in it.

'All right, then, what about you? Would you want your mum to find out what *you* done, Charlie?'

Charlie was silent. He wouldn't, but not because of any punishment he would get. Charlie's mum was gentle, she never hit him ever. But she would be shocked and grieved, and Charlie wouldn't like that. It would make him feel quite a bit uncomfortable, actually, to see his mum being shocked and grieved.

Charlie's mum lived for Charlie, he knew that because she was always telling him so. He was all she had, she said, and everything she did was for him. Charlie's mum lived for Charlie, and he wished she didn't, because it made him feel uncomfortable to think about. It was too much, it was too much to live up to. She never seemed to want anything for herself, it all had to be for him!

Just recently, Charlie's mum had gone back to work full time, so she could use her qualifications to earn more money for making a good home and getting more things for Charlie. He was old enough now, his mum said, to be trusted by himself until she came home in the evenings. He was a good boy, she said, she knew he could be trusted, and there was a telephone number he was to be sure to ring *immediately* if he didn't feel well. She could trust him to be sensible about that, she said, because he was such a good boy. Charlie tried not to think about how much his mum trusted him. 'I'm going to look for Jack,' he muttered.

'See you later, then,' said Leah.

Charlie struggled with himself. '. . . Wait a minute, OK?'

'Well hurry and make up your mind, because I think it can take half a hour to go all the way round to our road.'

Leah's feet went clump, clump, clump along the pavements. Her body felt heavy, her spirits still weighted with anxiety. Suppose she met that policeman on the way? Suppose that policeman had told other policemen, and they were all looking out for a black girl, a little bit fat, in a school dress. . . . And Darren and Joel, all by themselves in the house – she nearly forgot about them! Oh, she must hurry, she must hurry!

'Look!' said Charlie suddenly, behind her. 'There's Jack, down that street!'

'I'm not interested.'

But Jack was already prancing towards them. 'See what I found!' His eyes gleamed.

'I'm not interested,' Leah declared.

'*I'm* interested,' said Charlie. 'Show *me*!'

'Come on, Leah,' said Jack. 'You want to miss something good?'

His smile was radiant, captivating. '. . . What is it, then?' said Leah, weakly.

'Come and *see*. See if we can get inside.'

The attraction was a high-topped motor caravan, parked at the side of the road, and disappointingly locked so that Jack could not break into it.

'Is that all?' said Leah. 'I seen plenty of those before. Better ones than this. This one looks all knocked about and old.'

'It's good, though,' said Jack. 'I wish it was mine.' He stretched up to the window. 'Look – it's like a little house. With seats and a table and a upstairs and everything! Lucky we come this way, eh? To find such a good thing!'

Charlie climbed on to the bonnet, and peered through a long narrow window over the cab. 'There's a bed! Cor – fancy sleeping up here!'

Leah peered through one of the side windows. 'It's very messy,' she said, disapprovingly. 'There's clothes and things all over the place. They ought to keep it more tidier.'

'It's called *Hideaway*,' said Jack, reading the name along the side. 'I don't like that name very much. If I had one like this I should call it *Jack's Shack*.'

Across the pavement from the van were two front doors, one blue and one yellow, side by side and almost touching. An elderly man appeared out of the blue one. 'Kids again!' he tut-tutted. 'Hey you! Get down off that bonnet! Now! Do you hear me?'

'Is it your van, then?' said Charlie, not moving.

'No, it's not mine. It's George and Lil's. And George'll have your heart and liver for mucking it about, if he's in a bad mood.'

'Georgie, porgie, pudden' pie,' chanted Charlie. 'Kissed the girls and made them cry!'

He leapt to the ground smartly enough, though, when the yellow door also opened, and a burly figure with an angry red face appeared on the step. '*Scram*!' roared George.

Charlie and Leah began to run. 'Don't go!' Jack grabbed at Leah, and held her. 'He ain't going to do nothing to you!'

Charlie sidled back. 'I think your van is *great*,' Jack told George warmly. 'I'm going to have one like this, when I get some money. It's going to be called *Jack's Shack*.'

'*Is* it?' said George, glaring and baring his teeth at Jack. A wide gap between the two front incisors made the snarl quite menacing, but the only other noteworthy thing about George's appearance, not counting his red face and his bald head, was the size of his stomach. Huge and pendulous, the stomach distended the front of the badly ironed fawn sports shirt, and bulged over the waistband of the badly ironed fawn trousers.

Leah regarded George with wary eyes. I don't like him, she thought. It feels like there's something bad about him; I don't like him at all.

The man from next door seemed to like George all right. It didn't seem as though the man next door could see anything wrong with George. 'All ready to go, then?' said the man next door with a big bright smile. 'All ready for the off?'

George scowled. 'Soon as I can get her ladyship out!' He turned his bulk around, and bawled through the open doorway: '*Lil!* For God's sake get a move on!'

'All right, keep your scalp on!' A shrill voice sounded from somewhere inside the small house, and Lil emerged, grinning.

She was a tiny creature, as colourful as a tropical bird. Although quite old, she was youthfully arrayed in badly ironed loose flowered shorts, and a belted shirt of a different flowered pattern. Her hair was trendy too – short and spiky, and a wholly improbable red. There was a pillow under one skinny arm, and a saucepan under the other. 'Mustn't forget these.'

'Give me strength, you've had *all day!*'

Lil grinned again, showing worn teeth with lipstick all over them. Her lipstick, in fact, looked as though it had been put on in the dark – likewise her pencilled eyebrows, one up and one down, neither managing to follow the natural line. 'You seeing us off then, Arthur?' she said to the man next door.

'I suppose you're going on holiday,' said Jack to Lil. 'I wish I was coming. But I'm going to have a van like this one day, you know. It's going to be called Jack's Shack. Can I go inside yours? Just for a minute?'

'*Jack!*' said Leah, shocked. 'You're not supposed to!'

'No,' said George.

'Yes you can,' said Lil, her eyes gleaming. 'Go on, have a decko!'

'Are you mental?' George rounded on her.

Lil winked at Jack. 'Take no notice of my hubby. I think he got out of bed the wrong side this morning.'

'I don't like being held up,' George sulked.

'What's the big hurry?' said Lil. 'Our time's our own, isn't it?'

'You on the dole, then?' said Jack.

Arthur chuckled. 'They call it Early Retirement. *I* call it money for jam. They have a great time, these two . . . off on their holidays every few weeks. Go all over the country, they do. All right for some!'

'Come on,' Jack wheedled. 'Let me go inside for a minute!'

'*Jack!*' said Leah, urgently. 'You're not supposed to! You're not supposed to go inside strange people's cars! It can be worse than—' She had been going to say, 'It can be worse than getting caught by the police,' but she stopped herself just in time, and said, 'Bad things can happen if you go in strange people's cars,' instead.

'Oh, you don't have to worry about that,' said Arthur, reassuringly. 'Everybody in this street knows George and Lil. Aunty Lil to the kids all the time, and Uncle George when he's feeling like it. That's right, innit, George?'

It certainly seemed true that everyone knew the couple. Several people had passed, on this side of the road or the other, and all had a wave or a greeting for George and Lil.

'*Please* let me go inside,' said Jack.

'Are you deaf?' said George. 'Or just stupid?' He took something out of his pocket and pointed it at the front of the van. The van gave three bleeps, and the head and tail lights flashed.

'What's that?' asked Jack.

'Burglar alarm,' said George, grimly. 'Remote control.'

'What you got in that van, then, George?' Arthur joked. 'The Crown Jewels?'

Lil shrieked with laughter. 'That's a good one!' She shrieked again, and slapped the saucepan against her thigh.

George glared at her over his shoulder as he walked to the van. 'You can't be too careful these days, you know you can't!' He opened the cab door, and rounded on Jack, who was hopefully dogging his heels. 'What you want? I told you to get lost!'

'He's interested in the van and he wants to see inside,' said Lil. 'What's wrong with that?'

'He can't see it today.'

'What's wrong with today?'

'Nothing's wrong with today. We're just getting ready to hit the road, that's all.'

Lil climbed into the van, carrying the saucepan and the pillow. She turned to Jack, and winked. 'Come and have a peep, then, just for a minute.'

'One word from me, and she does as she likes,' said George, furiously. 'I don't know why we don't issue tickets, and make a charge.'

'Can my friends come too?' said Jack, with shining eyes.

'Why not, why not? And your brothers and sisters and cousins umpteen times removed while you're about it. Wheel 'em all in!' George snarled.

'Oh, don't pretend,' said Lil. 'It's your pride and joy, you know it is! You love showing it off. *You know you do.*'

I don't want to get in George's van though, Leah thought . . . doing it nevertheless. I don't care how many people know him, he makes me have a funny feeling. He makes me feel all prickly, like I don't want to be near him.

Inside the van, everyone was squashed against everyone else, while George stood in the doorway, huge and barring everybody's exit. 'Women!' he declared bitterly, calling over his shoulder to Arthur.

'Speaking of which,' said Arthur, 'I can hear *my* old trouble and strife calling. Have a good time if I don't see you again!' He chuckled, and disappeared into his house, and the door banged shut.

'Here it is, then,' said Lil, grinning proudly. 'Bit

untidy, but that's us.' She put the saucepan down on a sort of kitchen worktop, and threw the pillow on to the high-up bed.

'That's *her,* she means,' said George, sourly. 'Come on, you lot, let's have the conducted tour and get it over. It's one thing after another today. One blooming thing after another, holding us up.'

'All right, all right,' said Lil. 'Tell you what, *you* show the kids the works, and I'll just pop back and lock up, so we can go straight on after. . . . That please you? That make you happy?'

'You *are* mental!' said George.

'What's wrong now?'

'Nothing,' said George in a strangled sort of voice. 'Nothing at all. Just don't be too long, because I'm timing you. Two minutes, I mean it!'

Leah's uneasiness grew. There was definitely something that didn't feel right. She would be glad to get out of this van. She was glad she was only going to be here for two minutes.

George sat in the driver's seat to let Lil pass, then moved towards the back of the van and barked at the children: 'Right, sit! Sit down, all of you!'

He seemed to mean that they should sit on the sideways seats on either side of the table. It was not easy to push in. The table had to be swivelled on its centre pole to make room for Charlie and Leah on one side, then swivelled the other way so Jack could squeeze into the opposite seat. They sat, rather uncomfortably on top of odds and ends of clothing, securely wedged in place by the table.

'Are you looking, then?' said George. 'Are you all watching? You'd better be, because I shan't say anything twice! Beds, then. One up there, one down. Table comes off, and we fit it across. Too complicated to show you. Cooker? Under this lid, look.' To show them, he had to lift off the saucepan. 'Works on gas. Like this, see?'

He closed the lid, replaced the saucepan, and the bad-tempered monologue continued. The van was supposed to be George's pride and joy, but you would never have guessed that from the way he spoke. If anything, he seemed rather to dislike it.

'Sink? Under *this* lid. Fridge, you see, works on gas too, only not when we're moving. Cupboards? Plenty of them.' George waved his arms vaguely about. 'That's it, then. Right. Satisfied?'

'Are there lockers for keeping things, under these seats?' said Jack.

'Yes.'

'But I can't look inside, because there isn't enough room to move. . . . I'd like to climb on that high bed, though.'

'So would I,' said Charlie, who was longing to try it out.

'Well, you can't,' snapped George. 'Neither of you.'

'What's in there?' said Jack.

'Toilet.'

'Really? A real toilet? Can I look?'

'You can't see from there, the door opens the wrong way.'

'If you would open the door, I could see inside from here.'

'No you *couldn't*,' said George. 'The door opens the wrong way.' He swung the toilet door open and shut to demonstrate. The action took only a second, but in that second Jack moved. He twisted his slender body, whipping his long legs on to the seat, and climbed over the cooker top. Before

George could turn his bulk around, Jack had scrambled on to the high-up bed, knocking the saucepan on to the floor in the process – and was lying full length on his front, smiling his angel smile at the others. 'Get down!' George told him, furiously.

'All right.'

Jack dropped to the floor, landing on springy ankles like a cat. 'Now sit down again!' said George.

'I can't get past you,' said Jack.

'Sit in the front,' said George.

'All right.' Jack sat in the driver's seat and played with the steering wheel. 'How do you start the engine?'

'Sit in the *other* seat!' said George, grimly, yanking Jack out, and placing his own bottom firmly in the driver's place.

'All right,' said Jack. 'Oh, just a minute! I can look in the toilet now, can't I?'

He was too quick for George. In a moment, he had the door of the toilet compartment open, and was praising its contents with enthusiasm. 'It's brilliant! There's a shower as well.'

'That's right, there's a shower!' George had risen from the driver's seat, and was holding Jack by one arm.

'What's in that cupboard thing, at the bottom?'

'Nothing. Tools.'

'It looks like a nice little hidey-hole. Can I look?'

'NO! You can sit in the passenger seat like I said!'

'All right.' Jack sat down aimiably enough, and George sat beside him in the driver's seat again.

Jack twisted his body around, his eyes fixed longingly on the toilet compartment.

'Can I try that shower?'

'Certainly not. You can get out now and go home!'

'I want to try the shower, though. To see how it works.'

'I said OUT!'

There was real tension in the van now. Leah felt it, and worried that something was going to explode. But Jack did not move. Why wouldn't Jack just do as he was told, Leah wondered? Her own heart was beating painfully, and her hands had begun to sweat.

'GO!' said George, again. He turned his unfriendly gaze on the other children. 'And the rest of you!'

'Come on, Jack!' said Leah. 'George doesn't want us here any more. We have to go.' She half stood, willing Jack to agree.

'OUT, OUT, OUT!' George leaned across Jack, trying to reach the nearside door with the intention of opening it and pushing Jack on to the pavement – but Jack slithered neatly from under him and into the toilet compartment again. George lunged out of his seat, tripped over the saucepan and crashed to the floor. 'GET OUT OF THERE!' The fingers on the end of his outflung arm opened and closed, missing Jack's shirt by centimetres.

'It *is* a nice hidey-hole!' said Jack, appreciatively, scrabbling at the low-down door beside the toilet. '. . . oh, look! Everybody, just look what I found! In this bag!'

It was small, but it blazed in his palm like fire.

'What is it?' said Charlie, straining across the table to see.

'Jewellery,' said Jack. 'I thought it was a tool bag but it's not, it's full of jewels.'

'Well done!' said George, bitterly. He heaved himself off the floor, and sat in the driver's seat again, rubbing at his bruised knees and a badly knocked elbow.

'Didn't you know about the jewellery, then?' said Jack. 'Didn't you realise it was there? Are you pleased because I found it for you?'

'I'm talking to Lil. My ever-loving clever, *clever* wife.'

Lil had climbed through the cab door and into the high interior of the van, a large canvas hand-bag, decorated with yet another floral pattern, over one arm. Her face seemed suddenly to have sagged; fallen into folds over the sharp bones.

Leah was still gazing at the shining thing in Jack's hand. 'It's beautiful,' she marvelled, her fears overlaid for the moment.

'Is it real?' said Charlie.

'Of course it's not real,' said Lil. She gave a loud rasping laugh, and took the small object from Jack, holding it between finger and thumb. Her nails were short and bitten and varnished red. 'It's out of a Christmas cracker, can't you tell?'

'*All* of them?' said Jack, disappointed. 'All of them in that bag thing? All of them out of Christmas crackers?'

'*You're* crackers,' George muttered. 'If you think you're going to get away with *that*.'

'Take no notice of my hubby,' said Lil. 'He's at that awkward age.'

'What do you mean, awkward age?'

'Second childhood. Fantasies. Make-believe.'

'Oh,' said Jack.

'Off you go, then, the three of you. Nice knowing you. Cheerio!'

Suddenly there was the slamming of the cab door, and the engine roared into life. The van shot forward. 'Hey!' called Jack, indignantly, thrown off balance. He sprawled across the cooker top, holding on to the edges to avoid getting hurt, and Lil sprawled across *him.* 'Idiot!' Lil screeched at George.

'What's happening?' said Leah, her eyes round with bewilderment.

The van careered down the road. Lil slid jerkily to the floor, and began to make her way on hands and knees to the front of the van. Jack manoeuvred himself off the cooker top, and on to the table, shoving the corner of it without consideration into Leah's stomach, so he could squeeze into the seat opposite.

'Are we going somewhere then?' said Charlie.

'George is just taking you for a little ride,' said Lil. 'Out of the kindness of his great big heart. *Aren't you, George?*'

George said nothing.

'This is great,' said Charlie, as trees and houses and people sped past the window.

Leah's head spun. What *was* this, then? What was happening? Were they really only going for a nice ride? It didn't seem likely, but she must try to believe it, because anything else would be just too dreadful. 'Thank you, George,' she called politely. If she was good, and polite, perhaps that would make everything come all right.

George still said nothing. Jack leaned his elbows

on the table, and watched Lil's progress across the floor with a thoughtful look on his face.

Still desperately trying to make everything all right by pretending it was, Leah made a suggestion. 'As we're going this way,' she forced herself to say, 'do you think George might, like, take us to our road? . . . If it's not too much trouble?'

'I'll speak to him,' said Lil, still on her hands and knees. She hauled herself into the front passenger seat, and began hissing at George, cupping her mouth with her hand as she did it, so the children would not hear what she said – though she need not have bothered, considering the noise the engine was making.

'You forgot to ask the address,' Leah called. 'But anyway it doesn't matter, because we're just coming to our road now. Please, George, will you stop and let us out?'

George drove on. The saucepan slid about, on the floor of thc van.

'Oh dear, you've gone past it!' said Leah. 'Didn't you hear what I said?'

'George couldn't find anywhere to park,' said Lil, turning in her seat to shout the words.

Charlie sneezed. 'Do you mind?' said Leah, wiping Charlie's sneeze off her arm.

Charlie sneezed again. 'It's great this, innit. It's great, innit, Jack. We don't want to get out yet, do we!'

'We seem to be going rather a long way,' said Leah, faintly. She couldn't see George from where she sat, because the side of the toilet compartment was blocking her view, but she could feel the bad waves coming out of him. George's bad waves seemed to be filling the whole van.

'Don't worry,' said Lil from the front seat. 'George will turn back in a minute. *Won't you, George?*'

'I don't think he will, actually,' said Jack.

'What do you mean?' said Leah. 'Of course he will. He's only taking us for a little ride.'

'Huh!'

'What do you mean *huh*, saying it like that?'

'Where *are* we going?' said Charlie, suddenly alarmed.

'Don't ask me!' Lil's head jerked angrily from side to side, so that the long earrings she wore bounced against the side of her neck. 'Ask this lunatic behind the wheel.'

'I *thought* we're being kidnapped,' said Jack. 'I guessed it!'

3

Kidnapped!

I guessed it as well, thought Leah.

I didn't want to believe it, but it was true all the time. And it's all my fault this is happening to me because I shouldn't never have got in this van in the first place. And so what is going to happen now? . . . Oh, I can't think properly! It's like my thinking part has got all stuck up with glue.

Lil thumped her fist on the dashboard, and shouted at George. The children couldn't hear all the words, but the sense of it seemed to be that Lil wanted George to take them all home before they got themselves in deeper trouble.

The sense of what George shouted back seemed to be that he didn't want to go to jail, thank you very much!

And the sense of what Lil shouted back to *that*, seemed to be that they were now in danger of going to jail for kidnapping, as well as other things – and she didn't fancy that, thank *you* very much!

'They *are* real, aren't they?' Jack leaned across the table, and called eagerly to the two in front. 'Those jewels I found, they are real – they been nicked from somewhere, haven't they!'

George roared something about 'blabbermouth', and 'can't take *him* back!'

Lil turned round in her seat. 'Why don't you shut up?' she said to Jack. 'Mr Clever-dick!'

'Oh, I won't *tell* of you,' said Jack. 'You can trust *me!*'

'Don't be silly!'

'I won't, I'll be on your side. Are you robbers, then? Is George a cat burglar?'

'Don't be silly, look at him!'

'Are you in a gang, then? . . . Shut up crying, Charlie, this is interesting. . . . Are you in a gang, then? Can I join?' Jack's eyes shone.

George seemed in danger of bursting a blood-vessel. 'Look out!' Lil yelled. 'Do you know we shot that last lot of lights?'

The van went faster. The saucepan slid and clattered over the floor. Although the table stopped them from actually falling off the seats, every time they rounded a corner the children found their bodies thrown from side to side.

Leah came out of her daze. 'We can't be kidnapped though!' she shouted, in sudden anguish. 'I have to go home to look after Darren and Joel!'

Charlie began to scream. 'Shut up, Charlie,' said Jack. 'You'll get George in trouble.'

Charlie screamed some more. 'Do something!' George shouted at Lil.

Lil half stood, the flowered handbag still on her arm. The van turned another corner at crazy speed. Lil screeched at George, above the din of the engine and Charlie's yells, 'If you don't watch it, the cops are going to have you for dangerous driving anyway!'

The van slowed and steadied. Lil lurched to the back, holding on to the cooker top for support. She sat on the seat next to Jack, facing Charlie and Leah across the table, and spoke between her teeth. 'If you don't stop that noise, I shall give you something to make a noise *about*.'

Charlie stopped screaming, and gazed at Lil with fear in his narrow blue eyes. Lil took a small red bottle out of the flowery bag, and held it up for the children to see. 'Do you know what this is?'

'No,' said Jack, with interest. 'What is it?'

'If you get it in your eyes, just one drop, you will never be able to see anything again. Ever.'

'You mean you'll be blind,' said Jack.

'That's what I said.'

'Is it acid, then?'

'The most powerful acid known to Science.' Lil unscrewed the top slightly, and brandished the bottle under Charlie's nose. Charlie shrank back in horror. She brandished it at Leah, and Leah shrank back against Charlie.

'I didn't know acid was red,' said Jack. 'I didn't know that before.'

'Ordinary acid isn't,' said Lil, 'but this isn't ordinary acid. This is the most powerful acid known to Science. That means it also *hurts* more than ordinary acid . . . Do any of you want to find out how much this acid hurts?'

'Fasten it up,' Leah begged.

Lil unscrewed the bottle top some more. 'I think we'll leave it like this for now, just in case anyone gets funny ideas. Like, for instance, about grabbing it off me—'

'I ain't going to grab it,' said Jack. 'I'm on *your* side.'

'How can you say that?' said Leah. 'When you don't know what they're going to do with us!'

'I don't know what they're going to do with *you*,'

said Jack. 'But they're going to let *me* join their gang.'

Two large tears gathered in Leah's eyes. 'I don't want to be kidnapped, I want to go home! Darren and Joel are all by themselves. It's not safe to leave little children by themselves.'

'Tell that to my hubby,' said Lil.

'*You* tell him! Please, Lil! *Please* make George take us home!'

'I tried. Didn't you hear me, I shouted it loud enough!'

'But my mum's going to find out I left them, and she's going to *kill* me.'

'Well, well!'

Charlie sneezed, and clutched himself. 'I want to go to the toilet.'

'Bad luck,' said Lil.

'I'll watch him,' Jack offered. 'I'll watch him go, and see he don't try to escape.'

'Thanks, but no thanks.'

'If we could go back now,' Leah pleaded, 'like if we could start to go back now, I think we would be in time before my mum gets home from work.'

She wondered how far they had come really. She didn't recognise any of the streets, but she assumed they were still in London. London was a big place, Leah knew; London went on for miles and miles, and it was full of streets like this. It was comforting to think they were still in London, but terrifying to be aware that they were getting farther from home every moment.

There were lots of people about – millions of them. All those people doing their shopping, and going home from work, and not one of them knew that in this van were three children who were being kidnapped.

If only she could tell them! If only she could just open the window, and shout out to the people in the street, and make them get the police to come after the van with their cars, the ones with the flashing lights on the top and the sirens. If the police came after the van they would arrest George and Lil, and put them in prison probably, and serve them right! The police might find out about the Milky Ways as well, of course; but anyway they would take her home, and that was the main thing, and it could even be before Mum got back, it *could.*

They might even forgive her for the Milky Ways, and say she had had her punishment by being kidnapped.

... Only none of this was actually going to happen. It couldn't happen because of that dreadful little bottle, in Lil's hand....

'I think we're going on the motorway,' said Jack suddenly, sounding rather pleased.

'Really?' said Lil.

'Where are we going *to*?'

'When that one up front comes to his senses, I daresay we shall all find out. Personally, I've given up trying to guess.'

'I *do* want to go to the toilet,' Charlie moaned.

'Think about something else,' said Lil.

'Where was it you was planning to take the jewels in the first place?' said Jack.

'Do you expect me to tell *you*?'

'Of course, now I'm in the gang.... Oh, I get it, you don't want *them* to hear. I know, I know, why don't you just tie them up, and put a gag over their mouths, and leave them in a wood. Out in the country. Or I know something else we could do. We could drive to the seaside, and find a boat, and take the jewels to another country. Where the police can't get us.'

'You're full of ideas, aren't you?' said Lil.

'Well,' said Jack, modestly, 'I wasn't never in a gang before, but I have been practising.'

'I've wet myself,' Charlie announced, in a small shamed voice.

Leah inched away from him. 'You're disgusting, Charlie.' She hunched herself in her seat, and thought.

If she was going to be tied up and left in a wood, that meant there was no hope at all of getting home before Mum, and she might as well forget all about it. All that worry about whether the twins would tell – they wouldn't need to now, would they! There would now certainly be a beating from Mum, there was no escape from *that*, and another one from Dad most likely. And it was going to hurt! Leah knew from experience that beatings were nothing to joke about.

She deserved it, though, she couldn't pretend she didn't deserve it. She deserved it for leaving Darren and Joel alone, when it was her job to mind them and make sure they didn't come to harm.

And suppose they *had* come to harm? Leah grew cold and faint at the thought. She knew the dangers very well. The twins were only five, they could eat something they didn't ought to, for instance. Or they could play with the electrics and get a shock. Or they could set the house on fire. . . . Leah's fears grew inside her head; and now they were too many, and too enormous, to be voiced any more. She closed them into her private world, and suffered them all by herself.

The van was slowing down. 'I don't think this is a very good place to tie them up,' said Jack. The van veered off the motorway. 'Are we going in the Services, then?' said Jack. There was shunting and manoeuvring and bad language from George, and *Hideaway* was somehow persuaded into a parking space between two cars. George turned off the engine. 'No, no,' said Jack, earnestly. 'This isn't the place. There's too many people about.'

'Hold your noise,' said George, slumping in his seat and dropping his head into his hands.

'Well?' said Lil.

George made no answer.

Lil spoke in tones of extreme exasperation. 'If we've come here for any purpose, I presume it's to talk. Sort out this mess. Which you can't say you didn't get us into!'

'All right, I panicked. There. Satisfied now? I admit it, I panicked.'

'So what now?'

'Only one thing for it, as far as I can see.'

'Are you going to take us back, then?' said Charlie, hopefully. 'Are you sorry?'

'*You'll* be sorry if you make one move,' said Lil, waving the little bottle.

'Oh, no!' said Jack. 'This is good. Don't let's go back!'

'Of course we aren't going back,' said Lil. 'It's much too late for that. . . . Well, George? What *are* we going to do?'

George sat up and turned in his seat. 'We'll have to dump the lot, won't we? Dump the lot as soon as we can, and beat it . . . somehow.'

Lil snorted. 'It that the best you can come up with? Throw everything away?'

'You rather a stretch Inside?'

'What's the matter with you?' said Lil, scornfully. 'Lost your bottle?'

'Use your head, woman, we have to dump the van now – the police are going to be looking for it!'

'You mean, because of the kids?'

'Got it in one,' George sneered.

'You mean – these kids don't come home tonight, so the parents go up the cop shop and the police say right away, "Ah! They must have gone off in George and Lil's van!" Have a bit of sense, it'll take 'em days to get on to us!'

'Somebody might have seen.'

'Somebody in our street, you mean?'

'Where do you *think* I mean?'

'So let's say Arthur was looking out his window, and he saw us drive off with the kids, and he put on his shoes right away to go and tell the cops about it! . . . Is that what you mean?'

George was silent.

'You know as well as I do,' Lil went on, 'Arthur wouldn't think nothing of it. He knows us. *Everybody* knows us. That was the idea, in case you forgot.'

'Yeah, but—'

'Everybody's friends. Uncle George and Aunty Lil to all the kids. That was the idea.'

'Yeah – *your* barmy idea.'

'It was a good cover, George, and you know it!'

'All right, all right, it was a good cover. . . . What about when people know these kids are missing, though? What they going to think then? If they saw!'

'And when are they going to know that?'
'News gets round.'
'Not that fast. These kids were a goodish way from home, weren't they!'
'How do *you* know there they live?'
'Because the little girl said.'
'I didn't hear her,' said George.
'It helps to keep your ears washed out.'
'All right, what about the telly? . . . I mean, they often have missing kids on telly. Photos, weeping mummies, the lot!'
'Well, that won't be *tonight.* Nor tomorrow night neither, most likely.' They had been snapping and snarling at each other but now, rather unexpectedly, Lil's tone changed, and softened. 'Come on, hubby,' she comforted him, 'we got plenty to worry about, but the police aren't going to be after the van yet. . . . Unless—'
'Unless what?' George mouth dropped open, his eyes popped with fear.
'I was only going to say, unless somebody took the number when little Wet-Pants did his screaming act. . . . And don't have a heart attack about that, because the cops would have stopped us by now! Anyway, who takes any notice of a kid having a tantrum, in the back of a family camper van?'
'Yeah, well don't give me any more shocks.'
'And you pull yourself together!' Lil's voice was sharp again.
'Has George lost his bottle?' said Jack.
'Just strangle him for me, will you?' George exploded. 'All right, how about this then? Suppose one of those kids got a relative living in our street? I mean, someone that's going to hear about them going missing before it gets to be on the telly?'

'*I've* got one actually,' said Charlie. 'I've got a uncle living in your street, I forgot to say.'

'No you haven't,' said Jack. 'He hasn't, George, honestly. He's making out.'

'I'm *not* making out.' Charlie's blue eyes filled with tears. 'I've got a uncle that lives in your street, and he's going to tell the police of you!'

'All right, what's his name then? What's your uncle's name? What number does he live at? . . . See, you can't answer!' The tears rolled down Charlie's cheeks. 'None of us got no uncle in your street, George,' said Jack, reassuringly. 'Trust me!'

'There you are, hubby dear,' said Lil. 'We aren't done for yet. We got time yet.'

'Time for what?' said George, bitterly.

'Meet The Boss. As usual. Hand over the stuff.'

'What about the kiddywinks?'

'We'll sort that out on the way.'

'Little pests! Particularly *one.*' George bared the gap in his teeth at Jack. 'What a character to get lumbered with!'

'Well, *I* didn't drive off with him!' said Lil, tossing her head so the earrings bounced again.

'No, you just invited him in! Whatever possessed you, Lil?'

'To make up for you. You were acting suspicious.'

'I was *not.*'

'Yes you were. Arthur was giving you funny looks.'

'He was *not.* You're paranoid, you imagine things.'

'I was just being careful,' said Lil.

'Careful! Is that what it's called! Well, you gone

right over the top this time. What a crazy chance to take!'

'I thought you could control them. I thought, if there's one thing George is good at, it's controlling kids!'

'*That* is not a kid, though,' said George, shooting a look of sheer venom at Jack. 'That's a monster.'

'I rather like him actually,' said Lil. 'He's got guts.'

'You're saying that to get up my nose.'

'Oh, don't go on and on.'

'Don't *you* go on and on!'

'Are you two going to be quarrelling here all night?' said Jack. 'I thought we're meant to be meeting The Boss, to hand over the stuff.'

George glared his hatred at Jack again, and the van jerked its way back towards the motorway. 'Change places,' said Lil.

George protested, but not very hard. 'You can't drive this thing, Lil. You know you can't!'

'Well, *you* can't, you're shaking like a jelly.'

'I'm sensitive, aren't I? And I've had a shock. I mean, I've really had a shock.

'That's right,' said Lil. 'you're sensitive. And I'm the one with no feelings, so let me drive. I'll be all right on the straight.'

George muttered, and jammed on the brakes, and moved to the back of the van. He took the little bottle and brandished it, while Lil crawled over the cooker top to get past him. Once seated, George waved the bottle close to Jack's eyes; his hand was trembling visibly. 'You wanna be careful with that,' said Jack. 'You could have an accident.'

Hideaway chugged along in the slow lane of the

motorway. 'Is this the way home?' said Charlie, with forlorn hope.

'What you wanna go home for?' said Jack, brightly.

Charlie thought of the evening he would have been having. His mum would come in, somewhere about six o'clock, and find him watching television as though he had been doing that ever since he got back from school. His mum would put down the shopping she had done on the way home, and hug him, and kiss him, and say how much she missed him all day. Then she would go into the kitchen and start frying sausages, or fish fingers. The smell would waft into the living room, where the television was. 'I'm missing *Neighbours*,' said Charlie, just realising it.

'Charlie!' said Jack. 'This is a lot better than *Neighbours!*'

After their meal, Charlie thought, his mum would want him to sit beside her on the sofa. She would put her arm round him, and he would wriggle away a bit, because he didn't really like it when his mum put her arm round him. She knew he was old enough to be left, and that was fine, but she didn't seem to understand he was too old for his mum to be cuddling him like that.

He wouldn't mind if his mum was cuddling him now, though. He wouldn't mind a bit if his mum was sitting beside him now, instead of fat Leah from down the road. If only his mum would be there, she could cuddle him as much as she wanted to!

His mum wouldn't be nasty because he wet himself, Charlie was sure of that. His mum wouldn't say he was disgusting, like Leah did. His mum wouldn't tell him to shut up crying, when he was frightened.

Suddenly, Charlie ached for his mum. The ache was a fullness that started in his chest, and spread upwards and downwards: choking in his throat; making his head so tight he thought it would burst; sending nasty shivers through his tummy and his legs.

And then a new thought struck him. 'My mum's going to be worried about me!' Charlie said the thought out loud as it came to him, but nobody seemed to be listening. Everybody seemed to be thinking their own thoughts inside their heads. He might as well be all alone, he thought, despairingly.

Leah also was feeling alone. There was her guilt, of course, and all her fears, and as though these things were not bad enough, now she was beginning to feel sick! *Really* sick. How shaming, to be sick all over the table; she must keep her mind off it, so it wouldn't happen. She could keep her mind on how to escape, for instance. . . .

Hadn't there been a chance? Back there in the car park, hadn't there been a chance? Why hadn't she shouted through the window, when they were in the car park? The cars on either side had been empty, she thought, but there had been people walking up and down, in front of them and behind. She could have shouted, couldn't she, and told them to get the police.

No she couldn't, though; of course she couldn't. What was she thinking about? She couldn't shout in the street, and she couldn't shout in the car park. She couldn't shout because of the bottle, with the acid in it.

Couldn't there be a way, though? Suppose she

were to shout, and then duck under the table, quickly, before George had a chance to throw the acid at her? It was a pity the window was closed, so the people wouldn't hear her so well, but she could bang on it as well, perhaps. The plan might work; Leah practised doing it in her mind. She practised it over and over, until she almost thought she had done it already, but she went on practising it to stop the sickness from rising in her throat.

Jack came out of a pleasant reverie, all about his good fortune in having the luck to get in with a gang, so early in his life. He was not at all troubled by thoughts of home. The only shadow over a brilliant scenario, as far as he could see, was George's hostility towards himself. Jack set about putting that right. 'I can be very useful to you, you know,' he offered.

'Really?'

'Yeah, I can. I can watch out for you, when you do your burglaries. I can climb into small spaces, things like that.'

'Very good of you, but who says I do burglaries?'

'Don't you, then? Oh, I get it, you just *carry* the stuff. You and Lil. You pretend to be just an ordinary couple, having a holiday in your camper van, and really you're carrying stolen things all the time. For the Boss. Am I right?'

'You know it all, don't you?'

Jack regarded the florid face which had lost much of its colour, the haggard look, the shaking hand. 'I'm sorry you lost your bottle,' he said, kindly. 'Your other bottle, I mean; not the one you're holding. . . . I'm sorry you lost your other bottle, but I expect it could happen to anyone.'

'I daresay,' said George, ominously, 'you'll be losing your own before all this is over.'

'Why do you say that?'

'You're no fool – you figure it out!'

'. . . You don't mean you're going to tie *me* up, with the others?'

'What makes you think I'm going to tie them up?'

'I thought we decided it.'

'No, *you* decided that.'

Charlie began to cry again. 'I want to go *home.*'

'Oh, stop that!' said George.

'Yeah, shut up, cry-baby,' said Jack. 'We're all tired of your moaning.'

'I want to go home, though. My mum's going to be worried about me.'

'She'll get over it,' said Jack.

Leah wanted to tell Jack she thought he was really weird. She wanted to say she heard of people being kidnapped, but she never heard of anybody being on the same side as the ones that kidnapped them. But since she couldn't bring herself to criticise Jack quite so strongly to his face, she only said, '*Jack!* That is a hard-hearted thing to say! Don't you mind if *your* family gets worried?'

'Oh, nobody bothers about *me,*' said Jack, without resentment. 'All they're bothered about is for me to keep out of the way.'

'Surprise, surprise!' said George.

Jack gazed regretfully into George's face. 'Don't you like me at all, then?'

'Since you ask, no.'

'And you aren't going to let me join the gang?'

'What gang?'

'It doesn't seem like it's a *professional* gang,

anyway,' said Jack. 'It's probably not good enough for me to join.'

He lapsed into a disappointed silence, which no one else had the spirit to break. 'Anybody alive back there?' Lil called. She switched on the radio, flooding the van with pop music.

'Good old Lil!' Jack cheered.

But Lil turned the knob, seeking another station. A man's voice was reading the News, and they all listened, but there was nothing about missing children. 'Who's hungry?' said Lil. 'How about something to eat?'

Jack's face lit up. 'Good old Lil!' he cheered again.

'Are you mental?' said George.

'I'm getting a bit tired of being asked that,' said Lil. 'What's mental about not starving to death?'

'We shall have to stop. We'll have to go in the Services again.'

'So?'

'It's risky.'

'It'll be a disaster if we don't – we're running out of petrol.'

George said a bad word.

'Not in front of the children,' said Lil.

'Anyway, I don't know how you can *think* about food,' George growled.

Fighting her nausea, Leah agreed with George. Concentrate! Concentrate on her chance! Leah's heart beat faster, and her hands felt clammy, as *Hideaway* crawled between two rows of parked vehicles. 'There's a good space,' said Jack.

Lil began to haul on the steering wheel, grunting and straining. 'It's too heavy, give it to me,' said George.

Now, thought Leah. Now, while they're changing over. Turn, shout, bang, *duck*. . . . A young couple, walking towards the buildings, halted behind *Hideaway*, waiting for a clear way through. Turn, shout, bang, *duck*. . . . Why wasn't she doing it? Why was she just sitting there, letting the chance go by? The sickness came in waves; she couldn't hold it back much longer. . . .

The changeover was complete, the parking accomplished. George took the bottle again, and stood guard at the front. 'Right,' said Lil, 'who wants the loo?' She pulled the curtain that shut off the cab, and the one above the sink, and opened the toilet door. 'You won't have to be shy of me. One at a time, then, and no messing about!'

Leah vomited neatly into the toilet bowl. 'My, my!' said Lil, but she was kind enough to run some water into the sink, so Leah could wash her face. Leah felt much better, and vastly superior to Charlie now. 'I'll wait till you come back,' she told him. 'I'm not sitting in your seat. You're disgusting; you're all wet!'

There was more pushing and manoeuvring to change places. When everyone was seated again, Lil opened the cupboard over the sink. A few falling tins narrowly missed her head. 'You got a lot of stuff in there,' said Jack admiringly, peering round George.

'I got a hubby with a big appetite. If he doesn't get five meals a day, he's afraid he'll waste away.'

'Lies!' said George. 'And right now I couldn't eat a mouthful, so don't bother about me.'

'Nor me,' said Leah.

'How about Whatsisname?' said Lil. She took a

packet of sausages from the fridge, and began laying them out on the grill pan.

'Don't tell me you're *cooking!*' said George.

'Well, we aren't eating them raw.'

One of George's knees was jerking up and down; thump, thump against the table top, as though he could no longer control its movement. 'You must be out of your tree! Takes for ever on that stove, and anyway, I'm not sure it's allowed.'

Lil shrieked with laughter.

'All right,' said George, sulkily, 'you've had your laugh, now get some burgers from inside if we *must* eat, and let's get going.'

Leah thought, another chance! There's no excuse now I'm not feeling sick any more. I'll do it while Lil's gone and there's only George. . . .

. . . Why aren't I, then? Why aren't I shouting at those people going past now? . . . I don't want to be blind though, I don't! I'm scared of that stuff in the bottle, and I'm scared of George, and I'm scared of everything, I think.

I know, I'll do it when we go to get the petrol. I'll sit here while Jack is hogging his burger, and drinking the Coke that Lil has bought, and I'll give myself a good talking to and pull myself together.

But that opportunity also came and went.

I *can't*, Leah thought. I meant to, I really meant to, but I *can't*. I'm no good, am I? I'm all right for being sick in the right place, I'm all right for that. But I'm no good for saving myself from kidnappers. It seems like I'm just going to sit here, doesn't it, and not do anything, and just see what happens to me.

And it's getting late. The sun has gone; I suppose it will be dark soon.

Are we going to be in this van all night, I wonder?

What *are* they going to do with us?

Back on the motorway, Lil was driving again. 'I think we went past Bristol now,' said Jack.

'You got too much to say,' said George.

'Sorry. . . . Has your bottle come back yet? I don't mean the one in your hand, the other one!'

George looked murderous.

'I only asked. You don't have to be so nervous, you know. The police aren't after the van yet; we heard it on the News.'

George ground his teeth.

'You have plenty of time to meet The Boss, and hand over the stuff.'

George looked even more murderous.

'Have you got other things, besides the jewels? Like under the seats, for instance, have you got other things?'

George made a sort of strangled sound in his throat.

'I know where I think we're going,' said Jack. 'I think we're going to a seaside, like I said before. I think The Boss has got a boat, and he's going to take the stuff to another country. Am I right? Then I suppose you and Lil will make your getaway. Am I right?'

'You know what the first problem is, don't you?' said George.

'No. What is it?'

'The first problem is not the van, or the police, or the getaway, it's you!'

'*Me?*'

'Your mouth.'

'But I told you, I'm on your side! Even if you don't let me be in the gang, I'm still on your side. Us crooks have to stick together. Don't you trust me?'

'In a word, no!' said George.

'I suppose you're going to tie me up then, after all,' said Jack sadly. 'With the others.'

George was silent.

'So *are* you going to tie me up?'

George looked steadily at Jack, through narrowed eyes. His lips were a tight line.

'I know what he's going to do,' whispered Charlie in sudden horror. 'He's going to *kill* us! To stop us talking. He's going to kill us all!'

4

Escape?

The idea came as an unpleasant shock to Jack, that Charlie could be right. Up to this point, Jack had seen George as a glamorous figure – romantic, a member of the Underworld, no less! It was a pity he lost his bottle, but no doubt he would find that again soon enough.

Now, however, Jack saw a different George. Looking into those small eyes Jack saw a dangerous criminal, a sinister enemy, a nasty piece of work. And he didn't deny it, did he? When Charlie said that thing, George didn't bother to deny it. True, Lil said 'don't be silly,' from the front – but she could have been just trying to put him off.

Jack was not often frightened, but he was a bit frightened now. There was no fun in this! There was no fun in just waiting to be killed, he would have to find a way out. Jack did not doubt that there would *be* a way out. To have his life ended at age eleven was unthinkable; it just couldn't happen.

Escape would not be easy, though.

The windows were no good. By the time he got one open, and his head through, George would be pulling him back by his legs. The cab door was no good either, Jack thought. To reach that he would have to climb over George, or over the table. What if he moved quickly, when George wasn't expecting it? . . . But then what about the little bottle? However quickly Jack moved, George would surely have time to use that little bottle!

There was one other means of exit from the van, and Jack was sitting right next to it. At the back were big double doors, and they must open out somehow, otherwise why were they there? There were handles, and one of them turned but the doors wouldn't open. Jack's fingers travelled up and down the centre crack, but couldn't find a catch. He pushed, as hard as he could without attracting George's attention to what he was doing, but the double doors remained firmly closed. They must be locked from the outside, Jack thought. What a pity!

On the other hand, he considered, the van was probably going too fast for him to jump out anyway. So it was probably just as well he hadn't found a way to get out yet. He might have jumped, and hurt himself, and he didn't want to do that. He must wait until they stopped for something. They would have to stop for *something*, some time. More petrol or something. He would have to think quickly, and take his chance when it came.

Jack regarded Charlie and Leah, slumped against the cushions opposite. They were staring into space, their eyes vacant, their bodies slack. Come to think of it, neither Charlie nor Leah had uttered one word since Charlie had dropped his whispered bombshell. They seemed to have gone into a sort of trance, as though the horror of the situation had become too much, and they had just given up. What a useless pair! There would be no help from them. Whatever was to be done, Jack would have to do it himself.

It was beginning to get dark. Good. When the chance came, the dark would make it easier. . . .

Lil shouted abruptly, from the front. 'It's make your mind up time.'

'I know,' said George.

'So?'

'What do you think?'

'I think we'll have to let The Boss in on it. See what he says.'

'He'll kill us!' George's voice shook.

'He'll know what's best to do, though. He'll keep his head.'

'Meaning I don't, I suppose!'

'Now, now, hubby, I didn't say that.'

'You didn't have to,' said George, bitterly.

'So what about it? Shall we phone The Boss?'

'He hates us phoning!'

'Well, he'll have to lump it this time. Next Services?'

'All right, all right!'

We're going in a car park again, Jack thought. That's it, that's my chance! I wonder which one of them will go to the phone? I hope it's George, but I think it will most likely be Lil, because George doesn't really want to do it.

The van veered off the motorway.

'There must be some other way, there must be!' George's growl ended in a funny high squeak.

'You got a better idea?'

'*Yeah.*' The word came out hoarse and throaty, as George jerked his head round to glare his hatred at Jack. '. . . No, not really. The Boss, though, Oh, God!'

Jack did not like the sound of The Boss. The Boss sounded, if anything, worse than George.

The van slowed, and halted. 'Parking time,' said Lil. 'Needs a man's muscle, I suppose.'

'All right, give us the wheel.' They changed over, and *Hideaway* swung into a parking space. George climbed out of the driving seat.

'Where you going?' said Lil.

'Do the phoning. Get it over.'

'Are you sure? I'll go if you like.'

'What do you mean, woman, am I sure?' George bellowed. 'I said I'd do it, didn't I, what more do you want? . . . I got *some* pride left,' he muttered.

'Be careful what you say, though. You never know who's listening on these lines.'

'*Lil!* Give me credit!'

'Just say we got a problem.'

'All right, all right.'

Lil sat where George had sat, holding the little red bottle. Jack's eyes slid sideways, assessing the situation. Lil was tiny, and quite old; she didn't look very strong. She wouldn't be as strong as a boy of eleven, tall for his age, Jack thought. The bottle was the problem – could he possibly knock it out of her hand? Dared he try? His whole body was taut now, his pulse racing, his mind as clear as glass.

Jack took a deep breath. *Now!* His right hand swept across the table, striking Lil's, and the little bottle went flying. He pushed Lil with his left, and scrambled on to the table. Lil grabbed at his legs, but Jack kicked backwards into her face. 'You little brute!' Lil yelled, clutching her damaged nose.

Jack crouched on the table, flexing his knees. The little bottle lay on the floor, and some of the red stuff seemed to be oozing out. He must jump over it. He mustn't let any of the acid touch him, not even his shoes, because this was the strongest acid known to Science and could eat through the soles of his trainers for certain.

Jack was ready to kick Lil in the face again if he had to. What he was *not* prepared for was Lil's next action. Instead of trying to stop him from jumping, and making for the door, she dropped to her hands and knees on the floor and reached for the bottle. With her bare hands, not even wearing gloves, she picked up the leaking bottle and waved it at Jack. 'One move, and I throw it!'

Jack hesitated. He could jump over Lil, probably, but what might happen when he was in the air? What about if he crashed on to Lil, and the acid went in his face anyway? He couldn't escape if he was blind, and in any case he didn't *want* to be blind, that wouldn't do at all.

Lil hauled herself to her feet, still holding the bottle. 'Get down from there. . . . Go on, get down, get down, get back in your place!' Jack felt his hopes draining away. What could he do now? Lil was too far away to kick; it would be folly to try rushing her. She had beaten him, what a shame! But he had *nearly* made it, he had! Jack shrugged his shoulders and climbed into his seat again.

'Anyone else want to get smart?' said Lil, waving the bottle at Leah and Charlie. 'Anyone else thinking of getting above themselves?' Leah and Charlie went on staring blankly, as though they had not heard her, or had not understood what she said. As though they had not seen Jack make his bid for freedom, or grasped that his actions might have anything to do with them.

Jack sat, and brooded. It was going to be even harder to escape than he thought. He had messed up his good chance – well, not messed it up exactly

– whoever would have expected Lil to be so brave? Anyway, he wasn't likely to get a better chance, was he? And George was coming back. And they were going to meet this terrible person called the Boss, so soon he would have three of them to outwit.

How was he going to do it? How?

George returned, and climbed into the driver's seat. 'Well?' said Lil. 'How did it go, then?'

'Oh, he was delighted!' said George, bitterly. 'Overjoyed!'

'You mean he was wild, of course.'

'Of course.'

'And?'

'We've to meet him. At Number Four. . . . What you doing back here?'

'Young fellow-me-lad got stroppy.'

'Oh, did he?'

'I think we'll have to tie him up.'

'Best idea of the night – any string around?'

'Somewhere. Try the cupboard.' Lil moved back to the table, to give George room.

George fumbled, and swore. 'The cupboard's a shambles, Lil. I mean, why don't we have proper places for things?'

Lil grinned. 'I *like* a muddle. More homely. Oh – make do with something else. My belt, use that. Strap his arms to his sides, and buckle it behind, that'll do. Come on, you – *out!* You can squeeze past me, we're both skinny enough.'

Jack obeyed, because he had no choice. He stood between George and Lil in the centre of the caravan. 'Wait a minute,' said Lil. She opened the toilet door. 'Pull the curtains!' she told George. 'Probably not necessary, but just a precaution. Just in case anyone can see in!'

For a moment, Jack had a wild hope that maybe someone had seen before. Maybe someone saw him climbing on the table. But what if they had? They would only have seen a kid, messing about. Nothing sinister, or even unusual, in that.

Lil held the bottle under Jack's chin. He felt the leather biting against his bare arms, but he didn't dare struggle. With savage pleasure, and hands that still shook, George pulled the belt tight, tighter, to make it do up. 'What about the other two?'

'Don't worry about them, they've gone into a coma.' She swivelled the table so Jack could get into the seat, closed the toilet door with her back, and sat down next to Jack.

'Good.' George adjusted the curtains and took the wheel again. 'Another fill-up then, and off we go again!'

'We haven't used Number Four for a while, have we?' Lil called.

'I know. Hope I can find it again.'

'Don't we turn off just before Exeter?'

'Something like that.'

Being tied up, Jack found, was an unexpectedly disturbing experience. It was horrible, not being able to move his arms. He was really helpless now, wasn't he, really at the mercy of other people. For the first time, he recognised the possibility that perhaps he wasn't going to get out of this situation. Perhaps he wasn't going to escape after all.

He struggled to move his right arm, but only succeeded in getting his hand underneath his bottom. There was no way he could bend his elbow, or twist his wrist high enough to reach the buckle at his back. He tried again with his left arm, but with no more success. If he could get his back to Charlie now, or Leah. . . . But they were on the other side of the table, which might as well have been the other side of the world, and in any case they both seemed to have turned into zombies.

Jack looked down at Lil's hand. The headlamps of a passing lorry threw its light into the caravan, and Jack clearly saw a dribble, glistening on the side of the bottle. And Lil was *holding* it. Without a worry! She wasn't even looking, to make sure the dribble didn't touch her skin. And suddenly Jack thought – *I don't think that is acid at all.*

It can't be acid, Jack thought, because Lil isn't being careful enough. I think she tricked us. I think she just pretended. All this time we thought that Lil would make us blind if we moved, and I don't believe the stuff in that bottle would hurt us at all, really. I think I could have escaped all the time, really. If only I could have worked it out before!

I wonder what is in that bottle really.

I wonder why it's red.

Red. Something about Lil is red.

Lil's hands.

Lil's *nails.*

Lil has red stuff on her nails, I saw it a load of times.

I know what's in the bottle. I know what's in the bottle. It's *red nail polish.*

It's this rubbish thing of being tied up! If I wasn't tied up I could knock Lil down easy, and run out. . . . Well, not really, because the van is going too fast. And George is here as well now, which is another unlucky thing. We might stop again though. We might have a puncture. Or the van might break down – I wish it would!

Anyway, the first thing is to get untied, and then look for another chance.

Jack looked at Charlie, but Charlie's eyes were closed now, and his head had fallen to one side. His mouth was slightly open, and he was making little snuffling, snoring noises. What a time to go to sleep, Jack thought. He himself had never felt more alert, or more wide awake.

Leah's eyes were open, though still with that sightless glaze. Jack moved his long legs cautiously, and kicked her foot. Leah jerked her foot out of the way. Jack stretched further, and kicked Leah again. She looked at him then, and he tried to mouth a message at her. He leaned back, so Lil wouldn't by any chance see out of the corner of her eye what he was doing, and made the words *not acid*, with his lips. But Leah didn't seem to understand; either she was too far gone in hopelessness to be interested, or it was too dark in the caravan for lip reading. He tried *untie me*, with no more success.

Anyway, Jack reminded himself, there was still the problem of getting his back to her, and – oh, all sorts of difficulties. He decided to try something else.

'I want to go to the toilet,' he announced.

'*Again?*' said Lil.

'It's all that Coke. Can I, then?'

'No.'

'I'll wet myself.'

'Tough.'

'You won't like sitting next to me. I'll smell!'

'I'll hold my nose.'

Jack sighed. That was it, he had run out of ideas. He sat, and stared out of the window, and wondered where they were going. The van rolled on and on. . . .

Suddenly, they were turning. Suddenly there were no longer the lights of the motorway, and it was much darker inside the van. Then it was very dark inside the van. The headlights picked out the road ahead, but on either side were dense black shadows, with the outline of trees against a slightly lighter sky. No moon, no stars; just thick, dead night.

Jack was stiff, and desperately uncomfortable. The strap around his arms hurt, his back ached; and to make matters worse, he was beginning to be not just a little bit afraid, but very much afraid indeed.

Hideaway twisted and turned through the country roads. The passengers in the back seat were getting thrown from side to side again. Those with free hands could hold on to the table; but Jack was getting quite knocked about.

Occasionally, other vehicles passed them, but not very often. No one spoke. Now and again, Lil's head fell forward on to her chest and she jerked it back, looking anxiously around to make sure no child had done anything naughty, during her brief moment of unconsciousness. Is she going to sleep Jack wondered? The thought cheered him, filling him with new hope. If Lil went to sleep properly, there might be a chance after all – a chance to get untied, anyway!

They seemed to be on a straight bit of road. Lil's head nodded once more, and this time stayed where it had dropped, slightly askew, her jaw buried in the folds of the flowered shirt. Jack leaned his own head nearer, to listen to her breathing. Her breathing was a slow, regular hiss.

She was asleep!

Jack kicked Leah again, and nodded at Lil. 'Asleep!' he whispered. Leah gave no sign that she had understood, so Jack took a chance and said it louder. 'She's asleep. Untie me!'

'What?' said Leah suddenly, out loud.

'Sh-sh-sh!' hissed Jack. There was a moment of agonising suspense, while he waited to see if Lil would wake up. Then he whispered again, 'I'm going to try and stand up. When I turn round, you lean over the table and untie me.'

No answer.

'OK, Leah? Will you do it?'

No answer at first, and then, in a tiny whisper, 'What about the bottle?'

'It's nothing. It's nail polish.'

'*What!*'

'Sh-sh-sh! . . . It's not acid, it's nail polish. She tricked us.'

'How do you know?'

'Trust me!'

It was not easy to stand, without using his hands. Jack leaned forward, and pushed his calves against the locker behind them. Painfully, he struggled to his feet; the edge of the table ground into his tummy, but the pressure helped to steady him against the movements of the van. Now to turn round!

There was no room to stand sideways – the seat and table were too close together for that. If he could get one leg behind him, Jack thought, with his knee propped on the seat, he could swivel round on one leg, perhaps. He strained to do it. Now! Turn now!

But he needed his hands, and he hadn't the use of them. Losing his balance, as the van turned yet another corner, Jack fell against Lil and she woke with a start. 'What you doing? What you up to?'

'I told you,' said Jack. 'I want to go to the toilet.'

'You'll be able to go soon.'

'How soon?'

'Soon.'

'Why not now?'

'*Sit down!*' Lil screamed at him. 'You're getting on my nerves, you are!' She waved the little bottle at him.

At least she doesn't know I found out her trick, Jack thought. At least she doesn't know that! He comforted himself with the knowledge of this one small advantage, as he wriggled back into his seat. The small advantage grew, in his mind, into a really big advantage. There would be a chance to escape later, he was sure. Well, anyway, *nearly* sure.

'Everything all right back there?' shouted George, from the front.

'Just about,' said Lil, not admitting that she had fallen asleep when she wasn't supposed to. 'Everything all right up there?'

'Not sure. We should be near. Can't find the turning, though.'

'Something Farm, isn't it?'

'Cole's Farm.'

'That's right. I remember now. A nasty narrow road.'

'A nice *dark* road. No nasty snooping traffic.'

'Oh, we passed that,' said Jack. 'A long way back.'

'Don't listen to him,' said Lil.

'Actually I think we *have* passed it,' George shouted. 'Looks like we shall have to go back.' He grunted, and swore, as he turned the van in a gateway.

'There it is!' said Jack.

'Take no notice,' said Lil. 'He's not even looking. He's just trying to confuse you.'

'Wait till I get my hands round his neck!'

The road they drove down now was little more than a lane. There was a swishing, and a scratching, against both sides of the van. 'Where are we going?' said Leah, without much interest.

'To meet The Boss, of course,' said Jack.

'Shut up, Mouth,' said George. He sounded dreadfully nervous. 'Where's the gate? Where's that gate? They've taken the blasted gate away. They've moved it, they've done it on purpose!'

But as he said the words, *Hideaway*'s headlamps picked out a widening of the road, and two gates almost directly opposite one another. The brakes went on, and George climbed out to open both of the gates.

The van was still, the door was open, and George was outside! Jack toyed with the idea of kicking Lil off the seat, and making a dash for it. But how far would he get without arms? Not very far, he thought; and if he moved too soon, he could spoil everything. No, no, he must wait for the right moment. He would know the right moment when it came.

Probably.

And meanwhile, he'd make them think he'd given up. 'Is this it, then?' he said in a resigned sort of voice. 'Is this where we meet The Boss?'

'None of your business,' said Lil.

Back in the driver's seat George swung the van around so that its nose was right in the field beyond one of the gates. He switched off the engine and the headlights. Charlie woke, and muttered, and slept again. A heavy silence came down; a silence that was charged with tension and threat. Not far away, an owl hooted; and something alive, a fox perhaps, dashed out of the hedge beside them. Jack heard it for a moment, and then it was gone. From the darkness inside the van, he peered into the darkness of the lane and the field, straining to make sense of the shadows and the looming shapes.

Jack fidgeted, restlessly. 'What's the matter with you?' said Lil. 'Ants in your pants?'

'This is boring,' Jack complained.

'Make the most of it,' said George, ominously. 'There are worse things than being bored!'

At last there was another sound. Faint at first, but getting louder. 'There's a car coming,' said Jack. 'It must be The Boss!' His heart was thumping, but he was glad the waiting was over. Now, at least, something was going to happen. 'Hooray!' he said, with more courage than he actually felt. 'The Boss has come at last!'

Leah turned her head briefly, and turned it back again. 'You kids behave yourselves, now,' Lil warned.

George climbed out of the van. The car's headlights flashed into view. George stood waving his arms, the profile of his stomach clear in the yellow beam. The car turned into the gateway opposite, and stopped. Its lights went out, and now there was only inky blackness outside; inky blackness, and muffled voices.

The voices were indistinct; Jack could not distinguish words. He heard George's rumble, though, and the answer coming in a higher tone. He heard George's rumble, and the answer coming in a *sharper* tone. He heard George's rumble, and the answer coming in a furious burst of anger that raged, and spent itself – and suddenly stopped.

What now?

George climbed back into the van. 'He wants a stocking. Where's the torch?'

'He wants *what*?'

'You heard!' George blustered. 'The Boss wants one of your stockings. And hurry up, because he hasn't got all night!'

'What does he think I am? It's the summer. What does he want it for?'

Jack had a sickening feeling that the stocking was meant to go round his neck, and be pulled tight – but George only said, 'For a mask. So the kiddywinks don't see his face.'

'Well, I haven't got one. I don't wear stockings in the summer. Not on a camping holiday, nobody does!'

'He'll go spare, though. He'll kill me!' George had opened the door of the tall cupboard and was throwing everything on to the floor – shoes, underclothes, miscellaneous odds and ends. Out of the jumble, a ball of something rolled. George pounced on it in triumph, and shook out a pair of tights with trembling hands. 'What's this, then? What you call this?' He stuffed the mess back.

Lil grinned. 'Must have got mixed up with my knickers. Happy now, then?'

George disappeared in haste, and now the new voice outside was not quite so angry. Two torches waved about. One of them rapped three times against the double doors of the van, making an arc of light in the blackness. 'Open up, then,' came the muffled words.

George climbed into the van for his keys. Jack held his breath, and his heart banged against his ribs. The doors were going to be opened, and he was right next to them! Could he? *Dared* he? Without arms? With two grown men, four free arms between them, ready to grab him and put him back . . . if not something worse! No, wait, wait. This wasn't the moment. There could be a better chance later. . . .

Tormented by uncertainty, Jack hoped fervently that he wasn't throwing away the only chance he was going to get.

There was a fumbling at the rear of the van, and the doors swung suddenly open, letting in a flood of chilly night air. George was there, and a figure with no face, only Lil's tights pulled over its head, the stocking ends trailing comically down its back. The man with no face pushed roughly at Jack's shoulder, and his voice came through Lil's tights: 'Get a move on, then, George. Get this lot out of here, we haven't got all night.'

Was this it, then? Were they going to do the unthinkable thing now? Lil stood up. 'Where do you want us to put them?' In the actual presence of The Boss, she sounded almost as nervous as George.

'Why the hell should I care where you put them? Stick 'em in the front for now. We'll get the stuff out, and think about them later.'

'You kids move yourselves!' said George. 'Come on, chop, chop!'

'I can't see anything.' Leah groped with her hands at the toilet door.

'Well, you'll have to manage, girlie!' said the man without a face. 'We can't put lights on – not that you can see this spot from the farm, but you never know. Here.' He pointed his torch.

'What do I have to do?' said Leah.

'Sit in the front seat,' said Lil. 'And *you*!' she told Jack. Come on, *out!*'

'It's not easy without arms.'

'Since when has everything got to be easy?'

Jack shuffled to the edge of the seat. 'Are you going to kill us now?' he asked George.

'Probably.'

'How are you going to do it?'

'Wait and see.'

'Sit in that seat!' Lil ordered him. 'You and the girl together. . . . No, no, the girl on the outside. I want you next to me, and don't forget this!' She sat in the driver's seat and waved the bottle at them.

'This bloke's dead to the world,' said George, climbing into the van and dragging at Charlie. 'What shall I do with him?'

'Put him the other side of me,' said Lil. '*He* won't want any watching.'

'Are you really going to kill us, then?' said Jack.

'Don't be silly,' said Lil.

She was trying to put him off, of course; Jack wasn't fooled by that. He measured the door beside Leah with his eye, working out how to open it. Then he turned sideways to face Lil. 'Do you know something, I don't think you're a very nice person.' He kicked Leah gently, and she moved her foot away.

'Is that a fact?' said Lil.

Jack's foot pursued Leah's, and he thrust his back at her, wriggling very slightly. 'You're cruel, and you tie people up,' he said to Lil. 'I liked you at first, but I gone off you now.'

'Too bad.'

How frustrating it was, not being able to make Leah understand what he wanted her to do! Jack pushed harder against her, but didn't dare make his movements too obvious in case Lil twigged what he was up to. Bother Leah, what's the matter with her, Jack thought. What's the matter with Charlie, what's the matter with Leah, what's the matter with *everyone*? Am I the only person in the world there's nothing the matter with?

Behind the front seats, much strenuous activity was taking place. Jack twisted around and saw that the back seat lockers were open, and George and The Boss were busy lifting some quite large objects out of them. If he hadn't been so concerned with escaping, Jack would have been disappointed that the objects were all wrapped up, so you couldn't actually see what they were. He did notice that some of them had intriguingly knobbly shapes, though, and others were rectangular, and looked as though they might have framed pictures inside.

Then George came right up to the cab, and reached for something on the high bed shelf above it. Jack saw first one, and then another, large flat parcel being lifted down and handed out through the back doors of the van. The parcels must have been under the mattress.... As though it mattered! As though anything mattered, except getting out of this dangerous situation. Exasperated, Jack kicked Leah hard.

'Ow!'

'Sorry. My foot slipped.'

'Keep your feet still!' said Lil.

Jack twisted his wrist painfully, and managed to poke Leah painfully in the thigh. 'Sorry, I didn't mean to do it.' He poked her in the thigh again.

'Oh!'

'What's the matter *now*?' said Lil.

Jack drove his finger into Leah's thigh once more, and at last the penny dropped. She said, 'oh,' very faintly again, and with shaking fingers began to undo the buckle. Jack chattered excitedly at Lil. 'I don't think much of George, neither. He's too fat, and he loses his bottle. And doesn't keep his head. What's the use of a crook like that?'

'Oh, shut up, you mouthy little bore!'

Keeping them behind his back, Jack flexed his wrists and fingers to get the feeling back into them again. 'Do you think I'm a bore, then? My mum thinks I'm a bore. My stepdad thinks I'm a bore as well, but I'm not! *They're* the bores, not me!'

'Really?' said Lil.

'Yeah, really.' He clenched his fists, and opened them. '. . . Bye, then!'

'You come back here!' Lil screamed.

Too late. Much too late! In one movement, Jack had leaned across Leah, opened the nearside door, and disappeared into the night.

5

On the run

Leah watched Jack go without any great excitement. It was like watching a film, on television – a series of flat, moving pictures, unconnected with real life. Even untying Jack had seemed like something Leah's fingers did, while her real self looked on.

Lil's shrieks also, crashing about Leah's head, were only partly real. 'George! Get after him! Go on, find him, find him!' She turned on Leah. 'You *cow.* You sneaky, sly little *cow.*' She waved the red bottle, threateningly. 'Turn round! Go on, before I throw the lot in your face!'

'You mean the nail polish?' said Leah, tonelesly.

'*What* did you say?'

'Nail polish won't hurt me. Jack said that's all it is.'

'You want to find out if he's right, then? Shall we see?'

'No!' Leah cowered against the back of the seat, shielding her face with her hands.

'We'll just try it out, shall we?' Spitefully, Lil brought the bottle nearer.

'No, *please,*' Leah begged.

'Turn round, then, and put your hands behind your back.'

Leah felt something being wound round and round her wrists, and supposed it was the belt which had recently been around Jack. She wondered vaguely how Lil was managing to hold the little bottle, and tie her up at the same time, but she hadn't the fight to resist. When she was tied, Lil slapped her cheeks several times, but Leah made no sound. It did strike her then, that of course she *could* have escaped with Jack, who seemed to be on the right side now; she wondered why she didn't think of it when the chance was there. Now she was most likely to die, like people kept saying. The thought filled her with sick, mind-freezing dread – and yet, in a way, she was resigned.

Because, of course, she deserved it.

She deserved it because she had done a dreadful thing. She had left her little brothers for hours and hours, and *anything* could have happened to them. Now she was going to be punished. She was going to be punished, and she probably never would find out if Darren and Joel were all right after all. In spite of their sister's wickedness.

She just hoped that, when the punishment came, it wouldn't hurt too much.

Charlie woke, confused and whimpering. 'What? What is it? . . . What's happening?'

'We're kidnapped,' said Leah. 'Don't you remember?'

'I want to go *home!*'

'Jack just now escaped.' A tiny hope flickered. 'I suppose he might tell the police!'

Lil gave a harsh laugh. '*What* police? Do you see any police stations round here? Any police cars? . . . There's nothing here, and nowhere to go. They'll have him back in a jif, you'll see!'

Jack lay flat amidst quivering corn, and fought to get his breath back. He had plunged straight into the middle of the field, reasoning that if he kept close to the hedge, where it was easier to run, the car or the van would be able to follow him from the other side.

Now, however, he wondered if he had made a mistake. The corn was high and thick; ploughing through it was more like wading than running. He must move, he must get going! From where he lay, Jack could see a small light flashing. Someone was flashing a torch round by the gate; the torch would pick up his track. The torch would show where his feet had smashed the corn down – he must get out of here quick!

But where could he go? Where?

Whichever direction he went, he would leave a trail. And going through the corn was slow; whoever had that torch would catch up with him easily, once they found it. After all, they only had to follow the trail, not make it!

Supposing he doubled back? Supposing he were to lead his pursuer in a great loop, back to the hedge, where it was easier to move? That way he might stand a chance of outrunning whoever was behind the torch.

Outrunning them to where, though? Where was there to go, to be safe, in all this black emptiness, with no lights, and no houses? Never mind that now! Get to the hedge first, and then think. Jack scrambled to his feet and pushed on, keeping his head down, hoping he was going the right way.

A drop of rain touched the back of his neck, and another glanced off one bare arm. Way out to his left, Jack saw the waving torch. He couldn't tell if there was one person following his track or two, but he knew he would have to run very fast, and be very clever, if he wanted to stay free.

The hedge was getting nearer; Jack saw the black shape of it against the not-quite-black sky. I can see things better now, Jack thought. My eyes are getting to be like a cat's, I think. And it's coming good, my plan is working. . . . So now what? Where do I go from here?

Of course, of course, there's a farm! They said about a farm, I heard them! They said there's people asleep in the farm. I can wake the people up, and tell them there's kidnappers after me, that want to kill me. And they can telephone for the police.

So it's quite simple really. All I have to do is get to the farm.

Which *way* is the farm?

We came down the road from *that* way, so the farm must be *this* way. Will I get to it if I run along the hedge? I won't come to another hedge, will I, that I can't get over? . . . Perhaps it would be best to go back to the gate, and run by the road. But Lil is there, in the van! Lil can chase me, in the van! Lil has got quite nasty just lately, she might even run me over. . . . No, no, I'll go by the field. I'll go this way, as fast as I can. I'll run like it's the Olympics, they won't catch *me*.

Jack's long legs twinkled close to the hedge, invisible to everyone except the little prowling night creatures. His heart was pounding, and there was a stitch in his side, and – oh, *no!* There *was*, there was another hedge, right in his path so he couldn't get past!

Jack tried to force a way through the barrier, but sharp twigs tore his clothes, and there were some unfriendly leaves as well, which stung his hands, and his arms. Fear grabbed at him; but he sidestepped the fear, to stand in a pool of calm where he could think.

. . . I should have gone by the road. Never mind Lil, I should have took the chance. I should have gone by the gate, and got in the road. . . . Is it too late to go back? . . . Perhaps I ought to run by *this* hedge, away from the road! There could be another gate – but supposing there isn't? George can catch me if there isn't another gate, I can be just trapped. Or The Boss can catch me, I mean, or both of them. . . .

I think I better just hide. Not in the corn, because of the trail. . . . In the hedge! Not this one with the stinging leaves, the one by the road. . . . I'll run back and find a hidey-hole. I'll get right into the hedge, and lie still, and they won't find me.

. . . Where's the torch, where's the torch? When they follow my trail and get back to this hedge, which way will they go? They won't have a trail any more, they will just have to guess. I hope they don't guess right. I hope they don't shine that torch in the place where I am. I hope there will be a really deep hidey-hole, so they don't find me with that nuisance torch. . . . I think they *will* find me with that nuisance torch, though, I don't know if my idea is a good one after all.

. . . How about this, then, how about this? I think this hole goes right *through* the hedge. I can get through the hole and get in the road. I can, I can, I can do it, I can crawl through and I can do it! . . . Further, a bit further, I'm nearly there! I'm getting all scratched up, but never mind. . . . Ow, that hurt! Now my shirt's tore, but so what? . . . I'm through! I'm on the road, hooray!

Here I come, farm, here I come!

Another drop of rain hit Jack's nose as he stood erect, bleeding and tattered but still free, on the other side of the hedge. He began to run again, along the dark lane, with the high ragged hedges on either side. And however far he went, and however fast, the hedges stayed the same; so it began to seem as though he wasn't really moving at all, just running hard to get nowhere.

But the road *must* lead to the farm, because the notice at the turning said so.

And then he heard it.

Hardly a purring this time – more like an ill-tempered hiss. Jack turned to see, quite unnecessarily because the headlights were full on him now, throwing their beam over and beyond him on to the road. He hurled himself at the hedge, scrabbling desperately for another gap, so that he could squeeze into whatever sort of field there might be on the other side.

But there were thorns this time, as well as more stinging nettles. Cut, and smarting, Jack turned to face The Boss, who was just leaping out of his car. The body with the faceless head came charging for him, arms outstretched. There was a moment of sheer horror, then Jack put his own head down and butted it, *wham*, straight into The Boss's stomach.

The Boss grunted, and doubled over, but he had Jack by the arms. Jack drew his head to butt again, but The Boss held him out of reach. 'No, you don't!' said the voice inside the stocking. Jack kicked out, aiming for The Boss's ankle; The Boss side-stepped. Jack kicked out again. 'You don't know when to give up, do you?' said the voice inside the stocking.

With a sudden unexpected movement, The Boss threw Jack to the ground, and knelt over him. Jack found himself lying on his side, his arms and body gripped between The Boss's strong legs. It was like a particularly horrible nightmare, being held by a man without a face! The Boss put his hand on the back of Jack's head, and twisted it round, and down. Jack felt his cheek scraping against something rough, and the pain of it brought the tears suddenly to his eyes. He was beaten, he was beaten! His body went limp.

'That's better,' said The Boss, grimly. He spread his knees slightly, pushed Jack flat on his face, and wrenched his arms back, holding them in a vice-like grip. 'Now! You going to be sensible?'

'Are you going to kill me?' said Jack.

'Where did you get that idea from?'

'Are you, though?'

'If you don't behave yourself, I might have to.'

'What happens if I *do* behave myself?'

'You haven't given me much chance to think, have you? Running off like that!'

'Can't you think now?' said Jack. 'Because I really should like to know what it's going to be.'

'Yes, I can quite see that.'

'George said he's going to kill me.'

'George is an idiot.'

'You didn't go in that field with George, did you? You went up and down the road to look for me, didn't you?'

'Naturally. Divide and conquer!'

'Have you thought, yet?' said Jack.

'I have an idea, yes.'

'Will I like it?'

'Very much, I should think.'

'What is it, then?'

'If you come back quietly in the car with me, you'll soon find out.'

'Do you promise I'll like it?'

'It's a treat, I give you my word.'

'. . . All right, I'll trust you. Can I get up now?'

The Boss held Jack firmly, as they both struggled to their feet. The car door was still open; The Boss pushed Jack through, still holding him by one arm. Somehow or other, he then managed to squeeze in himself.

'Now,' said The Boss. 'What's your name, by the way?'

'Jack.'

'Right, Jack – the thing is this. Since I can't be sure you won't run away again, and since I have nothing handy to tie you up with, I have to hold you. Agreed?'

'Yep.'

'And since I have to hold you with one hand, that only leaves me one hand to drive with. Agreed?'

'Yep.'

'Which is just a little bit awkward. So how would you like to help me?'

'*Me*?'

'Perhaps you'd like to turn on the ignition for me for a start. . . . No, no, push first. . . . Right!'

'I never drove a car before,' said Jack with shining eyes. 'Is this the treat?'

'No. Now let's see if you're strong enough to put her in reverse. There's the gear lever. Now! Lift up, up, now to the right and *forward*. . . . Good man!'

'I thought you were going to be worse than George,' said Jack, as the car glided backwards. 'But you're not, you're better!'

'Oh, *everyone*'s better than George,' said The Boss, in a really friendly tone.

His mood changed abruptly, though, as soon as Jack was safely back in the van. 'Here he is, and we're not having this nonsense again. For God's sake let's find something to tie him up with. Properly, this time!'

'There's some string *somewhere*,' said Lil, humbly.

'Well, find it, find it!'

'The thing is,' said Lil, sounding really nervous, 'I can't look in the cupboard *and* watch the other two.'

'Giving credit where it's due,' said The Boss, 'you've got a point. . . . Where's George, still on safari?'

George stood in the doorway, huffing and puffing. 'It's her fault,' he accused Lil. 'I mean, it was her job to look after him, you can't blame me!'

'Who cares whose fault it was?' said The Boss. 'You take over from Lil, and Lil will find the string. Go on, Lil, you said it's somewhere. . . . Yes, I can see it's a jumble. Turn the jumble over, till you find the string. . . . *Good.* Now tie him. . . . Keep still, you little monster, or I shall have to clip you one.'

'You said there was going to be a treat,' said Jack.

'Did I? Well, I'm afraid the treat comes later. Just now you have to be put out of action. That's right, Lil, round his ankles. Now his wrists. . . . Now get the back doors locked, before we go any further. . . . *Right!*'

'You tricked me!' said Jack, reproachfully. 'I was getting to like you, and you tricked me!'

'Well, that's how it goes,' said The Boss. He scratched his hooded head. 'We'll put this one on the back seat and do the others. The young lady's done already, I see. Tie her ankles as well, just to make sure.... Now the sleeping beauty... you can stop that noise, young man! Tough guys don't cry!'

The Boss regarded the three children, trussed and silent on the back seats. 'Better gag 'em,' he decided. 'Come on, find me something: scarves, shirts, anything. Might as well blindfold 'em as well, while we're about it. Then I can get of this fancy dress.'

It was bad enough being tied and gagged; it was terrible not being able to see. 'Right!' said The Boss. 'Now let's get going! I'll lead, and you follow. I suppose you can manage to do *that* without making a shambles of it!'

'Er – *where*, exactly?' said George.

'Well, I don't know myself, *exactly*,' said The Boss. 'I'll have to work it out on the way.'

'But we're going to ditch *Hideaway*?'

'Naturally.'

'And we're going to ditch the kiddywinks?'

'Naturally.'

'They are going to be all right, though, aren't they?' Lil sounded as though she was half afraid to say it. 'I mean, we aren't actually going to hurt them!'

'We're going to do what we have to do,' said The Boss. 'No more, and no less.'

The children heard the banging of the cab door as The Boss departed, then the sound of the car engine, then the van starting up. *Hideaway* began to move. Once more there was the swishing of leaves against the side of the van, and soon after that the click-click of windscreen wipers, and the drumming of rain on the roof. From time to time, the van swerved; and the saucepan, which no one had bothered to pick up, slithered about the floor. Then the engine note changed, and it felt as though they were climbing. The children sprawled in their seats, and now and again flung painfully against hard edges and each other, waited helplessly for whatever the end of the journey might bring.

Charlie was no longer sleeping. Wide awake and frightened to death, he cried desperately inside – a lot for himself, a little for his mum, and even a little bit out of shame, because The Boss had reminded him that tough guys didn't do it.

Leah was not so much frightened as stunned. She had felt dazed and disconnected for much of the journey, but this was something more. Now everything had begun to seem very far away, as well as unreal. Cut off by blindness, Leah felt as though she were existing in a special space of her own, and the world outside had almost disappeared. Even the knocks and the discomfort of the string round her wrists and ankles hardly troubled her, because her body seemed to be part of that disappearing world as well. She didn't think any more about deserving what was to come. She didn't think any more about anything, really.

Jack was uncertain whether to be more frightened, or more angry. He was frightened because he didn't know what was going to happen, of course. But he was also *very* angry with The Boss, for cheating, and for tying him up like this. Being tied up was the worst part of it, really. It wasn't fair, it didn't give a person a chance! Jack hoped something really bad would happen to The Boss, only somehow his mind had got stuck on this being tied up rubbish, so he couldn't think of anything suitable.

The van climbed some more. George and Lil, sitting together at the front, were talking to each other. Jack strained to listen, but the noise of the engine drowned out most of what they were saying. Jack's sharp ears caught a few words, here and there. He heard: 'the kids' . . . 'us' . . . 'good riddance' . . . 'retirement'. It didn't make much sense, but then Jack heard George's great guffaw, as though he was pleased about something at last, and the words 'all over'.

There was a chilling feel about that last bit. What was all over? Or what was *going* to be all over? Jack's life, for instance, was *that* going to be all over? Or just George's career as a crook? There was no way of telling, and nothing to be done but wait, while this dreadful journey went on, and on, and on.

At last there was a turn, and after that no longer smooth road beneath *Hideaway*'s wheels; instead, the children heard the crunch, crunch of loose stones, and the van was lurching a bit, and swaying. The lurching and the swaying was going on for ever, it seemed. Then Lil's voice came sharply through the darkness, 'Stop! He's flashing his lights.'

Hideaway jerked to a halt, and was suddenly very quiet. Lil's voice came again, 'This must be the place.'

'It's deserted enough,' said George. 'Deserted enough for anything, I'd say. Wonder what he *has* got in mind!'

'We shall soon find out,' said Lil.

Yeah, right, thought Jack, we're going to find out now, aren't we. This is it, it's come now, and whatever it is, when I find it out, I'm going to fight. I shan't let them do it to me without fighting. I shall make a good nuisance of myself, so there!

It *is* real, thought Leah, in terror. It seemed like it wasn't, but now it seems like it is again. It isn't *possible*, but it is *real*.

Mum, Mum, Mum! thought Charlie.

Somewhere outside, a car door banged. 'Here he comes,' said Lil.

'Nervous?' said George.

'What do you think?' said Lil.

There was the crunching of footsteps, and a creaking noise as one of *Hideaway*'s doors swung open. Then came The Boss's voice. 'At least it's stopped raining. That's a good thing.'

'What's the plan, then?' said George.

'Come with me, and I'll show you.'

The children heard more crunching footsteps, dying away, then returning. 'I can't do it,' said George's voice, from inside the van.

'Do what?' said Lil.

'Take the van down the hill. Over the grass and stuff. I can't do it, it's too steep, we shall turn over.'

'George, you're pathetic!' The Boss was evidently inside the van as well now – or perhaps he had just poked his head through the door.

'Come on, hubby,' said Lil. 'Be a man!'

'Can't we just leave it here?' George pleaded. 'The police cars don't come along here, surely!'

'Probably not,' said The Boss, 'but you never know. Off the track is best. It's ideal here – there's a long grassy patch, and trees further down. That's speaking from memory, of course, but I knew this spot pretty well at one time. The idea is to get the van behind the trees if we can. That way it can stay hidden for days.'

'What about the kids?' said Lil.

'*I'll* deal with the kids,' said The Boss.

'I can't do it, though,' said George. 'I can't drive the van down there, I can't! To save my life I couldn't do it!'

'How did I ever get tied up with a jerk like you?' said The Boss, furiously. 'All right, *I'll* do it! The whole bang shoot, I'll do it myself! Lil, take your hero of a husband, and go and sit in my car. Come to think of it, climbing up afterwards would probably finish the old windbag off! A chap in his condition!'

Again, the banging of doors, and the crunching of footsteps. *Hideaway*'s engine sputtered, and sprang into life. The van began to move – crunching at first, then running smoothly over something soft, then bumping and lurching, then running smoothly again.

Suddenly, the van seemed to tip forward. Although they couldn't see, the children felt by the way they were thrown in their seats that they were really going downhill now. They seemed to be plunging headlong into something like a deep pit.

Down, down, down! Sometimes the going was smooth, sometimes bumpy. Once they seemed to get stuck, and The Boss shouted some very bad words indeed as *Hideaway* struggled, and tipped sideways, and righted itself.

Steeper, and steeper. They were moving very slowly now. Then they were levelling out. The children knew they must be levelling out, because they were no longer being thrown so hard against the cupboards.

Bumping, and more bumping, and they were tipping, and lurching, and there was fear, fear, fear, because something terrible was going to happen now, probably, only they didn't know what – they could only feel, and hear, and with wild imagination guess.

'Blast!' they heard. 'The blasted bracken's in the way!'

Hideaway seemed to turn, and veer to the right. They were going faster again – faster, faster, bumping and lurching. Then a wrench to the left, a roar from the engine, and – CRASH! *Hideaway*'s nose came up, the engine cut out, and all of a sudden there was stillness. Stillness, and silence.

They had arrived.

More stillness, and silence. There were a few grinding sounds from the front, The Boss doing something with the gears and the brake – and then the children heard his footsteps coming towards them, clumping over the lino on the floor. 'Must be a knife somewhere!' They heard the rattle as he turned over the cutlery in the drawer.

'This'll do. Right, which one of you?'

Three terrified hearts struggled inside three heaving chests.

'Young lady, I think.'

In a minute it'll all be over, Leah thought. Just a minute, and it'll all be over. She felt her arm gripped, and her body being turned around. 'OK,' said The Boss. 'We're nearly there, but first you have to listen. All of you. Are you listening? . . . I'll take it you are.' He paused. 'This is the treat. Jack knows about the treat, don't you, Jack? I said there was going to be a treat, and this is it.' He paused again. 'The treat is a holiday. You know what a holiday is, don't you? But this is a special sort of holiday because you're going to have it all by yourselves. *All* by yourselves! You see, we're right out in the wild country now, in a very wild place, miles and miles from where anybody lives. . . . You'll be all right. If I know Lil there's plenty of food, and the water will last if you're careful. Don't drink the tap-water if you can help it; there's a jerry-can of drinking water somewhere. The toilet will fill up, so you'd best use the bushes when you can, and don't leave the lights on for too long or you'll run the battery down and then you'll have no lights at all. You'll have to manage without the fridge or the water heater; they use up the gas, and anyway I'm not sure how to light them.

'There is one danger, and that is the wild animals. The wild animals are very fierce, but you'll be all right as long as you stay close to the van. Just stay by the van, and wait for someone to come and find you. . . . Do you understand?'

Since their mouths were tied, they couldn't answer, and in any case their heads were spinning. Was it true? Could they believe what they had just heard? The Boss went on. 'I'll take it you *do* understand. Now – in a minute I'm going to free the young lady's hands, and then I'm going. You won't see me again. You won't see George and Lil either. The young lady can untie the rest of you. And don't forget what I said about the wild animals!'

Leah felt something cold against her hand, and she jerked away. She twitched, and shivered, and her breath came in little gasps. 'Keep still!' said The Boss. 'I don't want to cut *you*.'

She tried to do as she was told, but she was too bewildered to make sense of anything. A minute ago, she had thought her life was about to end. Now someone said she was going to have a holiday. It was too much, she couldn't take it in.

The strands round her wrists parted suddenly, and Leah felt the blood flow suddenly, painfully, back into her hands. Before she could move them, or do anything with them, she heard the clumping of footsteps again, the banging of a door, and the faint sound of someone crashing about outside.

And after that, nothing.

Still trembling, Leah put her hands to her face and pulled off the blindfold. The Boss was gone, they were alone! One dim light burned above the cooker, showing her Charlie and Jack, still trussed and blind. Jack was wriggling, but Charlie was still – so still, that Leah wondered in a burst of anguish if he had died of fright, perhaps. She leaned over, and with shaking fingers undid his gag and his blindfold. He blinked at her, but said nothing.

Leah pulled off her own gag, and bent to cut the cords round her ankles with the knife. Jack's legs were thrashing impatiently against the centre pole of the table, but Leah couldn't help him until she had finished freeing herself. She remembered, with guilt, that poor Charlie's arms and legs were still tied. In a sort of dream, she lunged from one boy to the other and back again.

Freed at last, the children sat silently, rubbing at their wrists and stamping their feet. Every now and again their breathing turned to little shuddering sobs. No one looked at anyone else.

Jack was the first to move. Without a word, he

began to climb – over the cooker lid, across the sink lid, and on to the high-up bed. The mattress was piled high with clothing, but there was a quilt and a blanket under the clothes, and the pillow which Lil had thrown there, and another pillow besides, and a still-folded sheet. Jack pushed the clothes and the blanket and the sheet into a heap at the end, and crawled under the quilt.

He was more shaken than he had ever been in his life before. It had to be admitted, the events of this day had quite thrown him. He couldn't work out how to think about this amazing situation he was in; he would have to leave it until tomorrow. He must try to sleep. If he could sleep, then he would be able to work it out. He turned his face to the wall and lay rigid, trying to still the racing of his mind.

Leah followed Jack. She burrowed next to him, under the quilt, and listened to the rain which had started once more. She listened hard to the rain, holding on to the sound of it. The rain was something ordinary; the rain reassured her she was still joined to the ordinary world. Impossible things were happening in this van; but outside the rain still fell, and there was comfort in the sound of it.

Charlie sat numbly, on the seat below. Such a very few hours ago, he had so very much wanted to climb on that wonderful high-up bed. Now he had lost the will to do anything but sit, and stare with blank eyes at nothing in particular. But it was lonely on the seat, and dark as well because Leah had turned the light out. . . . With a great effort, Charlie forced his legs to move, and take him where the others had gone before. He snuggled in beside Leah, squashed up close because there was so little room.

It was warm under the quilt. The three children huddled together, and shuddered fitfully, and finally slept.

6

Wild animals

Charlie, who had slept so much on the journey, was the first to wake in the morning. There was a minute of confusion, three minutes of amazement and relief that he was actually still alive – and then an overwhelming flood of shame.

He had disgraced himself!

Most people who knew Charlie thought he was brave. In his heart of hearts, Charlie knew he wasn't all that brave really, but before yesterday he mostly managed to fool people. Much of the time he even managed to fool himself. It was important for Charlie to have a tough image for facing the world with.

The memory of yesterday filled him with bitterness and self-loathing. When real danger came he lost his bottle, didn't he, just like George. He actually cried, didn't he, he remembered it. What would Jack think of him now?

Jack was Charlie's ideal, his hero. Jack was everything Charlie would like to be himself. Jack was the person whose good opinion he valued above that of everyone else in the world, including his mum. Indeed, his mum hardly counted, since she would never scorn him whatever he did.

But Jack could scorn him, because of the things he did yesterday. Such shameful things! He had cried, and lost his bottle, and worst of all he had gone and wet his trousers.

They had dried in the night, but they smelled horrible. Curled up under the quilt, Charlie smelled himself, and was mortified. What could he do about it? He had no clothes to change into, but perhaps he could wash the ones he was wearing. Perhaps he could even get them dry, before the other two woke up.

Water! Where could he get some water?

There was a sink under that lid, wasn't there? There was a tap, as well, he distinctly remembered a tap. Moving with great care, so as not to disturb Jack and Leah, Charlie crawled down from the high bed to investigate. He lifted the lid, found how to clip it back, and turned the tap. Water! Plenty of it! Charlie fitted the plug, and watched the sink filling up.

He sneezed, stifling the sneeze against his sleeve. There was a soreness in his nose, and at the back of his throat. He thought he might be going to have a cold, which wasn't really fair since it was the middle of summer. He was bruised from yesterday, as well. Miserable, and sorry for himself, Charlie watched the basin filling up.

The basin was full. Charlie took off his trousers and his underpants, and dipped them. He couldn't see any soap, and didn't know where to look for some. In any case he was in a hurry to be done, so he just swished the garments around in the cold water, and hoped for the best.

Now – where to dry them?

Outside somewhere? Spread them over the bonnet of the van, perhaps. Charlie squeezed as much of the water out of the jeans and underpants as he could, and bundled them in his hands – and it was at that point that he remembered something else.

Wild animals!

The Boss said there were wild animals, didn't he! Charlie had been too terrified to listen to everything The Boss said, but he had caught the bit about the wild animals. Supposing the wild animals were near, right at this moment? All Charlie could see through the window over the sink was some sort of tree, or bush. Now for the first time since waking, his eyes went with awareness to the back of the van – and his spirits dropped with dismay at what he saw.

No animals, to be sure. No anything really, it seemed at that first sight. Just a vast dismal greenness, stretching up and away, filling the window, filling the world.

Charlie sneezed again, three times in rapid succession. This time he forgot to catch the sneezes in his sleeve, and the noise woke Leah. 'Why are you bare?' came her disapproving voice, from aloft.

Embarrassed, Charlie dragged at his tee-shirt, and tried to distract attention from his nakedness. 'Look at this horrible place we come to!'

'I'm looking at *you*, and you look *rude!*'

'Well, I can't help it. Had to wash my trousers, didn't I?' The humiliation of it tightened his throat, making it hard to say the words.

'Oh yeah, I remember.' Leah fumbled at the foot of the bed. 'There's a pair of trousers here, I think. There's a load of clothes, actually. . . . Here!' She threw down a large pair of shorts.

'They're too big.'

'Well, of course they're too big. They're . . .

his . . . you know!' This morning, Leah found, she couldn't bring herself to say George's name.

'They're no good for me, though. They're going to drop.'

'Well, use your brains, Charlie. Tie them up with a bit of string. One of those bits on the floor, look!'

She thinks she's big, thought Charlie fiercely. Just because I cried yesterday, she thinks she can talk to me like I'm nothing. With his back to her, hating her, he nevertheless did as Leah said.

Jack stirred. 'It's *cold*,' he complained.

The morning was, indeed, raw and chill and cheerless. Charlie shivered, realising for the first time how cold *he* was. 'It's because of this horrible place,' he said. 'It's meant to be summer, but it seems like it's winter here.'

Leah scrabbled about some more, and found him a cardigan. 'I can't wear that, it's a lady's one,' said Charlie. 'It's got all pink flowers on it.'

'All right,' said Leah. 'Freeze if you want to.'

Charlie put on Lil's cardigan, and thought how much he would like to spit in Leah's face.

'I'm starving,' said Jack, with his head still under the quilt. 'What time's breakfast?' His face felt sore, and there were itchy bumps all over his arms.

'I'll see what there is to eat,' said Leah. It would be good to have something nice and ordinary to do. She pulled a huge brown pullover from the pile on the bed, and wriggled into it. 'That's better. That's more warmer.' She climbed down, with difficulty; her shape was not designed for climbing. The pullover hung to her knees, below the hem of her skirt. The sleeves flapped; Leah rolled up the sleeves, and opened the cupboard, searching for cornflakes. 'Here we are, now we just want plates and spoons.' A dreadful thought struck her. 'I suppose they really *went!*'

'Who?' said Charlie.

'You *know!*'

Filled with sudden panic, Charlie cowered against the toilet door, afraid to look out of the window. 'Don't say that! Don't say things like that, Leah!'

'They went,' said Jack. 'Of course they went!'

'How do you know?' Leah's voice was fearful. 'How can you be sure?'

'Because that was their plan. You know, for how to make a getaway. That's why they put us here, so they would have time to make their getaway. . . . Hey! Look at that!'

Jack had propped himself on his elbow, and was gazing through the high front window. 'He tricked us! That Boss tricked us again! Some treat! Some holiday place, I *must* say!'

Leah was anxiously scouring the scene outside for signs of George and Lil. 'It's not important if it's a nice place; it's important if they won't come and catch us again.'

'They don't *want* to catch us,' Jack insisted. 'They want to get rid of us. Trust me!'

'That's right,' said Charlie, much relieved. 'They want to get rid of us.'

More or less convinced, Leah began fussing over the breakfast arrangements again. She gathered up the mess of clothes from the seats, and stuffed them into the lockers out of the way.

'Come and look at this, though!' said Jack.

Leah climbed to look, and so did Charlie. Three unsmiling faces peered through the high-up window. 'Did we come to another planet, then?' said Charlie.

'Actually, I think it's called a wilderness,' said Jack.

It was certainly like nothing they had seen in all their lives before. Across a valley, and all around them, the great slopes rose. One high mound away to the left had a sort of rocky point to it; the rest swept in grey-green curves, curve behind curve, into a lowering grey sky. The grimness of the scene was heavy, overwhelming. The grimness would crush them if they looked at it too long.

Charlie cleared his throat, and found a shaky voice. 'Anyway, somebody is going to find us, aren't they? Do you think they might find us today?'

'We can't tell *what's* going to happen today,' said Leah.

She would keep very busy, she decided, and not think very much. There were all sorts of things she didn't want to think about. Almost everything in the world outside was frightening and confusing; but inside this van were lots of comforting, ordinary things. Things like getting breakfast, and finding plates, and putting the clothes away. She would make a shield for herself, out of those things, against all the terrors of the world outside.

Jack moved suddenly. He grabbed an outsized jacket, rolled across the other two children, and dropped gracefully to the floor. '*Food*! Come on, *food*!' There were long disfiguring scratches on his face, but his eyes were bright from sleep, the smile coming back. 'Hey, Leah's found some! Good old Leah!'

'There was only two plates,' said Leah. 'So someone will have to eat out of the saucepan.'

'That can be Charlie,' Jack scratched at the lumps on his arms. 'You don't mind, do you, Charlie?'

Charlie did mind; he minded very much. He didn't mind eating out of the saucepan, but he did mind taking second place to Leah. Sulking, he shuffled his bottom into the corner.

The floor of the van sloped slightly downwards towards the front, but not enough to make the plates slide off the table. His spirits rising, Jack's gaze travelled round the little home. 'Anyway, lucky we got the van!' He tossed back the too-long hair and smiled approvingly. 'This is a good van I found, innit!'

'It's messy,' said Leah. 'I'm going to clear it up, after.'

'Yeah, you do that. . . . I think I'll go outside, and explore.'

'Is that sensible, Jack?' said Leah, cautiously. 'I know – *they* aren't coming back, but what about the wild animals?'

'Oh yeah, them.'

'*I* ain't scared of the wild animals,' said Charlie bravely, from his corner.

Jack ignored him. He was pretty disgusted with Charlie, after yesterday. He really found Charlie out yesterday, didn't he! Leah was a bit of a drag as well sometimes, of course, but at least she was making herself useful. 'I suppose they'll come with helicopters,' he said.

'Who will?' said Leah.

'The police. They going to be looking for the van, aren't they? Like George and Lil said.'

Leah shuddered slightly at the mention of the hated names.

'That's right,' said Charlie. 'They going to be looking for the van.'

Jack ate noisily and with enjoyment. 'I know what we can do, we can listen to the radio again! See if there's anything on the News.' He crammed the final spoonful of cornflakes and milk into his mouth, and shoved the corner of the table into Leah's stomach so he could make for the driving seat. A blast of pop music filled the van. 'Oh, *look*,' Jack shouted, above the din. 'Look what I found!'

'What have you found?'

Jack turned the volume down. 'The little red bottle! She left it behind.'

'The acid?' said Charlie, horrified.

'It's not acid, Charlie,' said Leah. '. . . Anyway, I don't think so.'

'How do you know? How do you know?'

'Jack told me.'

Jack had told Leah, and not him! That really hurt. It was his own fault, for losing his bottle – Charlie accepted that. But it was Leah's fault too, it was. He knew what she was up to! Always trying to push herself in, and push him out.

'It's nail polish, like I said,' said Jack, triumphantly. 'It says it on the bottle, I was right all the time!'

'Let's forget about that, now,' said Leah. 'Yesterday is over – let's not talk about it, eh?'

'Why?' said Jack. 'It's interesting. It's fascinating, actually.'

'Yeah, it is,' said Charlie. 'It's interesting. It's interesting and fascinating.' His voice came thickly, through the stuffy nose.

'I wonder if they made their getaway yet,' said

Jack. 'Their real getaway, I mean. They only had the night so far, but I expect they made a start.'

'Where do you think they're going to?' said Charlie, encouraged that Jack was actually talking to him.

'Oh, to another country, of course,' said Jack. 'In a boat. In The Boss's boat, I expect.'

'That's what *I* think, as well,' said Charlie. 'They must have went in The Boss's boat, to—'

'Shut *up*, Charlie!' Jack interrupted. 'The News is coming now!'

He turned up the volume, and they all listened. There was a lot of boring stuff about The Economy, and The Pound, and Interest Rates. There was some stuff about hungry people in Africa, and fighting people somewhere else, and there was a hurricane going to come, in the Caribbean. Nothing at all about a van called *Hideaway*, and three missing children.

'The radio people don't know about us yet,' said Leah. She wasn't sure whether to be glad or sorry. It was frightening being in this wilderness, but there were frightening things to do with home as well; things Leah didn't want to think about; things she had decided *not* to think about.

Jack was restless. 'Let's go outside, now.'

'*Jack!*' said Leah. 'The wild *animals!*'

'*I'm* not scared of no wild animals,' said Charlie, eagerly.

Jack regarded Charlie, and considered. All right, he decided, he would be kind to Charlie, he would give him one more chance. 'Let's just have a look for these wild animals, then. Let's look out the windows. You do the back ones, Charlie, and I'll do the high-up one over the bed.'

They looked, very carefully, and in the dark light of a rain-sodden sky saw only the emptiness and desolation they had seen before. Jack tried the nearside door, but there was a tree or something blocking it. He opened the door by the driver's seat, where there seemed to be a space. 'Who's coming, then?'

'I think we should turn the radio off first,' said Leah. 'You know – to save the electricity. And I wish you would take those wet trousers with you, Charlie. They're all dripping, and making a mess.'

Charlie's cheeks flamed. She said that on purpose, didn't she! Just to shame him in front of Jack. If they had to be kidnapped, why did *Leah* have to be in it? Why couldn't it just have been him and Jack?

Jack jumped off the high step and on to the ground. It was not actually raining, but everything outside was very wet. Grass and leaves spattered water drops; the air was damp, and very raw. Jack moved round the van, and the sound of his footsteps was the only sound there was.

Hideaway had come to rest in a slight hollow, lodged with her nose buried in a clump of small trees. On its descent, the van had crashed so hard against the trees in its path as to smash them partly down, making a sort of prop for the front end. *Hideaway* was tipped slightly forward, and slightly to the left, with her rear on mossy grass, her white top rising nobly above a mass of leafy branches.

Charlie emerged, and scurried into the trees to spread his washing carefully out of sight. His disgrace thus hidden, and hopefully soon forgotten, Charlie's cockiness began to return. 'Come on, Leah, come on out! What's the matter, Leah, you too scared?' He hoped she was. It would really put her in bottom place, wouldn't it, if she was too scared to come out. '*I'm* not scared, am I, Jack?'

'I don't think there's anything to be scared *of*,' said Jack. 'I think that Boss is a liar. He's just a liar; he made it up. Just to keep us from finding our own way home. To give them more time for their getaway.'

'Can we find our way home then, Jack?' said Charlie, a great hope leaping.

'I dunno. Let's look down the bottom of this hill.'

'I don't think we should go so far,' said Leah, nervously.

'Don't take no notice of her,' said Charlie.

'I'm not,' said Jack. 'We can't find out if we don't look. There might be a house down there. Or a road.'

'But it's a wilderness,' Leah objected. 'There's nothing here for miles.'

'How do you know?' said Jack.

'Yeah,' said Charlie. 'How do you know?'

'. . . I think somebody said.' Leah knew very well who had said it really, but found she still couldn't bring herself to pronounce any of those names.

'Well, I'm going to find out for myself,' said Jack.

'Yeah,' said Charlie. 'I'm going to find out for myself as well.'

The boys ploughed downhill, through a sea of ferns. Leah trailed behind them for a few metres, then stopped. 'I think I best get back and do the washing up.'

'You just say that because you're scared,' Charlie jeered. 'Leah's scared! Leah's scared!' He was delighted that it was Leah who was scared now, not him.

'All right, I am. . . . But I got to do the washing up as well. Somebody has. I don't see you offering, Charlie.' She turned to climb again, and gave a sudden scream. 'The animals! The wild animals, they're coming!'

They had appeared out of nowhere – two groups of four-legged creatures, way up towards the skyline, and seemingly not moving. The children raced for the van.

Safely inside, they peered through the back window, but the angle of the slope outside cut off their view.

'Did you see them, Jack?' said Leah. 'Did you see what sort of animals they are?'

'Not really.'

'Perhaps they're lions,' said Charlie. 'Or tigers.' Faced with the reality of wild animals, he was not sure how brave he was expected to be; but surely it was all right to be scared of lions and tigers.

'I don't think they're lions,' said Jack. 'They looked more like horses to me.'

'I think they're lions,' said Leah.

'I think they're horses,' said Charlie.

'Well, you can think what you like,' said Leah. 'I think they're lions, and I'm not going outside no more, no way. I don't want to be ate for their dinner!'

Jack's fingers drummed restlessly on the table top. 'We can't stay inside all the time, though, it's going to be boring.' He went to the front and switched on the radio again. 'It's boring,' he said, again.

'Well, *I'm* not bored,' said Leah. 'I got plenty to

do. I got the washing up, and all these cupboards to sort out.' Enough to keep her from thinking about anything else all day, she comforted herself.

'What you wanna sort out the cupboards *for,* though?'

'Because they're all messy. I would be ashamed, you know, to have messy cupboards like this. My mum wouldn't have messy cupboards like this, we have everything all neat and tidy in—' Leah stopped, suddenly. Home was one of the things she didn't want to think about, wasn't it? 'Anyway, I got too much to do for wasting time in chattering!' she finished.

Jack played with the radio, switching from station to station. There didn't seem to be any more News. Charlie sat at the table, watching the window anxiously, and pretending not to. 'I'm going out again,' said Jack.

'You want to be ate, then?' said Leah.

'I can keep a lookout. You coming, Charlie?'

Charlie sneezed. He was grateful to the sneeze, because it gave him an idea; he tried to make another one come. 'Actually, I think I best stay inside. I've got a cold, actually.'

'Fresh air is good for colds, though,' said Leah.

'No, it's not.'

'I think it *is*. Because of the germs.'

'A cold is nothing anyway,' said Jack. 'Fancy making a fuss about a little thing like a cold!' He opened one of the back swing windows. 'That's a good idea,' said Leah. 'Get some fresh air for Charlie's germs. . . . Mind the lions don't put their heads in, though!' she added, in some alarm.

Jack leaned out, so he could see right to the top

of the slope. 'It's all right, they're not coming any nearer.'

'They might, though,' said Charlie.

'You chicken, then?' said Jack.

Charlie wished he hadn't said that about the lions coming near. ''Course I'm not chicken!'

'I think you are.'

'I'm not, I'm not. OK, I'll prove it, I'll come out with you! I'll go out *first!* . . . Are they really still, then, are you sure? . . . OK, watch me! Are you watching? . . . Right, I'm going out *now!*'

Charlie tumbled out of the van, and Jack followed. Their eyes scanned the horizon all around, but the animals were where they had been, small in the distance, unthreatening. Jack ran, and jumped, and cartwheeled over the grass, and Charlie tried to copy.

Leah watched them through the window. She was uneasy that the boys were outside, and hoped they wouldn't go far. One good thing, though – now the boys were gone, she could take the opportunity to have a good wash. She worried about using too much water, but you have to be clean! She went back to her cupboards, and her feverish busy-ness.

It was going to take a nice long time to get those cupboards really organised, Leah thought. Already she had sorted out the tins from the packets, but there was plenty left to do. There were the knives and forks and spoons to be collected, for instance, and put all together in the drawer underneath the cooker. There was the tall cupboard next to the toilet to be tackled. Inside that was more food, mixed up with plates and shoes and various odds and ends. And when all that was finished, something must be done about the piles of clothes on the high-up bed, so she and Jack and Charlie could sleep comfortably tonight . . . If they didn't get rescued . . . which they probably wouldn't.

The sleeves of George's pullover were a nuisance. They kept unrolling themselves, and Leah had to keep stopping to push them back. As she did so for the tenth time, her eyes went to the back window – and widened, in sudden terror. For a moment, she was too frightened to move. Then she opened her mouth, and screamed, and screamed, and screamed.

There were three of them, and they were very near – just a few metres beyond the open back window of the van. Leah ran to pull the window shut, then cowered at the front of the van, covering her eyes from the dreadful sight.

Horses! They *were* horses, not lions or tigers, and that was some comfort. They were not even very big, as horses go. But horses could bite and kick and trample, couldn't they? Even little ones could do that. Perhaps they could eat people as well, she didn't really know. Wild ones could eat people perhaps, fierce ones! Leah screamed again, but there was no one to hear her.

Jack and Charlie! What about Jack and Charlie! They hadn't come running back; where were they? Had the horses eaten Jack and Charlie? Oh, no, don't let Jack and Charlie be eaten! *Please* don't let Jack and Charlie be eaten, to leave me all alone in this wilderness!

She crept to the back again; she made herself look.

The horses were still there, but moving steadily away now. There was a black one, and a sandy one, and a white one with dark patches. They were shaggy, with short legs, and although they were small for horses, they were large enough to be very alarming. There was no sign of the boys at all. Trembling, Leah climbed on to the bed, but there was no sign of them from the high-up window either.

They were gone! They were eaten! She was never going to see either of them again!

As a matter of fact, Jack and Charlie had *not* been eaten. As a matter of fact, they had not even seen the horses, yet. 'Let's go down the hill again,' Jack had said.

'OK.' There was a sinking feeling in the pit of Charlie's stomach, but there was no way he was going to let Jack see that.

'Let's go all the way down. Let's see what's at the bottom. Let's really find it out this time.'

'OK.'

Charlie wanted to remind Jack that they should keep a lookout for the wild animals, but decided it would seem braver not to mention it. His head turned nervously this way and that, and he lagged slightly behind, so Jack wouldn't see him looking.

Down they plunged, through the bracken. The going was very steep; Charlie's head swivelled right around – *Hideaway* was completely out of sight now, hidden behind a mass of trees. Charlie's uneasiness grew, but he managed to force a sort of whistle as they went. Don't let Jack see he was scared, don't let Jack see!

'Get that!' said Jack, suddenly.

'What is it?'

'Are you blind or something? It's a *river*!'

'Oh, yeah, I can see it now.' Charlie tried really hard to concentrate on Jack's river. 'It's good. It's a good river. Yeah, I like the look of that river.'

'Come on, let's go right down.'

Charlie wanted to say he thought they should turn back now. He wanted to say he was happy about the river, but saw no need to see it closer. He wanted to say he thought it was very likely going to rain again. He wanted to say that his throat was sore and he wasn't, as it happened, feeling very well. He wanted to say all those things, but what he actually said was, 'OK, that's a good idea.'

Down, down, down. Furtively, Charlie turned his head once more. The scream came before he could stop it.

'What's up?'

'It's them! It's the animals!'

'Oh, *sugar!*'

'What shall we do? What shall we do?'

Jack bit his lip, and frowned. 'Run, I suppose.'

'Where to, where to?'

'Where do you think? Back to the van.'

'I don't know where it is. I can't see it. And the animals are in the way; they're coming after us. They're coming after us, Jack! They're coming, they're coming, what shall we do?'

'Get down!' said Jack.

'What?'

'Get down! In the ferns. Crawl along in the ferns, so they don't see where we go.'

'I can't!'

The three horses were still some way off, but advancing steadily. Jack threw himself full length, and began to wriggle along on his stomach. He turned to see if Charlie was following. 'What's the matter with you, stupid? Get down!'

'I can't!' Charlie wailed. 'It's no good, they're going to get us anyway!'

'All right, stay there!' Jack was on his hands and knees now, and making faster progress through the bracken. 'Stay there and let them catch you!' he threw at Charlie, over his shoulder. 'I'm getting out of here!'

Helplessly, Charlie watched him go. His own legs had turned to stone, paralysed with fright. Charlie watched Jack getting farther and farther away, and *still* he couldn't move. He saw the horses coming nearer and nearer, and he closed his eyes against the terrifying sight. With pounding heart he stood there, waiting without resistance for the attack.

He heard their hooves in the bracken, and one of them made a neighing sound. Charlie's breath came in great shuddering sobs. This was it, it was coming now. Now!

. . . *Now!*

The sound of the hooves was fainter. . . . Was it possible? . . . *Was* it? Shaking all over now, his knees like wobbly jelly, Charlie dared to open his eyes.

They were gone!

They hadn't attacked him at all. They had walked right past him. They were going after Jack instead! If Jack thought the ferns were hiding him he was wrong, because the ferns were doing no such thing. His back and his bottom were clearly visible, bobbing up and down, as he scuttled along. And the horses were moving steadily in his direction.

Did Jack realise it? Had he seen?

Charlie wanted to scramble for the van. He

could have done it now – the horses were no longer in his path. But his legs, no longer frozen with fear, were still too weak for running. Fascinated, and horrified, Charlie watched the horses gaining ground on Jack.

Suddenly, Jack stopped. He had seen the horses all right, or heard them. What would he do? What *could* he do? Sick with dread, Charlie watched.

For a few moments, Jack did nothing. Then his long graceful body sprang into action. He leapt to his feet, and even from this distance, Charlie heard him shouting. 'Go away! Go away!'

The moving horses stopped in their tracks, and looked at Jack. 'Go *away!*' The horses went on standing, and looking at Jack. Jack bent. He picked something up, a stone perhaps, and threw it. The horses backed nervously. Jack waved his arms and yelled. 'Go away, *go away!*' He threw another stone and, amazingly, made a few lunging steps towards the fearsome creatures. 'I SAID "GO AWAY"!'

The horses, all three of them, turned tail and galloped off.

Jack danced in the bracken. He clapped his hands, and yelled his triumph at the wet grey sky. 'I did it! Yippee! I made them go, I did it!'

Slowly, with a new dread now, Charlie made his way towards Jack. 'I wasn't *really* scared,' he tried to say. 'I know it *looked* like I was scared, but I wasn't really!'

Jack barely glanced at him.

'I was going to shout at them myself, actually,' Charlie insisted. 'Only you done it first.'

Jack shrugged. 'Yeah!' he said, pityingly. 'I *bet!*'

'I'm not scared of them really.' Shame tugging at his heart, Charlie pleaded to be believed.

Jack shrugged again. 'Why should you be? It's them that's scared of *us.*'

'Next time,' said Charlie. 'I'll be the one to drive them away.' Jack began to climb the hill, and Charlie trailed miserably after him. 'Shall I, Jack? OK? Shall I be the one to drive them away next time? . . . Anyway, I bet Leah will still be afraid of the silly old wild animals. Only me and you know they're not really wild at all, don't we, Jack?'

Jack did not bother to answer. They climbed in silence. Charlie struggled to keep pace, but the effort was too much for his frail physique, and laboured breathing. He lagged farther and farther behind.

When eventually he pulled himself into *Hideaway*, panting and lonely, Jack was already explaining things for the fourth time to a disbelieving Leah. 'I tell you we're *free.* We can go out when we like. We can go wherever we like . . . we can go home, in fact.'

'Home?' said Leah, faintly.

'Well, we don't want to stay here, do we?' Jack waved his arms at the windows, indicating the bleakness all around them. 'Not in this wilderness! No way.'

7

A good try

Leah was confused. 'I thought we supposed to wait till they find us.' She wasn't sure that was the right thing to do, but it was what she would have preferred.

'That's only what The Boss said,' said Jack. 'Forget about that liar, we don't have to be ruled by *him*!'

'But it's a long way. We can't walk all the way.'

'Well, we won't have to. Not *all* the way. We just have to walk till we find someone, that's all. And tell them what happened. And they will tell the police, and the police will take us home in their car.'

'But it's miles and miles to find anyone.'

'*That's* only what The Boss said, as well. That liar. There might be a house quite near, really. We just have to walk till we come to it. It'll be easy, trust me!'

'*I* trust you,' said Charlie.

Leah frowned. '. . . I dunno, though . . . I haven't finished tidying the cupboards, actually.'

'Don't be stupid!' said Jack.

'Yeah,' said Charlie. 'Don't be stupid, Leah!'

Jack turned on him. 'Don't you call Leah stupid! Leah's not stupid, actually. She's in my class at school, so I ought to know if she's stupid or not, and she's not, she's very intelligent, so there!'

Humiliated again! Charlie turned his head, and swallowed the lump in his throat.

Leah was mildly flattered by Jack's compliment, but the effect of what he had said was mainly to bring a vivid picture of school into her mind. She loved school, and she loved her teacher. She thought about her friends, and all the lessons she most liked. Was it really possible that only this time yesterday she had been safe in school? How wonderful, if she could be back in school this minute!

Home, now – that was a different matter. There were frightening things waiting for her at home, weren't there? Leah wasn't letting herself think about what they were, but the awareness of bad things waiting for her at home hung like a dark menacing cloud at the back of her mind. If she went home, she would have to face those nameless troubles, whereas if she stayed here, she could put them off. Besides, she was beginning to feel rather safe in *Hideaway*. Why leave it, for all sorts of unknown perils?

But Jack said they were to go, and there was really no arguing with that. With a sigh of resignation, Leah rolled up the sleeves of George's pullover once again. 'Did we ought to, like, take some food for on the way?'

Jack was impatient to be off. 'Don't be silly, Leah, we won't need any food! The police will give us some dinner. The police are good for that, you know. Even the criminals get their dinner at the police station, didn't you know?'

'That's right,' said Charlie, still desperately trying. 'Didn't you know that, Leah?' He retied the string to stop George's shorts from falling down. Jack's slender frame was lost in George's jacket.

The three scarecrows in their borrowed clothes tumbled out of the van, and regarded the wilderness and each other.

'Which way?' said Leah. Not that it mattered, she thought. Whichever way they went, they were bound to come to something unpleasant.

'Well, we already been down,' said Jack. 'There's nothing down there, only a river.'

'That's right,' said Charlie. 'There's only a river down there.'

Leah peered upwards. 'It's very steep,' she said, doubtfully.

'But we know there's a road up there,' said Jack. 'We know there's a road up there, because of yesterday.'

'I don't want to think about yesterday,' said Leah.

'Well you don't have to think about it. I'll do the thinking, and you just trust me!'

They climbed. Leah's legs began to ache; she paused to look around her. 'I can't help thinking about one thing. I can't help think about how did the van come down here? Like, I know there's a road up *there*, but there isn't a road *here*, for it to drive on.'

'It come over the grass,' said Charlie. 'It come over the grass bits, didn't it, Jack?'

'You got it!'

He had said something right! Jack had praised him, for something he said! Charlie felt his spirits rising, and he made a great effort to keep up with the others. The effort took all his strength, but he managed it for a while.

Jack began to bound ahead. 'Come on! Come

on, you two! Who says we'll be back in London today?'

Since neither of the others had any breath to reply, Jack answered his own question, calling back over his shoulder. 'Anyway, I say we'll be back in London today, and I just thought of something else good. Know what I thought? . . . Guess what I thought! . . . All right, I'll *tell* you what I thought: WE'RE GOING TO BE FAMOUS!'

Leah looked up in amazement. '*Us*?'

'Yeah, us, us! We're going to be on the telly!'

Leah panted, then drew a deep breath to shout with. 'I don't believe it!'

'Trust me! We'll be famous because we got kidnapped. People that are kidnapped always get famous afterwards, so how about that, then?'

'Fancy us famous!' Leah marvelled.

Charlie had dropped a long way behind, but he heard the bit about getting famous, and being on the telly, and that cheered him greatly. Things were getting better and better now. He would like to be on the telly, he would be proud. His mum would be proud to see him on the telly, as well.

His mum.

Charlie had hardly thought about his mum today; he had been too busy thinking about his wet trousers, and about being attacked by wild animals, and about Jack liking Leah better than him. Indeed, he didn't often think about his mum's feelings at all, being mostly concerned with his own. He thought about his mum's feelings now, though, and was surprised to find how much it hurt to do that. His mum would be worried just now, wouldn't she! His mum would be crying. And he didn't want his mum to cry, he *didn't.*

The grass patch veered off at an angle. Leah thought it would be quicker to the top if she went through the ferns. She made to carve a short cut, but found her feet sinking into bog. 'It's all squelchy, I don't like it!' She tried to extricate herself, and her feet sank deeper still. 'Help me!' she was alarmed, now. Visions of people being sucked into quicksands rose before her eyes. They got sucked right down, didn't they, even their heads, and were never seen again. 'Help me!' she called, again.

Jack stood at the top and laughed at her. 'You stuck, then?'

'It's not funny!'

'It looks funny from here. Come on, I found the road!'

Leah dragged first one foot and then the other out of the bog. She was much relieved to find she was not going to be drowned in mud after all. With difficulty, she plodded back to the grass patch, and scrambled to the top. 'It's not a road, though, it's just a sort of track.'

'It's the stony bit,' said Jack. 'Remember the stony bit, when we come off the proper road? Well, this is it.'

Leah shied away from the memory. 'It's starting to rain,' she said.

'Don't matter. Look what I just seen. There's a house!'

'There can't be!'

'All right, what's that, then? Down that hill, what's that?'

'It's a house,' Leah admitted.

'Come on, let's go and tell the people about we were kidnapped.'

'In a minute. Wait for Charlie. Charlie's not come yet.'

'Oh, *him*!' Jack turned, and began sprinting, alone, along the track. Leah hesitated a moment, then stood looking down the way they had come. Far below was *Hideaway*, its white top and rear end sticking out from among the trees. And not quite so far was Charlie, struggling slowly, slowly, more slowly – staggering as best he could up the slope.

At the top, he collapsed entirely. His breathing came in noisy gasps. He gasped, and gasped, and couldn't seem to stop. Leah regarded him with some concern. 'You OK?'

Charlie found his breath. 'Course I'm OK. Don't go on about if I'm OK, of *course* I am.'

He was OK, Charlie told himself, he *was*. There was a nasty little fear, a new one, twitching away at the back of his mind. But Charlie pushed the fear away.

That wasn't going to happen again. It wasn't. He was a big boy now, he was growing out of it. Anyway, of course he couldn't tell anyone because that was his secret.

'I don't usually get out of breath like this,' he claimed.

'Oh, right,' said Leah, doubtfully. 'Is it because of your cold then?'

'Yeah – well, don't make a fuss about my cold. A cold is nothing to make a fuss about.'

'All right, I won't make a fuss about your cold.' Leah set off along the track after Jack. The rain was coming down quite steadily now, and she couldn't see Jack at all. She began to run; then, conscious that he was not with her, she glanced over her shoulder to look for Charlie. He was coming, but moving slowly through the rain, a long way behind. Leah turned back. 'You all right?'

'Course I'm all right.' He coughed as he spoke, though, and again Leah felt uneasy.

'You going to get all wet if you don't hurry.'

'Don't matter. I *like* getting wet. That's why I'm walking slow, because I like getting wet.'

'You didn't ought to get wet with a cold, though.'

'Why don't you mind your own business?'

'Oh, all right, *be* like that!'

Leah ran ahead again, then turned once more. Charlie was still plodding, his hair soaked now, the rain trickling over his small sharp face. Leah stood, and waited for him to catch up. 'Can't you walk any faster than that?'

'Course I can if I want to. I don't want to, though. I *like* walking slow.'

'I don't believe you.'

'Do you want me to spit in your face?'

'How rude!'

Much offended, Leah charged ahead. She wished she could see Jack. She knew she was going the right way, because the house they were aiming for was still just visible through the rain, but it wasn't very nice having to walk all by herself, with only that nasty little thing tagging on behind.

Charlie wished he could see Jack as well. He was pushing his legs as fast as they would go, but he was exhausted from the climb, and beginning to feel quite unwell. The soreness at the back of his throat was worse; his throat felt as though someone had been scraping it with sandpaper. And to make matters worse, there was the rain trickling icily down the neck of Lil's cardigan, and fat Leah annoying him, and sticking her nose in!

The path curved to the left, and dipped suddenly. Leah's feet skidded over the stones. She began to wonder what sort of people lived in the house they were going to. They must be funny people, actually, to want to live in the middle of a wilderness. Come to think of it, they must be very strange people indeed.

Perhaps they were witches, or something like that. Perhaps they were vampires – she had read about vampires in a story once, and the idea had sickened and horrified her for weeks afterwards. Perhaps the people in the house weren't people at all, perhaps they were ghosts! Or aliens from another planet. Perhaps the aliens, or the ghosts, had captured Jack, and that was why she couldn't see him any more.

Leah turned her head for a reassuring look at *Hideaway*, down below, and found that now *Hideaway* was out of sight as well. She stood alone in the rain, and felt the fear closing in.

Charlie also, just beginning the downhill bit, had discovered that *Hideaway* was out of sight, and his pride trickled away with the rain. In spite of his tiredness he began to run, slithering and slipping over the stones, and calling to Leah, 'Wait for me, then; wait for me!'

I suppose she's better than nothing, Charlie thought. And Leah thought, I suppose Charlie's better than nothing. She held out her hand, and Charlie took it. Together they went, in silence down the hill.

They were almost there. The building in front of them was very still. 'Jack must have went inside,' said Leah, speaking at last.

'Yeah, he must have.'

'What shall we do, Charlie?'

'I dunno.'

There was a tumbledown low wall, and a rusty gate, and a patch of weeds overgrowing what had once been a path. There were no curtains at the windows, some of which were broken, and all of which were filthy. 'It must be very poor people live in this house,' said Charlie, hoping they were only poor, and not cruel, or wicked, or weird.

'Perhaps they're just lazy,' said Leah. 'And can't be bothered to keep it nice.'

'Did we ought to knock at the door?'

'Actually, I'm a bit nervous, Charlie. Are *you* a bit nervous?'

'What, *me*? Nah!' With thumping heart but bravely, Charlie stumped over the weeds and banged with his fists on the door. What a pity Jack couldn't see him, being braver than Leah. He must make sure Jack found out that Charlie had been brave, when Leah was afraid.

There was no response to Charlie's knock.

The door was slightly ajar. Really daring now, Charlie put his head round and shouted, 'Anybody at home?'

Still no response.

'It's ghosts, it is!' said Leah, in sudden panic. 'The ghosts have got Jack! Come on, Charlie, let's run!'

They ran, hand in hand again, scuttling like frightened rabbits down the path. Charlie began to stumble and gasp, and Leah dragged him faster.

'Come back!'

Leah turned. 'Jack! . . . Didn't the ghosts get you then?'

'Don't be silly, Leah, there's no ghosts.'

'What about the people?'

'There's no people.' His poor scratched face showed hurt, and disappointment. '... I suppose they could have gone shopping.'

Leah looked again at the cracked and dirty windows, and reality dawned. 'It's a empty house, isn't it?'

'No, not empty. Not really *empty*.... There's some chairs, come and see!'

Inside the house, the cobwebs hung like net curtains everywhere. There was dirt, and holes in the floorboards, and paper hanging off the walls in damp strips. There was a musty smell – an old, dead sort of smell. The few bits of furniture were falling to pieces.

'It's a deserted house,' said Leah, sadly.

'I know,' Jack admitted. '... What did they want to desert it for? What did they want to go and do that for?'

'It's a tumbledown house,' Leah pointed out. 'The rain is coming in.'

'They could mend it! I hope their new home is a lot worse than this one. I hope their new house got mice in it. And rats. And blackbeetles.'

'Anyway,' Leah sighed. 'We come all this way for nothing.' It was better than finding ghosts, she supposed, but a big let-down after all that excitement.

'Aren't we going home after all, then?' Suddenly Charlie felt colder, and smaller, as though his whole self had shrunk with his hopes.

'Yes, we are, we *are*!' said Jack.

Leah frowned, and stuck out her lip. 'How, though?'

'Trust me!'

'I wish you wouldn't keep saying that! Why do we have to trust you all the time?'

'Because I'm the one that knows what to do. We just have to walk some more, that's what!'

Charlie sat down heavily on a dirty chair with the springs coming through. Water ran down his shins, and into his shoes. There was nothing inside him, he thought, but emptiness and dread.

'It's raining,' Leah pointed out.

'That's nothing to make a fuss about,' said Jack.

'What are we supposed to do, then?'

'All right, I'll tell you. It's all right, I can see it now. The first thing is, we have to go back the way we come.'

'You mean you made us come the wrong way.'

'It was only a little mistake.'

'You told us wrong, though. And you said to trust you.'

'Well, you *can* trust me. For instance, did you notice this is the end of the track?'

'No,' said Leah. 'It's raining.'

'See? You can trust me to notice things. You didn't notice it, and I did. That means you can trust me.'

'All right, you noticed it's the end of the track. What about it?'

'Well what about it is, what about it is – if we go the other way, and keep going and keep going. If we do that we're going to come to the real road, aren't we?'

'It's raining though . . . And I think it's going to be a long way.'

'But we know the road is there. We know it for definite, because that's the road we must have come off of yesterday. When we was tied up in the van, remember? And there can be cars, and people in them. And we can tell somebody that we been kidnapped. And they can tell the police and the television people. And it will all happen just like I said.'

'It's raining a lot,' said Leah. 'And Charlie's not well; he's got a cold.'

'I'm OK,' said Charlie. 'A cold is nothing to make a fuss about.'

'You didn't ought to get too wet. It's bad for the germs.'

'I tell you I'm all right!' Charlie struggled to his feet, swallowing on the emptiness and dread, clinging desperately to thoughts of home. He ached for concrete and traffic fumes; for bright lights and fire-engines and police sirens; for the comfort of close horizons instead of all this horrid space.

'Let's go, then,' said Jack.

Outside the tumbledown house, the rain was without pity, really heavy now. The rain made all of them slow, not just Charlie. In seconds, it was whipping the children through their ill-fitting clothes, beating on their heads and against their faces. It stung their eyes, blurring the landscape into a sea of grey-green ripples, without shape or meaning.

'I'm hungry, actually,' Jack admitted.

'That's because it's dinner time,' said Leah.

'Why didn't we bring any food with us?'

'Because you said not to. You said the police would give us some dinner. Only we haven't found any police yet.'

'All right, all right.'

They trudged on.

'Look,' said Jack. 'I can see *Hideaway* down there!'

'I can see it too,' said Leah.

'There's food in *Hideaway*,' said Jack, thoughtfully.

'I know. A load of it.'

'. . . I had an idea. How about we go down and have some dinner, and come back up again after.'

'Oh, *no*!' Charlie wailed. It was too much. Not that hill again, not that dreadful hill!

'I think it's not a bad idea, Charlie,' said Leah.

'I don't want to, though. I want to go home!'

'After we ate,' said Jack.

'No! I wanna go now!'

'Go on by yourself, then. No one's stopping you.'

Jack slithered and jumped down the hillside, through the lashing rain. Leah plodded after, not sure if she was doing right or wrong, but following Jack anyway. And Charlie came too, a long way behind.

Charlie wasn't hungry. In spite of his tiredness, all Charlie wanted was to be on his way. But he couldn't do it alone; there was no way he could brave this wilderness all by himself. This wilderness was like a great wavy sea, washing over him, trying to suck him under. If he didn't have the others to hold on to, he would drown.

The van was warm, though, and cosy. Even Charlie was conscious of its warmth and cosiness. The seats were a shabby grey, but there were yellow and red cushions, and the curtains had a bright yellow and red pattern on them. There were dry clothes as well, plenty of them. Jack and Leah quite enjoyed themselves, deciding who would wear what, and laughing at one another's peculiar appearance. 'It's good we come back,' said Jack. 'I bet you're glad we come back now, Charlie. Come on, say you're glad!'

'All right, I'm glad,' said Charlie, not meaning it.

Leah foraged in the food cupboard. 'There's a very lot of tins. Shall we have stewed steak and mashed potato with it?' She was happy to be useful and busy, with the rain and the cold and the fear shut safely away outside. 'And we can have cake for afters.'

Leah found matches in the drawer, and after a few mistakes managed to get the gas jets alight. There was a tin opener, which Leah didn't know how to work. 'Give it here,' said Jack. He got the lid off the tin without difficulty, but said the rest was Leah's job. Leah didn't mind; she *wanted* the rest to be her job. She found forks and spoons, and enough plates after all. There was only water to drink but then Leah had the brilliant idea of making tea, which was really warming and nice, with lots of sugar. There were even, surprise surprise, enough cups for them to have one each, and Leah said it was a good thing she made tea really, since the water from the can might have germs in it, you never could tell, but tea was safe to drink because the water had been boiled.

Charlie drank his tea, but pecked at his food. 'When are we going, then? Are we going soon?'

'Not yet,' said Leah. 'I haven't done the washing up.'

'You don't *have* to do the washing up,' said Charlie. 'We aren't coming back, so you don't have to do the washing up.'

'Course she has to do the washing up,' said Jack. 'Don't be stupid, Charlie, 'course Leah has to do the washing up.' He was warm, and full, and comfortable, and in no hurry to move. He sat in the driver's seat, and was about to switch on the radio when he noticed something interesting – The Boss had left George's keys in the ignition! Could he start the engine, perhaps, *could* he? He turned the key, but there was only a reluctant grumbling noise. He turned it back and tried again, but the same thing happened. Jack looked for other knobs and levers to play with. He found the switch for the headlights and amused himself for a few minutes flicking them on and off until he remembered about not running the battery down. Not that it mattered now, or did it . . .?

'Are we going now, then?' said Charlie.

'In a minute,' said Jack. It was still raining. They could hear the rain drumming on the roof, and see through the windows how it sliced through the greyness outside.

'When we get to the road,' said Charlie, 'will we wave to a car and make it stop?'

'Yeah,' said Jack, still fiddling with the knobs on the dashboard. There was one that could be pulled out and pushed back again. Jack did that a few times, but there was limited fun in the exercise, and he finally left the knob half in and half out.

'Oh, *Jack*!' said Leah, in sudden dismay. 'I just now thought.'

'What?'

'We can't stop a car, there can be Strangers in cars!'

'Oh, *them*.'

'But it's true, we could get kidnapped again!'

Jack considered. 'We shall have to take a chance.'

Leah was shocked all over again. '*Jack!* We not supposed to go in cars with people we don't know! Look what happened when—'

Charlie was sick with anxiety. 'How we going to get home, then?'

'Oh, we'll find a way,' said Jack, not terribly interested for the moment. 'Somehow.'

'Not in a car,' said Leah, firmly.

'All right, we don't have to go *in* the car,' said Jack. 'We can just tell the people, and they can tell the police. Or we'll find somebody that's not in a car. Or we'll find a house – a real house this time, not a tumbledown house.'

But Leah's fears were falling over themselves to multiply. 'Don't Strangers live in houses, then? There might be Strangers in the houses.'

'Nah – people in houses are all right,' said Jack.

'Yeah, they are, they are,' said Charlie. 'People in houses are all right, they *are*.'

'Actually,' said Leah. 'I don't think we're supposed to speak to Strangers at all!'

'There might be a police car,' said Jack. Hadn't The Boss or someone mentioned police cars?

Charlie felt the relief flooding through him. It would be all right, they could find a police car. 'Shall we go now, then, and look for one?'

'It's raining,' said Leah.

'Yeah, wait till it stops raining,' said Jack.

Charlie peered hopefully through the window. 'I think it's stopping now.'

Leah peered through the window as well. 'It's not stopping, it's worse than ever. It's getting dark, too. It looks like it's getting to be night again.'

His mum would have come home from work, Charlie thought. His mum would have come home from work, and found him not there! Tears pricked in his eyes. 'It's not night, it's the rain. It's only the rain, making it dark.'

'Hang about,' said Jack. 'There's a clock here.'

'What time is it, then?'

'You'll never guess!'

'Well, it can't be late really, we only just now had our dinner.'

'I think we had our dinner at tea time. I think we got up at dinner time and didn't notice. . . . It's nearly six o'clock!' He flicked the ignition key over one last time for luck – and to his amazement and delight the engine sputtered, then roared into life.

Charlie's heart leapt with sudden hope. 'It's going! Are you going to *drive* us home then, Jack?'

'No don't, don't!' said Leah, in alarm. 'Don't try to drive the van, Jack, we can have an accident!'

'I would drive it if I could,' said Jack. 'But the thing is, I don't know how. I mean, I don't know how to make it move. You have to do things with the pedals and the gears, and The Boss only learned me some of it.'

In his heart, he didn't really want to *drive* the van. At any rate, not at the moment. He would be just a little bit frightened to do that, all by himself. Another day, perhaps. . . . For the moment it was exciting enough that the engine was running. It was so exciting, Jack could hardly believe it. Here he sat, in a real van, holding a real steering wheel, and feeling a real engine going because *he made it go*. What power! What delicious power!

His engine! *His* steering wheel! *His van.*

Jack felt lit up; every bit of him tingled with joy. London was all right, but what was there in London compared to this? What was there to go back for, actually? A home where he wasn't really wanted, that's what. A stepfather who didn't like him, and a mum who cared a lot more for his stepfather than she ever had for him. . . . All right, there were some good things in London, but they could wait. He couldn't give up this engine, not just yet.

'Tell you what,' he said to the others. 'Let's not go home tonight after all. Let's wait till tomorrow!'

8

The miracle

Leah awoke.

What? . . . What? . . . Where was she?

For a moment she lay confused – then suddenly, everything flashed into place. What was more, she found her thoughts untangled, all the threads lying neatly side by side.

Yesterday she had been muddled, but this morning she was not muddled at all. This morning she saw quite clearly that she had been wrong to want to stay in this place and wait to be found. Of course, of *course*, the three of them must do all they could to get home as soon as possible, because their mums were going to be worried about them. Granted, there was a beating to come, and Leah wasn't looking forward to that; but it was right to go home and face it, because she deserved to be punished, after all. And now she started thinking about it like that, she couldn't wait to be done with the punishment and have it over.

And if Jack wanted to delay the start, playing with his silly old engine, she would hide the keys or something, she *would*.

Her eyes still closed, Leah turned on the high bed, and was instantly aware of golden light playing over her face. 'It's too bright,' Jack muttered, half asleep.

Charlie lifted his head. Because there wasn't room for the three of them to lie comfortably side by side, Charlie had spent the night curled up at the feet of the other two. He had cried himself to sleep, softly and privately, longing for morning to come. And what a morning! Charlie shielded his eyes from the glory, and sneezed.

Jack propped himself on his elbow to look out of the high-up window. 'It's a miracle!' he said, in awe.

'What happened?' Leah squinted through half-opened lids, and saw how the sunbeams slanted over her, and into the dimness below.

'It must be a miracle,' said Jack. 'It's come all beautiful in the night.'

The great outside was not grey and rain-soaked any more, but green and gold and blue, and bathed in brilliant light. The sky was dazzling; tree-tops glistened and sparkled; the slope beyond the valley swept cleanly into a radiant distance. The scene which yesterday had been unutterably dreary, had turned to enchantment while they slept. The children stared and stared. 'How funny,' said Leah, but Charlie sniffed and turned away. He didn't care about the miracle, he didn't want the miracle. Right now, there were only two things Charlie wanted; to have Jack for his friend – thinking well of him like before – and to go home to his mum. Yesterday the two things Charlie wanted had been at war with one another, but it would be all right today. They were going home today, they *were*.

Jack crawled over Leah, and dropped to the floor of the van. He foraged in the cupboard and the fridge. In too much haste to sit properly at the table, he stood at the cooker top, cramming his face with cornflakes. 'You took all the milk,' Leah accused him, coming after.

'First come, first served,' said Jack. He left his dirty plate and spoon on the cooker top, and pushed past Leah to plunge out of the cab door.

'*Now* where's he off to?' said Leah, crossly.

She found a tin of dried milk, and mixed some of that for herself and Charlie, but it wasn't the same. '*Charlie*,' she scolded him. 'Your nose is all running, and you didn't even wash your hands yet!'

She ran water for him, and found a tissue which he took without thanks, blowing his nose and rubbing at the tears which would keep coming. She's trying to boss me, he thought with fierce resentment. I bet she wouldn't talk to Jack like that.

'What's the matter?' said Leah, in a kinder tone.

'Nothing.' Charlie turned his head to hide the shameful tears.

'Yes there is, there's something the matter.'

'I think my cold has got worse,' he muttered.

Yesterday's soaking had not helped. Charlie's eyes prickled; his head felt full, and too heavy for his neck; and his nose streamed uncontrollably.

'Never mind,' said Leah. 'We'll soon be home – that's if we ever get going! Jack is a nuisance; he never thinks of anybody but himself.'

'Don't say bad things about my friend,' said Charlie, loyally.

'He's not your friend, Charlie. I don't think he's anybody's friend, really. I don't think he's got feelings like other people.'

'He's my friend,' Charlie insisted. 'He *is*. Anyway, he's a lot more my friend than yours!'

Charlie waited for Leah to dispute that, but she only shrugged and said, 'Well, I think we better go and find your friend. Because we got a long journey, I think, and we need to start early – which reminds me, we better take something to eat this time.'

She found a plastic bag, and began stuffing it with packets of biscuits. Charlie, not interested in food, scanned the sunny slopes through the windows. 'Can you see Jack?' said Leah.

Charlie didn't feel like bothering to answer fat Leah, so he didn't.

'I wonder where he went.'

'Probably the river,' Charlie mumbled, mostly to himself.

'What did you say?'

'I said "PROBABLY THE RIVER!" . . . You deaf?'

'I don't know why you're being so horrible to me,' said Leah, exasperated, 'when I'm trying very hard to be nice to you!'

Charlie sniffed, and turned his head away.

'Come on,' Leah coaxed. 'Come and look for Jack with me.'

The sun was warm on their heads as they began the descent. 'I'm too hot,' said Charlie, pulling off Lil's other cardigan, which had mauve flowers on it for a change. He tied it round his waist by the sleeves, adding to the bulk of George's shirt stuffed into George's other shorts.

'I think I'll do the same as you, Charlie,' said Leah, pulling off George's other pullover, and revealing yet another flowered shirt and flowered pair of shorts belonging to Lil.

The golden light played on her arms; she felt the magic of its touch. Sunshine was never like this in London. There was a steamy sweetness coming from the damp earth and newly washed bracken; Leah breathed it, and marvelled. I didn't know there was a place like this in the world, she thought. All these years I been alive, and I didn't know! . . . Perhaps I can come back here one day. When I'm grown up – perhaps I can come then.

The children tripped, and slid, and stumbled their way down the steep moorland slope, totally ignored by a group of ponies away to their right, and another group away to their left. 'I'm still frightened of them, you know, Charlie,' said Leah. 'I don't trust them, whatever Jack says!'

Charlie was pleased that Leah was still frightened of the horses. 'You *must* be chicken!' he said, with satisfaction.

'I expect I am – oh, look, is that the river?'

'Something wrong?'

'That's not a river! No a *proper* river.' Rivers were broad and muddy, like the Thames in London. This was nothing but a strip of shining water, winding gently between the slopes. 'I suppose it's a baby river, I suppose that must be it.'

There were smooth boulders, like stepping stones, and clumps of reeds at the water's edge. 'I can see Jack!' said Charlie, brightening visibly.

He was on the far side of the steam, away to the left, and close to where the silver-blue curved, and disappeared into the green. '*Jack!*' Leah shouted. 'We have to go!'

The distant figure waved, but made no other move. 'Looks like he took his clothes off,' said Charlie.

'JACK!' Leah called again. 'WE HAVE TO GO!'

The figure on the opposite bank waved again, and began to wade into the water. 'What a pest he is!' Leah scolded. 'We shall have to go and get him! . . . Now, how we going to get across this baby river?'

'I see how to do it,' said Charlie. 'You walk on the stones.' He stepped on to the nearest boulder, and began picking his way across the stream. Less sure-footed, Leah tried to follow, but half way over her foot slipped on wet rock. She tottered, trying to get her balance – and found herself sitting on pebbles, up to her waist in cold water.

Unkindly, Charlie laughed.

'Don't be rotten, Charlie. I could have hurt myself!'

'You look like a fat hippopotamus!'

Leah answered him with an offended silence. She had always thought he was rather a horrid person, and now she knew it for certain, she decided. She felt sore and ill-used; her bottom was bruised, and so was her dignity. With some difficulty, she hauled herself to her feet. The shorts stuck to her legs; the waterlogged pullover attached to her waist dragged and flapped as she moved.

'Look!' said Charlie. 'Jack's swimming!' He wiped his nose on his arm, and Leah turned her head so she wouldn't have to see.

'What are you doing, Jack?' she called. She stood on the bank, next to the rock where Jack had left his clothes, and called again. 'What do you think you're doing, we're meant to be going home!'

Here the stream had widened into a sort of pool – not very deep, but deep enough to swim in. Jack covered the width of the pool in graceful overarm strokes. Stripped to his underpants, he stood up at the far side. His face, disfigured as it was by long red scabs, was as radiant as the morning. 'Come on in!' he called to Leah.

'I shall do no such a thing.'

'It's good. It's not cold!'

'Yes, it is.'

'It's good anyway.' Jack ducked, and swam underwater. His head came up in the middle of the pool. 'Come on, Leah. Come on, Charlie!'

'Nah!' said Charlie. 'Don't feel like it.'

'Chicken!'

'I'm not. I'm not!'

'Come on, then, prove it!'

Charlie hesitated, then began to undress. He wore no underpants; Leah pulled a face and averted her eyes.

'Come on, Leah,' Jack enticed. 'And you!'

'I haven't got a costume.'

'Don't matter.'

'Yes it does, I'm not going to be all bare like Charlie.'

She untied the heavy wet pullover, though, and took off her shoes. She dabbled her feet in the water, and it seemed less cold than before. She took a few steps into the pool; Jack swam up and splashed her.

'Leave off!'

He splashed her again, and she splashed him back; the water drops were rainbow-coloured in the sunshine. Jack seized Leah's wrist, and pulled her right in. Her legs came up and she floated, kicking, and threshing the water with her free hand. Jack let her go and she stood; the water was chest high, and clear so you could see right to the bottom.

The water didn't seem at all cold now. Leah began to dog-paddle. She was not a good swimmer, and the shirt hampered her a bit, but she managed to get the other side of the pool without putting her feet down. Filled with pride, she began to dog-paddle back. 'See, I told you!' said Jack, with shining eyes. 'It's good, innit!'

Standing waist-deep near the edge of the pool, Charlie splashed ineffectually with his hands. 'Come on in, Charlie!' Leah called. In the happiness of the moment, she had quite forgiven him for being unkind.

'I am in!'

'Come on and swim, though.'

'In a minute.'

'I don't think he *can* swim,' said Jack.

'All right, I can't,' said Charlie. 'What about it?'

'I'll teach you,' said Jack.

'No.'

'Me and Leah will teach you, all right?'

'*No!*'

'He's got a bad cold,' said Leah.

'What you want to say that for!' Charlie snarled. 'What you want to make a fuss like that, for?' He was still trying to be a success with Jack. He was still trying, but he had lost so much ground already that there wasn't much left now to lose. Charlie felt the remains of his success slipping, sliding, rushing away from beneath his feet.

'Come on, let's make him!' said Jack, ignoring the bit about the cold anyway.

Well, why not, Leah thought. He deserves it, for being horrid again. Between them, she and Jack dragged Charlie into the middle of the pool. He struggled, and gulped, and went under. They heaved him, and held him up. The water level here was over his mouth; Charlie threshed in panic. He coughed, and gasped. Leah was uneasy. 'I think we best take him back.'

They dragged him to the shallows and left him there, sitting miserably on a boulder. 'Never mind him,' said Jack. 'Let's me and you have some more fun!'

They swam, and played, and the sun shone. The wilderness was a place of magic and sharp delight. Nevertheless, there was a niggling shadow. 'You know, Jack,' said Leah reluctantly, 'we really do have to go!'

'In a minute.'

'No, now! I think we ought to go now!'

She waded back to the bank, and sat down next to Charlie. 'Are you cold, Charlie?'

'No.'

'I think you are.'

'I'm not. I'm not. Leave me alone!'

Leah shrugged. Jack came to the bank too, and sat down next to Leah. He picked up a stone, and threw it into the stream. Dark rings rippled out; little lights flickered and danced over the water. 'Are we going home now?' said Charlie.

'In a minute.' Jack threw another stone.

Charlie got up, and began to dress. 'Is it a minute now?' he asked.

'I got an idea,' said Jack.

'What idea?'

'Let's not go today. Let's go tomorrow!'

'*Jack!*' said Leah.

'I wanna go *today*.' Even to keep in with Jack, Charlie couldn't pretend otherwise. He *couldn't*.

'*You* don't want to go today though, do you Leah?' said Jack. 'Not really. You're having a good time like me, aren't you? . . . Go on, say it! Say you're having a good time!'

'I'm having a good time,' Leah admitted.

That wasn't the point, though, was it? The point was, they ought to be getting home. It was wrong to stay here enjoying themselves, when their mums didn't know where they were.

'See, Charlie?' said Jack. 'Me and Leah's enjoying ourselves, so it's two to one.'

Leah was silent, wavering just a little bit. She had made up her mind to face the beating, and she still wanted to get that over. . . . It would be nice to stay here, though. . . . And now, suddenly, other fears came surging back into the front of her mind, out of the dark mists where they had been hiding.

Darren and Joel! She left them alone, didn't she? That was what she was going to get the beating for. And suppose something *had* happened to them? Suppose they hurt themselves, or set fire to the house, or a bad person came to the door and they answered it, like they weren't supposed to . . . ?

'Only till tomorrow,' said Jack. 'We'll go tomorrow! Just stay one day, eh?'

'No!' said Charlie. 'Let's go now!'

. . . And what if my mum and dad don't really want me home, Leah thought? What if they can't forgive me for the wicked thing I did? Nobody wants Jack, after all, so I suppose it could happen to me. . . .

'One day here, eh?' Jack's eyes were shining, his whole face alight. 'Just the rest of today, eh? Eh?'

It was hard to say no, when Jack coaxed like that. It was almost impossible to say no, when Jack enticed. This morning she might have said it, this morning early. But this morning she was only thinking about the beating, and now she remembered all those other things. Things that made her feel sick to think about. Things she certainly couldn't bring herself to talk about. . . .

'Just one more day, then.' There! She had committed herself. And it wasn't such a terrible thing to do, was it? To want just one more day, before she must find out exactly *how* bad things were going to be for her, at home?

'*Not* one more day,' Charlie pleaded. '*Please*, not one more day!'

'Shut up, you!' said Leah, fiercely. 'Just because you don't like swimming.'

'I hate you, Leah. I shall spit in your face in a minute.'

'Temper, temper,' Jack teased.

'Yeah – temper, temper,' said Leah, quite nastily.

She knew she was behaving badly, but somehow she couldn't stop herself. However horrid Charlie was, it was cruel to make fun of him when he wasn't well. And besides that, Charlie was in the right and she was in the wrong, and she didn't ought to tease him for that. The trouble was, the more wrong things Leah did, the more she found herself doing to cover up the first ones.

'So now that's settled, let's have a game,' said Jack. 'Let's have a game of Monsters.'

'All right. How do you play it?' Any game would do. Any game that would use up all of herself, so she didn't have to think about the wrong things she was doing.

'I hide, and you two come and find me, and I shout at you and make you jump.'

'Go on, then.'

Jack ran off, the drops of water on his white body gleaming in the sun. Leah pulled on her shoes; the wet clothes were uncomfortable, and she hoped the sun would dry them soon. 'Come on, Charlie!' Leah ploughed into the bushes, and Charlie dragged unwillingly after her.

Jack pounced. Leah shrieked, and shrieked, and went on shrieking. 'Now me!' she screamed, jumping up and down and waving her arms in the air. 'It's my turn to be the monster; it's my turn!' She was never this boisterous in London, nor this noisy.

'Let Charlie have a go,' said Jack.

Charlie stood listlessly, a little way apart. 'Don't want to.' He knew he should make the effort. If he wanted to save anything at all of his standing with Jack, he should make the effort to join in Jack's game; but somehow he couldn't summon the spirit.

'Come on, it's fun!'

'I said I don't want to.' Charlie kicked at the turf. 'I wanna go home, don't I?'

'Well, you are going. Tomorrow. Tomorrow is tomorrow, and today is today.'

'I don't like it here.'

Jack grinned. 'Let's cheer old Charlie up a bit! Let's tickle him, make him laugh.'

He seized Charlie's arms, and held them behind his back. Leah tickled his ribs, and Charlie wriggled and squirmed but did not laugh. He sneezed, and his nose streamed. 'Wipe your nose,' said Leah, in disgust.

'I can't. Jack's holding my arms.'

'Try and get free,' Jack teased. 'Come on, try and get free.'

'Leave me. I don't want to play.'

'I didn't ask you what you *want!*'

Inside Charlie, something snapped. '*I hate you, Jack!*'

Jack laughed. He dropped Charlie's arms, and danced around to face him. 'Come on, then, hit me!'

'No.'

'Come on, you hate me, so hit me!'

'I *don't* hate you. I didn't mean it.' Of course he hadn't meant it. Whatever had made him say it? It was Leah he hated, not Jack.

'Yes you did. You did mean it.' Jack presented his cheek. 'Come on, hit me. I dare you!'

Suddenly, all the pent-up misery and frustration in Charlie's heart came out in a burst of fury. He lunged, and Jack dodged neatly out of the way. 'Again!' Jack taunted, skipping back into range.

Frantic with rage now, Charlie threw the whole of his meagre weight into a punch which missed Jack's face, but brought Charlie himself crashing to his knees. He sprawled on the ground, sobbing and thumping the grass with his fist.

'Serve you right,' said Leah, not liking herself very much. 'Serve you right for being a spoilsport.'

'Oh, come on!' said Jack. 'Get up.' He had only been teasing; he hadn't meant any real harm.

'No.'

'Get up, you little worm!' Jack was irritated now. This was supposed to be a happy day, and Charlie was casting a blight over it.

'Yeah,' said Leah. 'Get up, you little worm!'

'No.'

'All right then, stay there. Come on, Leah, let's me and you explore this wilderness a bit more.'

Charlie dropped his head on to his arms and waited. Would they really leave him? Would they really go off and leave him alone? Cautiously, he raised his head. For one moment he glimpsed their retreating backs, just rounding the next bend in the river – then they were gone! Desolation gripped him, and something like panic. He got up and began to run, back to the only security he knew.

Back to *Hideaway*.

The sun shone warmly on his back as he went, the stream rippled and sparkled round the stepping stones as he crossed. The wilderness shimmered with light and colour, and Charlie saw none of it. Charlie saw only the hatefulness of boundless space, when all he wanted to see was damp-spotted wallpaper, closing him into a small room with too much furniture in it. And *Neighbours* on the telly. And his mum, coming in from work.

His mum!

His mum *must* be missing him; he was all she had, she told him that lots of times. His mum must be as miserable as he was. At that moment, his mum's miserableness hurt him almost as much as his own. Once again, Charlie found himself surprised at how much the thought of his mum's miserableness hurt.

He climbed the hillside, stopping every now and then to catch his breath. His nose streamed and he let it run, too unhappy to care. *Hideaway* coming into sight was a small comfort; Charlie hurried, but stopped again when he began to gasp. Slowly, laboriously, he dragged his way upwards.

His trousers and underpants were still spread on the little trees. They had got soaked again in the rain, of course, and were far from dry. Nevertheless, Charlie decided to put them back on. He didn't like George's shorts; he wanted his own clothes. He felt better in his own clothes – more himself. Almost brave again. He sat in the sun, outside the van, and made up a story in his head.

In the story, Charlie saved Jack's life from the wild animals, the horses. The horses were not dangerous really, of course – they had found that out yesterday – but you never could tell, one of them might turn vicious. In Charlie's story, the vicious horse attacked Jack. The horse rushed at Jack, baring its great big teeth, when Jack had his back to it, and didn't notice. But brave Charlie leapt out of the bushes and drove it away, waving his arms and shouting. 'Thank you, Charlie,' said Jack, in Charlie's story. 'You saved my life.'

'It's nothing,' said Charlie, modestly. 'Don't think about it.'

'*You* will be my friend for ever,' said Jack, full of gratitude. 'But that Leah is a fat, bossy pig.'

'I agree,' said Charlie.

'Let's me and you not talk to Leah any more,' said Jack, in Charlie's story.

Leah!

It was all Leah's fault that Jack had turned against him. In his heart, Charlie knew it was not Leah at all who made that happen; it was his own shortcomings. It was not being brave enough, and being a misery, and not being willing to play. But it was more comfortable to blame Leah; Charlie felt a lot better, having someone to blame.

The thing was now, how could he get his own back?

The cupboards!

Leah had spent all of yesterday morning tidying up the cupboards. She had made a great fuss about the cupboards, as though anybody could care about cupboards, compared with being kidnapped, and tied up, and left all by themselves in a wilderness.

Charlie climbed into the van. Very deliberately, he began to mess up Leah's cupboards. He mixed the packets with the tins, and hid the plates and cups in the lockers under the seats, so she couldn't find them. He pulled out the shoes and odds and ends from the tall cupboard next to the toilet, and scattered them in a jumble, all over the floor. Then he went back to the food cupboard, and emptied a whole packet of spaghetti into the sink. Some of that went on the floor as well, and Charlie stamped it into the rest of the mess.

Satisfied now, he curled up on the seat by the table, and went to sleep.

Hungry, and healthily tired, Jack and Leah raced each other up the hillside. Jack gave Leah a good start to make it fair, but he still won. In any case, Leah was hampered by the large bunch of pink foxgloves she had gathered in the valley.

'Dinner, dinner, dinner time!' Jack chanted, happily. 'Dinner, dinner, *dinner time!*' He was looking forward to the meal which, of course, Leah would cook. Leah was good at things like cooking and washing up. Besides, she seemed to enjoy these things, so everyone was happy except for drippy Charlie, and really it was lucky they got kidnapped; it was the best thing that ever happened.

Except for that rubbish thing of being tied up, of course! Jack very much hoped someone would tie George and Lil up some time, and The Boss, to show them what it was like. He also hoped he would be there to see, and have a good laugh. And meanwhile he had the laugh of them anyway, didn't he, because he had the van. It wasn't George and Lil's van any more, it was *his*. Jack walked all round *Hideaway*, surveying it proudly.

Leah climbed through the cab door. 'I'm going to do the sausages today,' she announced. 'Because otherwise they might go off, seeing the fridge isn't working.'

Jack followed her, licking his lips. 'But I must wash my hands first, because I've been touching these dirty flowers,' Leah went on. 'Oh, *Jack!* Look! We've had burglars!'

Jack snorted with annoyance. 'It ain't burglars, Leah. It's Charlie!'

'What?'

'It's Charlie. He's done it for spite.'

'He can't have,' said Leah. 'Nobody wouldn't be so spiteful as that!'

Jack shook Charlie roughly. 'Come on, wake up! Come on, you little rat, you got work to do!' He was greatly annoyed now; Charlie was really spoiling the day.

Charlie opened his eyes. For a moment he was bewildered, not sure where he was. 'What? . . . What you doing to me? . . . What?'

'You know what! You clear it!'

'Clear it?'

'You heard! Or do you want my foot on your bum to help you!'

Humiliated beyond all telling, Charlie crawled on the floor, and began picking up the things he had thrown there. Why had he done it? Whatever had made him? Things were bad enough before; now they were ten times worse! Jack stood over him, kicking this item and that towards his groping hands. Charlie coughed, and his nose ran. Leah pushed a tissue into his face. 'Wipe it!'

He grabbed at the tissue, but Jack kicked a tin against his knees; the edge of it struck painfully, through the thin jeans. 'Get on with the clearing, don't stop!'

'I ain't got three hands.'

'That's your problem!'

Leah began picking things up herself. The three of them kept colliding, in the small space. 'No!' said Jack. 'Let Charlie do it!'

'I'm not doing it for him; I'm doing it for us. So I can get on with cooking the dinner.'

She was furious with Charlie, more angry than she remembered being, ever. Her anger was a red mist, blurring her vision, filling her mouth and her throat with a choking thickness. When she opened the sink top, and saw the spilled spaghetti, her anger exploded. 'You're wicked, Charlie! That is the wickedest thing you done!'

'What is?'

'You wasted food. You wasted all that spaghetti!'

'He can pick it up,' said Jack. 'Go on, Charlie, put it all back in the packet.'

'We can't use it now,' Leah stormed. 'It's been in the sink; it's got all germs.'

'We can wash it,' said Jack.

They could, of course, but Leah was beyond reason. 'We can't. It's too dirty now; it's spoiled.' She began gathering the spaghetti in armfuls, and stuffing it into the waste container under the sink.

'No, don't,' said Jack. 'Don't throw it away.'

Leah went on putting the spaghetti into the waste container. Jack picked up the empty packet, and pushed Leah out of the way. 'Best save it,' he said. 'We could be glad to have it, later.'

'Actually, we don't need it,' said Leah, her anger cooling. 'Charlie's wicked to waste it, but we don't actually need it – we got plenty enough food for one day.'

'Best save it, though,' said Jack, putting the spaghetti very carefully back into the packet.

9

Camouflage

I really, actually, *do* hate Jack now, Charlie thought.

In fact, he was confused to find that he had two quite different feelings about Jack, both at the same time. He longed, with a passionate longing, for Jack to be his friend; he also wanted him a hundred miles away.

And Leah with him!

Jack and Leah. Both ganging up on him, both against him. At first, they wouldn't even give him any dinner. Charlie didn't too much mind not having anything to eat – he wasn't very hungry – but being left out made him feel dreadfully lonely. He didn't know where to look, so he cowered in the corner, and pretended to be very much interested in something outside, while Jack and Leah scoffed grilled sausage and mashed potato.

But then Leah decided that Charlie ought to eat. 'If you don't eat, Charlie, you'll get really sick,' she said; and she piled his plate high with mashed potato, stone cold now, and a whole tin of baked beans, also cold.

The sight of so much unappetising food put him off completely; but Leah stood over him, and forced him to swallow it, so he felt ready to vomit, as well as being stuffed up with cold.

Leah washed up, and afterwards Jack wanted her to come swimming with him again right away; but Leah said no, first she must find the ball of string and make a washing line outside, so they could dry their wet clothes from yesterday, and put their own things on again tomorrow. And they must take the drinking can, because the water in it was getting used up, and they would have to fill it full again from the river. The water in the river was so clean it couldn't possibly have germs in it, she said, so it would be quite safe to drink.

'And then we go swimming!' said Jack with shining eyes.

'All right, then we go swimming.'

I hope they both drown, thought Charlie. I hope they both drown, and that's the end of them! I mean – I hope *Leah* drowns, and that's the end of *her.*

It wasn't that he wanted to go swimming, but it would have been nice to have been asked. As it was, they were behaving as though he just didn't exist.

After the others had gone, Charlie sat miserably at the table, and wished the time away. He didn't know what the time was, and was too despondent to get up and look at the clock on the dashboard, but he knew it couldn't be more than halfway through the afternoon. That meant there would be hours and hours before tomorrow, when they were going to go home. Hours and hours more in this hateful camper van – how was he going to stand it?

There was that long climb to come, as well – the one that made him so out of breath. If anyone said the word 'holiday' to him ever again, Charlie thought, he would definitely spit in their face.

It occurred to him to turn the radio on, but he decided he couldn't be bothered to get up. Then he changed his mind, and thought he would go and sit in the front after all.

In the driver's seat, where she had thrown them

and forgotten them, were Leah's foxgloves. Horrible flowers! Horrible Leah and her horrible flowers! Charlie didn't care if he never saw another flower in the whole of his life. He would like to pull Leah's flowers to pieces, actually, and throw them out of the window. Only if he did that, there would be another fuss, he supposed, and he didn't want any more of that; he'd had enough already.

He twiddled the knob on the radio; but there was only pop music, which didn't interest Charlie very much. He twiddled the knob again, and there was a boring person talking about some boring walk she had done, out in the boring country. Charlie twiddled the knob, and found another station.

More pop music. Charlie was just about to switch the radio off altogether, when he heard somebody say something about 'News on the Hour'. He would keep it on for that. There might be something about *them*.

He listened patiently through all the tedious stuff about the Pound, and bombs, and some people in the Houses of Parliament quarrelling with each other. And at last it came!

'... In connection with three children, missing from their London homes since Tuesday,' Charlie heard. At this point, his heart started hammering so fast he almost missed the next bit, but he clenched his fists against his chest, and strained everything he had to concentrate. '... Police are anxious to trace the whereabouts of a motor caravan on a Ford Transit base, registration number TGU 823X, believed to be touring somewhere in England or Wales—'

Charlie did not wait to hear more. He rushed

outside before he should forget the number the radio said.

It was true! Expecting it, he could nevertheless hardly believe that his luck had turned at last. TGU 823X as plain as anything on the number plate! Hooray, hooray, he was going to be rescued!

The police were looking for the van. That meant they would be coming with their helicopters. Charlie looked into the blue sky, expecting to see helicopters there and then. No helicopters yet, but they would come soon for certain. This evening, perhaps. Tomorrow morning at the very latest.

He wouldn't have to do that horrid climb after all!

Charlie sat on the grass, and watched for helicopters, and waited for the others to come back.

When they came, they were laughing and joking, and carrying the full water can between them. They took no notice of Charlie; they didn't even look in his direction. 'I know something you don't know,' said Charlie.

'What?' said Leah.

'Something important.'

'Well, come on! Tell us if you're going to!'

'You have to be nice to me, first.'

'He doesn't know anything,' said Jack. 'He's putting it on.'

'No I'm not, then. I know something very important, and very exciting, so there!'

Leah sat down beside Charlie, and put her arm round him mockingly. 'All right, I'm being nice to you, now tell!'

Charlie pushed her arm away. 'Get off me!'

'Leave him!' said Jack. 'He's just putting it on.'

Jack and Leah climbed into the van, and Charlie

followed, less confidently now. 'Do you want me to tell you, then?'

Jack shrugged. 'Please yourself.'

'OK, I will. It's the police are coming!'

'*What?*' Jack didn't sound just surprised, he sounded quite dismayed.

'The police are coming,' said Charlie. 'I heard it on the radio. They're looking for the van; they got the number and everything.'

Leah turned away, and began fussing over the contents of the fridge, to take her mind off what she had just heard. It wasn't that she was sorry about the police coming, it was just that she didn't want to think about it today.

'Are you sure you heard it right?' Jack demanded.

'Of course I'm sure. I listened and I heard it. And I went right outside to see, and the number was the same.'

Jack turned abruptly, and went outside. He stared thoughtfully at the number plate on the back of the van. He kicked it, stared again, then kicked it once more. He bent, and pulled at it with his hands. He climbed into the van again, and found a hammer in the little tool cupboard. 'What's that for?' said Charlie, mystified.

Jack took the hammer outside, and a moment later there was the sound of banging at the rear of the van. Bang, bang, bang! Leah began to sing. In the middle of summer she sang 'We wish you a merry Christmas,' loudly and all out of key. She's gone mad, thought Charlie. They've both gone mad, they must have!

Outside, Jack stopped trying to knock the number plate off, and started wrenching at it with the hammer. He wrenched and wrenched, till the sweat came out on his forehead, but the number plate wouldn't budge. He struck futilely at TGU 823X, trying to obliterate the letters, but that was no good either. He threw down the hammer, and retreated up the hillside a little, where he sat in the bracken, gazing at *Hideaway* with brooding eyes.

A group of ponies grazed nearby. They weren't the same ones he had seen before, at least, Jack didn't think so. One of them was smaller than the others, and especially pretty. Its body was white, with brown patches, but its face was all white – white as featherdown against the green hill. And looking out of the long white face were dark eyes, like pools of treacle.

Jack looked at the horse, and the horse looked at Jack. Without really thinking what he was doing, Jack held out his hand to the horse. The horse stared, but made no move. 'Come on, then, come!' The horse backed, nervously. It turned and mingled with the others, its head well down, nibbling at the grass between the clumps of fern.

With a heavy heart, Jack went back to the van, and turned the key in the ignition. This time the engine started almost at once. It sounded a bit noisy and rough; but the main thing was, it was going! Jack wondered why he had had so much trouble with it before, and thought the cause might be something to do with the knob on the dashboard – the one that pulled out and pushed in again. He couldn't be sure of that, of course, but he left the knob as it was for luck, half in and half out.

They were rushing away from him, though, his van and his wilderness. In the deepest parts of him,

Jack felt them going. They were the best things he had ever found in his life so far, and soon the police were going to come and take them away from him.

Suddenly, a brighter thought struck him. He switched off the engine. 'They may not come for a long time, you know! The police may not come for a really long time yet!'

Leah was getting their tea. She had discovered some cold chicken that certainly ought to be eaten today, and she was cooking a packet of savoury rice to go with it. She wanted to think about her cooking, not the police. She hummed, 'We wish you a merry Christmas,' as she stirred.

'Did you hear what I said?' said Jack.

Charlie looked up from his corner. 'I heard, but it's not true. They *will* come, it said it on the radio. It said they're looking for the van.'

'How do they know where to look, then? Tell me that, how do they know?'

Charlie faltered. 'They'll come with the helicopters. You said so.'

'Did the radio say about the wilderness?'

'No . . .' Doubt appeared, like a yawning pit, right at Charlie's feet.

'Did the radio say where they think the van went?'

'. . . They said somewhere in England or Wales.'

'There you are, then; there you are!' said Jack, triumphantly. 'England is a big place. And Wales. The police can't go everywhere with the helicopters . . . not all at the same time. How will they know to look in *this* part? They may not think of this part for a long time. They may not think of it at all!'

'They will. They will!'

'They won't, you know. This wilderness is so far from everything else, they most likely won't *never* think of coming here!'

He didn't sound sad, he sounded delighted. And Leah went on humming 'We wish you a merry Christmas,' as though the police not coming could be no possible concern of *hers.*

'So you see,' said Jack, 'we don't have anything to worry about!'

Nothing to *worry* about? They *had* gone mad. He was in this caravan with two mad people. Charlie looked from one to the other with stricken eyes.

'And *you* can cheer up!' said Jack, impatiently. 'Come on, Charlie, we don't want no miserable faces in this van, we want happy ones. And you can eat up your tea, can't he, Leah! And after tea, I know a good game we can play . . . *all* of us!'

Through a fog of deep anxiety, Charlie did his best to comply. He must do as they said because they were almost certainly mad. It was the wilderness, or the sun or something, that had done it to them. And mad people could be dangerous, you never knew which way they might turn.

At bedtime, Charlie began to cough. Not much – just a little, wheezing sort of cough. Leah frowned. 'You know something, Jack. I don't think me and you should sleep with Charlie tonight. We might catch his germs.'

'I was going to say that anyway,' said Jack. 'I was going to say there's no room in our bed; Charlie will have to sleep down here.'

'It's all right,' said Charlie. 'I don't mind.' Who wanted to sleep with mad people, anyway?

'Should we try to make a proper bed for him?'

said Leah. 'With taking the table out? I know there's a way to do it. Should we try to find it out?'

'Can't be bothered,' said Jack.

'Actually, I can't be bothered neither,' said Leah.

'It's all right,' said Charlie. 'I don't mind.'

He wasn't very big, he could manage curled up on the little seat – he had slept there this morning, after all. 'It's a bit cold, though.' He coughed again, and his nose streamed. Leah dragged down the blanket, and threw it over him with no particular kindness.

'There! Don't say I never do anything for you!'

Charlie tried to make himself comfortable. It was no worse than last night really, when he had had to sleep at the feet of the others. Indeed, it was better in a way – at least here he was in no danger of being kicked. But it was a lot more lonely. Charlie listened with faint hope, as darkness deepened, in case the helicopters should be coming after all.

Then the coughing began again. 'Shut up coughing!' said Leah crossly, from aloft. 'You're stopping me going to sleep.'

Charlie felt the tears welling up, and really it was a relief to let them go, when no one could see, and scorn him for it. He groped for a drink of water, and that helped, but he could hear himself wheezing, and there was a worrying sort of tightness in his chest.

Charlie tried to pretend the tightness wasn't there. He tried to pretend he couldn't hear the wheezing. The wheezing and the tightness frightened him, but he wasn't going to tell anyone he was frightened, because that would mean giving away his secret. No, no, he wasn't going to tell anyone about *that.*

He propped himself up on the cushions, to make the breathing easier, and fell asleep at last.

Next morning Jack was up before any of them, and crashing about outside the van. He came in for his breakfast, and immediately afterwards made for the door. 'Come on, you lot, we got work to do!'

Leah followed slowly. She didn't know what was in Jack's mind, but she was beginning to have her suspicions.

And Charlie came too, because you had to humour these mad people. He didn't feel much better this morning, but at least he didn't feel any worse. Anyhow, the coughing and the wheezing had more or less gone away, thank goodness!

Outside, Jack was doing another mad thing. For some reason, he had climbed on the bonnet of the van, and was trying in vain to get on to the roof. He reached with his arms, but even Jack's arms were not long enough for the purpose. He dropped to the ground, and walked round the van, looking upwards and frowning. Suddenly he began to climb one of the little trees, the one just outside the kitchen window. The tree was weak; it bent and swayed, and wouldn't hold his weight properly. But eventually Jack stood precariously on, or rather amidst, the tree's leafy top. His feet slipped as he changed position, and bits of branches and twigs snapped as he moved, scattering themselves over the ground and lodging themselves on the branches of other trees.

But he made it!

Triumphantly, Jack stood on *Hideaway*'s high

top, and waved his arms at the sun. Then he lay full length, and stretched his arms downwards. 'Bring me leaves and branches,' he instructed. 'Anything green. Bring them to me.'

'What for?' said Leah, though she knew the answer already.

'What do you think for? So the police won't see the van, when they come with their helicopters to look for us. I mean, they most likely won't come, but just in case.'

Leah opened her mouth to say, 'Jack, we *have* to go home today, you know we do' – but found herself saying, 'Will ferns do?' instead.

What was she doing? What was she *thinking* about? She was making the wrong things she did already a lot more wrong, that's what! The punishment that was waiting for her at home was going to be a lot worse now, because of what she was doing today. Feverishly, she gathered ferns and stood on tiptoe to pass them up to Jack. Jack lay on the roof, leaning perilously over to take the greenstuff from Leah, then spread it carefully over the top of the van. 'More!' he called. 'More!'

Leah pushed her misgivings to the back of her mind, where they grew, and multiplied, and hung like threatening monsters. She wasn't just afraid to think about the bad things at home now – she was afraid to look inside herself at all. She began to run, and jump, and shriek with a raucous voice as she darted here and there, gathering armfuls of mostly ferns, hugging them to her chest, and passing them up to Jack.

To pacify them, Charlie made some show of joining in the antics of the mad people, but in his heart there was only desperation. Out of the corner of his eye, he kept watch for the helicopters that just *might* come before the van was completely covered; but he didn't really expect to see them. It was no surprise that there was no sign of them, in the cloudless blue sky.

'Let's have those branches that broke for on top,' said Jack. '. . . All right, it's finished now.' He climbed down, found a sharp stone, and scratched JACK'S SHACK on the side of the van. 'I say, Leah, I just thought of something else!'

'What's that?'

'You know George—'

'Don't say that name. Don't say it!'

'All right, all right. That big fat creep that brought us here, then. Something he said. He said the police might come in their *cars.*'

'Looking for us, you mean?'

'I don't know. I don't think so. I wasn't listening properly, because I had, like, a few other things to think about just then, but I remember he said about the police might come on the wilderness in their cars. . . . I think what he meant was they sometimes come anyway. . . . I don't know what for.'

'Will they come close, then? Will they see us?'

'Only if they come along the track. You know – where we went to the empty house that time.'

'You can see the van from the top,' said Leah. 'We know you can see the van from the top, because we looked.'

'Yeah . . . that's why you-know-who said to get the van behind the trees. So the police can't see it if they come with their cars. But then he *couldn't* get the van behind the trees. So the end of it sticks out, and if the police come, they can look down and see it after all, they can see the side of it.'

'So we done all that work for nothing.' Don't think, Leah told herself. Don't think, oh, *don't think* what can happen now! Perhaps even today!

'No, we never. We never done all that work for nothing, we just have to cover the side as well. Like, at the back, where it sticks out.'

'We can't!'

'Yes we can.'

'We can't, then. How we going to make the leaves stick on?'

'I don't know exactly yet,' said Jack. 'But I know we can do it. I mean, we have to do it, because otherwise the police might come and take us back to London, so there has to be a way. Wait a minute, let me think. . . .'

They could break off more branches, he said, and plant them in the ground all round the rear end of *Hideaway* – he meant *Jack's Shack.*

'They won't come high enough,' said Leah.

All right, all right, Jack had another idea. They could open the back doors a tiny bit – the keys were on George's key ring, it wouldn't take long to find the right ones – and they could close the back window, the one facing up the hill, so it was only open a tiny bit. Then they could find some really big ferns and poke them in the cracks, so they hung down, and stretched across, and they could weave them together, or tie them together perhaps, so they joined up.

It was very hard work. Jack and Leah laboured tirelessly; but Charlie's efforts grew more and more feeble, and eventually he sat on the grass by himself where, trembling with apprehension, he made himself think about the unthinkable.

'Charlie's not helping,' he heard Leah call.

'Oh, leave him alone. He's not worth bothering about.'

'What a misery!'

'Yeah – what a face for us to look at!'

Don't worry, thought Charlie, you won't have to look at it for very much longer. . . .

'Let's go up the hill now, and see how well we hid my van,' said Jack.

He scrambled up, with Leah following; and the two of them stood on the track, gazing down at *Hideaway*.

'It looks a bit peculiar,' said Leah, doubtfully.

'It looks good!' Jack insisted. 'It looks like it's part of the little wood.'

'*I* think it looks like a van,' said Leah, 'that somebody covered over with ferns and branches, on purpose.'

'Not if you look quickly. Like this, see? Look quickly and then away. . . . See? It don't hardly notice at all that way.'

'Yeah – anyway, perhaps the police won't come.'

'That's right. Most likely they won't come anyway.'

'I hope you're right.'

'Trust me.'

They began to wander down the hill. 'Oh, look, Leah, here's my horse!'

'*Your* horse?'

'Yeah, I seen him yesterday. The one with the brown patches and the white face. I'm going to have that one for *my* horse, I think.'

Jack stood still and smiled his most winning smile – but the horse didn't seem to understand smiles. He held out his hand, but the horse only snorted and backed. 'Come on, Jack,' said Leah, nervously.

'If I had something nice to give it,' said Jack, 'it might come to me.'

'It might bite you, though. Come on!'

'I'm going to call it Treacle,' said Jack. 'Because of its eyes.'

'Come on,' said Leah. 'It's getting to be dinner time.'

'Oh yeah – *food!*'

Jack's eyes lit up in anticipation, and he pranced down the hillside with Leah stumping behind. 'Food, glorious food!' Jack sang. A thought struck him – there was plenty of food in *Jack's Shack*, might there be something that horses like? Something sweet! What about biscuits? Jack began rooting in Leah's cupboards to find some. 'Where's Charlie?' said Leah, coming after.

'Who cares?'

'He's not in the van, and I can't see him nowhere outside.'

'Probably gone to find somewhere for toilet.'

'Oh, yeah. . . . Where *you* going?'

'Just back up the hill a minute. Just while you're making the dinner.'

'You're going to look for that horse again, aren't you?'

'Who says that's what I'm going to do?'

'Well, mind you don't get bit!'

'Trust me!'

'Besides,' said Leah, uneasily, 'I'm a bit worried about where Charlie's got to. He's taking a very long time.'

'Good!' said Jack, leaping to the ground with his

handful of biscuits. He scrambled eagerly up the hillside, carried on a wave of excitement and hope.

The horse was browsing along now, at some distance from its companions. Jack stood a little way off, and held out a biscuit. The horse looked at Jack's outstretched hand, but did not move. 'Come on, Treacle, come on,' said Jack, softly.

The horse stood squarely on four legs, still very suspicious of this strange being on two. 'Come on, Treacle, I won't hurt you. Look, there's a nice biscuit for you. Come on, *please* come.'

The little horse took one hesitant step forward. Jack was delighted. 'That's right, that's right,' he coaxed. 'Come on, it's nice, look! Nice biscuit! Oh, come on, Treacle, *please!*'

Jack took a small step forward himself. The horse lifted its head and whinnied. Jack stood still again, the biscuit on his open palm, his eyes beseeching.

And slowly, very slowly, the horse walked towards him.

Jack held his breath. He didn't risk moving, or speaking any more; he just waited, and willed the horse to keep on walking towards him.

He smelled it. He felt its warm breath on his hand, and the incredible softness of its lips, as it took the biscuit from his hand. Still careful to make no sudden movement, Jack offered another biscuit, and the little horse took that as well. For the third and last biscuit, the pony allowed the boy to stand really close. With his heart in his throat, Jack reached up and gently, very gently, stroked the horse's nose.

There was a warm feeling, starting in Jack's chest and spreading all over him. A feeling of being all choked up – excited and contented, both at the same time. Jack had never felt anything like that before, ever. It was as though something that had been asleep in him, suddenly in this wilderness had woken up.

Jack put his cheek briefly against the horse's side. 'Now don't you forget me, Treacle, because I'm coming to see you again!' He began to run down the hillside, turning now and again to wave at his horse. 'Don't forget me, mind, don't you forget me!'

He ran for his dinner, through colours that were somehow different – more brilliant, yet softer, than he had seen them before. He felt light as air, almost *part* of the air. He was utterly, utterly happy.

It was Leah who pulled him down to earth.

'Do you know something, I think Charlie's gone!'

'What you mean, gone?'

'He's disappeared. I think he's tried to go home.'

'*What?*'

'I told you I was worried, but you wouldn't listen.'

The light had gone out of Jack's face. 'He'll tell!'

'I know.'

'He'll tell that we're here, and they'll come and find us.'

'I know.'

'They'll come and find us, and take us away! They'll take us back to London.'

'I know,' said Leah, sadly. 'I think it's all over, Jack.'

'No, it's not. It can't be, it *can't.*'

'What is there to do about it, though?'

'Get after him, of course, and fetch him back!'

10

Traitor

Mr Gosling drove his rattling old red Mini over a high road, in the heart of Dartmoor. He was pleased with himself, and pleased with the world. 'What a beautiful day,' he said, as he drove.

'Not a cloud in the sky,' said Mrs Gosling, who was pleased with Mr Gosling, and pleased with the world as well.

'A beautiful day for a picnic.'

'Not a cloud. Not one!'

'*A beautiful* day.'

'Wonderful weather! Not a cloud!'

'Let's go to our special place,' said Mr Gosling.

'That's just what I was going to say, Teddy Bear,' said Mrs Gosling, beaming all over her round rosy face.

Charlie thought he had really been rather clever. He knew he couldn't tell mad Jack and mad Leah what he was planning, because if he did that they would stop him; so he waited till he could sneak off without them seeing. His chance came when the two of them went up the hill, to get a better view of the mad things they had been doing to the van.

Charlie was no less frightened than before at the idea of going off on his own – the difference now was that he was desperate. This whole business had been a nightmare, and the nightmare was getting more dreadful all the time. He must get out of the nightmare, he must – before something even worse should happen.

He scuttled parallel with the stream, until Jack and Leah were out of sight, and then a bit further to make absolutely sure. Then he began to climb – the same hill, but farther along.

He took it slowly. No use hurrying, and getting out of breath! His nose streamed, and his chest was beginning to feel tight again, but it would be all right because he was going home, he was going home, he was going *home*. He must think about that. He mustn't think about his chest, or about being alone, or about his secret, or about not knowing what was going to happen at the top of this hill.

When the climbing got too much, he sat beside a prickly bush to rest. He took deep breaths, and looked down over the valley, to see how far he had come. *Hideaway* was out of sight here; all around were only sweeping green slopes and open sky. He was a tiny dot in the middle of all that vastness. The sense of his smallness, and weakness, terrified him.

There was a lump of panic, filling his throat. He tried to swallow it down, but it kept coming back. He was scared to go on, and scared to stay where he was. His heart began to thump. Light-headed now, he pushed himself to his feet and began to climb frantically – up, up, and this was the steepest bit – up, up, faster and faster, till his legs crumpled beneath him and he collapsed into a gasping, wheezing heap.

'I can't see him,' said Leah, looking upwards and around.

'Come *on!*' said Jack.

'Perhaps we're too late. Perhaps he got to the road already. Perhaps he found somebody to tell.'

'That Charlie has turned into a traitor!' said Jack, indignantly. 'I never thought he would do such a thing – did you, Leah? Actually, I thought he would be too scared.'

Charlie recovered his strength at last. He dragged himself up the last bit of the slope, and stood trembling and overheated at the top, trying to remember which way he was supposed to go. *This* way for the house, and *this* way for the road – or was it the other way around? His head spun, and he couldn't think straight. The sweat trickling into his eyes, he turned right and trotted blindly along the track. . . .

Oh no, oh *no!* No, he thought, I remember it now. That other day, in the rain – that day the slope was the same side it is now. I'm going the wrong way! I made a mistake; I'm going the wrong way; I wasted time and made myself more tired for nothing.

He turned, and the sun beat down on his head. He wiped his streaming nose on his arm, then blinked to clear his vision. He was vaguely aware of things he hadn't noticed that other day – a rough stone wall on his right now, and tawny sheep nibbling at the grass beside the track and on the other side of the wall. How far to the road, though, how far?

What was that! Away in the distance, there was a splash of red, amongst the green; what was it? . . . It was a car! Charlie was sure it was a car – yes, yes, it *was.* There was somebody else in this wilderness besides mad Jack and mad Leah, and him! Somebody had come in a car, to save him and take him home. With new hope in his heart, Charlie began to hurry.

Mr and Mrs Gosling were getting the picnic things out of the car. 'Oh look!' said Mrs Gosling. 'There's a little boy!'

'Oh dear,' said Mr Gosling, 'Somebody else found our special place.'

'I suppose we shouldn't be selfish.'

'The trouble with you is, you're not selfish *enough*,' said Mr Gosling, fondly.

'So you always say, Teddy Bear.'

'Never mind, it's still a beautiful day.'

'Beautiful! Not a cloud in the sky.'

'We'll sit on the grass down there, shall we?'

'I made your favourite pickle sandwiches,' said Mrs Gosling, with a happy smile.

'Bless you!' said Mr Gosling, smiling back.

Suddenly, a terrible thought struck Charlie.

Strangers! You weren't supposed to speak to strangers, particularly strangers in cars! Bother Leah! If Leah hadn't said about the Strangers that time, the bad ones, he probably wouldn't have thought about it now. Bother Leah, what did she want to say that for? What did she want to make it harder for? Charlie wished Leah was here now, so he could spit right in her face!

He sat behind a bush, out of sight of the car, and shook all over as he struggled to make up his mind. . . .

'The little boy's disappeared,' said Mrs Gosling.

'Good,' said Mr Gosling. 'His family must be over that way. He must have gone back to them.'

'I didn't really *want* to share our special place, I must admit,' said Mrs Gosling.

'Quite right. You can't share everything.'

'I do love all this peace. Don't you love this peace, Teddy Bear?'

'I do, I do.'

'It's a perfect day as well. Not a cloud in the sky!'

Jack pelted along the track, with Leah puffing far behind. Suddenly he pulled up short. He turned, ran back to Leah, and pushed her over the low wall. 'What's the matter?'

'There's a car!'

'And people?'

'They might be inside the car; it's too far to see.'

Jack and Leah crouched low, behind the wall. 'I wonder where the traitor is?' said Leah.

'That's what's worrying me.'

'Jack, I just thought . . . perhaps the people in that car are Strangers. They might have kidnapped Charlie and tied him up. Like . . . you know, like that thing happened to us, before!'

Jack's eyes lit up. 'That would be lucky! It would be really lucky, if that happened!'

'*Jack!*'

Charlie's heart hammered, and his head buzzed. His thoughts tipped, down and up and down again like a see-saw. He would go, he *wouldn't* go. He would risk it, he was too scared.

Those two people he saw getting out of their car – suppose they were like George and Lil? Suppose they *were* George and Lil? They might not have gone away after all! What should he do? What should he do?

Suddenly there was a wave of unbearable homesickness. His mum, he wanted his mum! And his mum was missing *him*, he kept forgetting that. Choking on tears, Charlie scrambled out from behind his bush, and began to run towards the car – and the people who might be Strangers, or might not.

There was a shout behind him. *Two* voices shouting! Charlie turned his head fearfully, and saw them coming – Jack and Leah, running at full speed along the track, and gaining on him every moment. 'Help!' Charlie shrieked. 'Help me! Oh, help me, *please!*'

'What's that shouting?' said Mr Gosling, and he stood up to look.

Mrs Gosling stood up too. 'It's that little boy again. And two other children.'

'What a noise they're making,' Mr Gosling sighed. 'Spoiling our lovely peace!'

'I suppose they have to have their fun.'

'A pity they can't have it somewhere else.'

'It *is* spoiling our peace,' Mrs Gosling sighed.

'It's spoiling our peace, like I said.'

'. . . Teddy Bear,' said Mrs Gosling. 'Do you think that little boy's all right?'

'He looks all right to me.'

'You don't think he sounds a bit frightened?'

'You worry too much,' said Mr Gosling, with a fond smile for his wife. 'That little nipper's as right as rain – they're only playing!'

'Yes, Teddy Bear, I expect you're right.'

Mr Gosling found a smile for Charlie also, as he ran towards them. 'Having a good game, then?'

Charlie tried to speak, but his breath was coming in great gasps, so he could only make whooping noises. 'I think you've been overdoing it,' said Mrs Gosling, with motherly concern.

Jack caught up and grabbed Charlie from behind. Charlie writhed, and struggled, and whooped. 'Hey, hey!' said Mr Gosling, with mild reproach. 'Not so rough!'

'I can't let him go,' said Jack. 'I have to take him back to our mum.'

At that point, Charlie's whoops subsided. Jack held him against his own body with one arm, and covered his mouth with the other hand. Charlie struggled harder. He couldn't breathe through his nose because of the cold, and now he couldn't breathe at all. 'Hey, hey!' said Mr Gosling again.

'He was naughty,' Jack improvised. 'He run away from our mum, she said to fetch him back.'

Leah reached them, panting. 'That's right. We have to take him back to our mum.'

'No need to suffocate him, though,' said Mr Gosling, frowning just a little bit.

'Yeah, Jack, let him breathe,' said Leah, anxious for herself but uneasy about Charlie too.

'If I take my hand away from his mouth,' said Jack, 'he will most likely say bad words. . . . All right, Charlie, breathe!' he released Charlie's mouth just long enough for him to take one gasp.

'That's better,' said Mrs Gosling.

'Having a picnic like us, are you?' said Mr Gosling. 'Whereabouts, then?'

'Oh – back there.' Leah gestured vaguely, wondering how she ought to regard Mr and Mrs Gosling. They were undoubtedly strangers, people she didn't know – but were they *Strangers*, the bad sort? Certainly they didn't have bad feelings coming out of them; in fact they were giving out very *good* feelings. Leah felt the good feelings coming out of Mr and Mrs Gosling, and knew in her heart that these were kind people.

'A *long* way back?' said Mr Gosling, hopefully.

'Yeah,' said Jack. 'A long way. This one said bad words to our mum, and she said to fetch him back.'

'Oh, dear,' said Mrs Gosling. 'That won't do!'

'He says the worst bad words of anybody I know,' Jack claimed. 'Our mum says she don't know where he learns them from. . . . All right, Charlie, breathe!' Jack released his mouth for a moment again, then wrenched him round and began to frogmarch him in the other direction.

'Goodbye,' said Leah politely, before she turned to follow.

'You have to wash your mouth out, Charlie,' said Jack.

'You be a good boy, Charlie!' Mr Gosling called, chuckling. 'You mind your language, now!'

'He's got a nasty cold,' said Mrs Gosling.

'Ah – these kids are tough, you fret too much!'

'I expect you're right. . . . Teddy Bear, did you notice that little girl is black?'

'I did, actually.'

'But they all seem to have the same mother. The girl must be adopted.'

'I was just going to say the same thing.'

'I think it's rather nice, don't you? A nice idea.'

'It is a nice idea. Yes.'

'To bring them up together. Part of the same family.'

'We're *all* part of the same family. The *human* family.'

'That is a lovely thing to say, Teddy Bear,' said Mrs Gosling, beaming.

'Just a thought I had,' said Mr Gosling, modestly.

'Breathe!' said Jack grimly to Charlie, for the tenth or eleventh time.

'I think those people can't hear, now,' said Leah. 'I think we can let his mouth go, now.' She didn't quite like the look of Charlie, she thought he was going a funny colour.

'If you shout again, Traitor,' said Jack, 'I shall tie up your mouth with my shirt.'

But Charlie had no fight left. Limp and unresisting, he let them drag him along the track and down the hill. There was a boiling cauldron of hate inside him but he had no strength for expressing it. All he could do was rage silently and inwardly at the person he had once idolised. He had never hated anyone as much as Jack in all his life, Charlie thought, and he never would. If he ever got out of this, if he ever got home, he would never want to see Jack again, ever!

Inside *Hideaway*, Charlie sat at the table with his head cradled on his arms.

'We have to make sure he doesn't do it again,' said Jack.

'Yeah, right,' said Leah.

'We have to tie him up.'

'Yeah, right.'

'What happened to that string?'

Leah opened the cupboard. She reached for the ball of string, and stood fiddling with it, winding loops around her fingers.

'Come on, then, give it to me!'

'Jack. . . .'

'Come on, Leah, I already wasted a lot of time on him, I don't want to waste no more.'

'. . . I think we didn't ought to tie him up, though. I think he's not very well.'

'That's his problem.'

'Well don't tie him too tight. We don't have to be cruel.'

'*Cruel?*' Jack was surprised and indignant. 'Who's being cruel? Who said anything about *cruel?* . . . Actually, I'm going to be very kind to him. You watch. You just watch how kind I'm being to Traitor!'

He took the end of the string, and knotted it into a loose collar round Charlie's neck. Then he stepped with the ball, unwinding it as he went, to the front of the caravan. He unwound the rest, pushing the great loops of slack into a heap behind the driver's seat, then tied the end of the string round the gear lever. 'There!' he told Leah. 'Who says I'm not kind? He can walk about and go to the toilet and everything!'

'He can undo that easy enough.'

'That's all right. One of us can watch him all the time.'

'. . . It's like he's a dog, though. You tied him up like he's a dog!'

'So? Serve him right!'

'And anyway, you didn't ought to tie him round his neck, it's dangerous.'

'No it's not. How is it dangerous!'

'He could catch the string on something, and choke himself.'

Jack shrugged. 'All right, I'll tie it round his waist.' Neck or waist, it was all the same to *him*. 'See? I'm undoing his neck, and tying it round his waist.'

Leah did not answer. Returning to abandoned

preparations for the meal, she began heating tinned Irish stew in a saucepan. 'Oh, good,' said Jack. 'I'm starving!'

Leah said nothing.

'What's up?'

Leah said nothing, but she stuck out her lip, and frowned as she worked.

'Anyway, I'm starving!' said Jack, cheerfully.

Leah heated tinned peas, and reconstituted mashed potato. 'That's most of the potato gone,' she observed.

'We got other things, though,' said Jack. 'Biscuits, and cake, and spaghetti and things. And some bread, still. There's plenty things in that cupboard, I can see all the way from here!'

Leah said nothing. She piled Jack's plate and her own. Then she put a small amount from each saucepan on to a third plate, and sat down next to Charlie. 'Come on, Charlie, have some dinner.' She put the plate in front of him, but he pushed it away with his elbow. 'Come on, Charlie, you must have something to eat!' She tried to lift his head, but he held it stubbornly down. Losing patience, she grabbed him by the hair and yanked back. Charlie's chin came up, and Leah pushed a spoonful of stew against his mouth. The food smeared his face, and dribbled down the front of his neck. 'Don't bother,' said Jack. 'You're only wasting your time.'

Leah tried again anyway. 'Come on, Charlie, it's tasty. Look, Jack's eating his, and I'm waiting to have mine. Come on, there's a good boy. . . . Will you do it if I let your head go? Will you do it then?'

She released Charlie's curls, and immediately he

jerked his head round, away from her, and dropped it on to his arms.

'Oh, all right, *be* like that!' Leah snapped. She attacked her own dinner, stabbing aggressively with the fork, but found she wasn't all that hungry after all. She couldn't very well leave it, though, because that would be wasting food, so she forced it down, then gathered the plates and dishes for washing up.

'Leah,' said Jack. 'Give us some biscuits for my horse!'

Leah threw him the last packet. 'There you are, and don't blame me when they're all gone!'

'You watch Traitor then, all right?' said Jack.

Leah clattered the dishes, and sang 'We wish you a merry Christmas,' in a hard voice.

Running and skipping to find his horse, Jack's conscience was perfectly easy. He had done nothing wrong, he reflected, he had even been kind. Look how kind he had been to Charlie, who had behaved with such treachery. It was Charlie's fault I nearly lost my wilderness this morning, Jack thought. It was Charlie's fault I nearly lost my van with the engine that really goes. I nearly lost Treacle as well, and all because of Charlie.

But was I cruel to him in return? No, I wasn't! I gave him a long string to move about on. I didn't stop Leah from giving him his dinner. I just tied him up so he won't run away again, that's all. That's all I did. Because I'm a kind person, and not a cruel one.

Contented, and full of goodwill, Jack struck out for the place where he had last seen Treacle. The horse was not there, which was disappointing – but never mind, it could be somewhere around. Jack wandered, his eyes scanning the hillside and the distant slopes, where some small groups of ponies clustered.

Suddenly, he heard a rustle behind him. He turned, and to his overwhelming joy he saw! There was his horse, standing a few metres away, looking at him. His horse had come to find *him*.

This time it came without hesitation for the biscuits. With trembling and excited fingers, Jack took them one by one from the packet. He stroked the pony's neck, and laid his cheek against its side, and once again there was that marvellous feeling, the one he had this morning. The feeling flooded him, and poured out of him, all over his horse.

Jack fed Treacle until he realised that the packet was half empty. And it was the last packet, wasn't it! Jack thrust the remains of the biscuits into his pocket. 'That's it, now,' he whispered to his horse. 'That's your lot – we have to save the rest for tomorrow.'

The horse whinnied and pawed the ground. It nuzzled Jack's chest, trying to find the biscuits – then gave up, and let Jack fondle it anyway. For a few minutes, the horse accepted Jack's caresses, then whinnied again, and began to walk away.

It ambled off, towards one of the far off groups. Tiny in the distance, it mingled with the group, and the group blended into the rest of the wilderness. 'See you later, Treacle!' Jack called after it. He had not the slightest doubt that they would meet again. They had to meet, it was all part of the pattern. This wonderful new pattern that had just lately come into his life.

Jack threw himself down in the bracken and lay on his back, gazing up at the sky. His feeling for

Treacle swelled and swelled, only now it wasn't just for Treacle, it was for everything around him. And it seemed like the feeling was somehow coming back to him, from outside! It was outside and inside, or so it seemed. It was everywhere; the wilderness was alive with it. Jack lay on his back, and felt the wilderness, and knew that he was happy.

He turned, and the biscuits in his pocket jabbed uncomfortably against his hip. The last packet! And the food in the cupboard was disappearing fast! There was plenty left still, but it wouldn't last for ever; something had to be done. . . .

He had an idea. He jumped to his feet and began a leaping run back to *Hideaway*, eagerness carrying him without effort through the bracken. He was so elated, it was like flying. Sitting on the grass outside the van, Leah greeted him without enthusiasm. 'Where have you been?'

'I told you. To see my horse.'

Leah said nothing.

'What's the matter?'

'It's all very well, innit? You go off to do exciting things, and I have to stay here and watch Charlie.'

'So? What's wrong with that?'

'It's not very interesting for me.'

'Don't you like sorting out the cupboards any more then?'

'*Jack!* I finished that ages ago!'

'All right, don't worry. I just now thought of something good for us to do!'

'*Really* good?'

'Trust me!' Jack climbed into the van, and came out carrying the hammer and a screwdriver.

'What's that for?' said Leah.

'A spade would be more better, but I couldn't find one.'

'What you want a spade for?'

'Don't be stupid! The usual thing people do with spades is dig, isn't it?'

'OK. What you wanna dig for?'

'Trust me!' He found a patch where the grass was short and springy, and began attacking it with the claw end of the hammer. 'You do some with this.'

'I can't dig with a screwdriver.'

'It's better than nothing.'

'But what's it *for*?'

'Leah! You are not being very intelligent this afternoon. It's to make a garden, of course.'

'Is that it, then? Is that the good thing?'

'I bet *you* couldn't think of it.'

'I don't see the point,' said Leah. 'I don't see the point of a garden.'

'To grow things in, of course.'

'What things?'

'Things to eat. Like carrots and potatoes and things.'

Leah gaped at him. 'What are you talking about?'

'I'm talking about carrots and potatoes. You know what carrots and potatoes are, don't you?'

'But *we* can't grow carrots and potatoes!'

'Why not?'

'It takes a long time. We won't be here for long enough. For them to come up.'

Jack hacked away with his hammer head. 'Come on, you're not doing your share!'

Leah poked half-heartedly with the screwdriver. 'Anyway, we haven't got any seeds to plant.'

'I'll find a way to get seeds. There must be some seeds somewhere.'

'Where, for instance?'

'Somewhere. In the van, perhaps.'

'Get real, Jack!'

'All right, all right, I'll tell you what. In the tumbledown house – there's probably some seeds there!'

For all Leah knew, there might be. She poked again with the screwdriver, her unease growing. 'Jack – we can't stay here for always, you know.'

Jack went on hacking away at the turf. His muscles ached, but he kept going. Leah dutifully stabbed alongside him with the screwdriver, and wondered how much longer she was expected to keep this up. Finally, Jack straightened his back, and reviewed their progress. 'We don't seem to have done much,' said Leah.

'Yes we have, we made a good start. We can have a little rest now, if you like.'

'Good, because I must say I'm not enjoying this wonderful thing you thought of very much.'

They sat side by side in the sunshine. Jack took out a biscuit, put it to his mouth, and regretfully put it back in his pocket. 'I have to keep them all for my horse,' he explained. 'Would you like me to tell you about my horse?'

'Jack—'

'Don't you want me to tell you about my horse?'

'I have to tell *you* something. . . . It's about Charlie.'

'Do we have to talk about Charlie?'

'I think there's something wrong with him.'

'There is. He's a cry-baby and a traitor.'

'I think he's sick.'

'He's got a cold, that's all. A cold is nothing.'

'He's not *doing* nothing, though. He's just sitting there, with his head down. Didn't you see him, when you went inside?'

'I didn't bother to look. I'm not interested in traitors.'

'Aren't you? Well anyway, he won't eat nothing, and he won't talk.'

'He's sulking. Because we wouldn't let him give away our hiding place.'

'I don't like it, though.'

Jack frowned, considering. Leah was making an unreasonable fuss about Charlie, and a fairly unreasonable fuss about having to mind him. Nevertheless, it wouldn't do to let her get too dissatisfied; he made her an offer. 'Would you like to go swimming?'

'By myself?'

'Well, we can't both go!'

'It's no fun by myself, I don't want to do it.'

Jack considered again. '. . . I know, we'll take him with us! We'll take Traitor with us!'

'We can't, he's not well.'

Annoyed, and irritated because Charlie was *still* spoiling things for him, Jack climbed into the van. 'What's the matter with you, then?'

Charlie, his head still on his arms, did not move.

'See what I mean?' said Leah, in the doorway.

'Come on, get up!' Jack grabbed Charlie by the arm, and yanked him to his feet. Something fell to the floor, beneath the table. Jack pounced, and held it up in triumph. 'What's this, then? What's this I found?'

'What *is* it?' said Leah.

'Only a empty packet of crisps, that's all! And

crumbs all over him! He's ate a whole packet of crisps when nobody wasn't looking, and then he tried to hide it!'

'Charlie!' Leah reproached him.

Charlie turned his head, and said nothing.

'See? He's a cheat! You don't have to be sorry for him, he's just making out!' Jack climbed out of the van again, and untied the lead from the gear lever. 'Come on, Charlie, walkies!'

Leah was not comfortable about what they were doing, but she was angry with Charlie as well, for not being as ill as he was pretending to be. She found a tissue and thrust it into his hand. 'And wipe your dirty nose, you look disgusting!'

Jack's smile was quite untroubled as he dragged Charlie down the hillside. And Charlie came because he had no choice, the string tugging painfully at his waist whenever he flagged. His nose streamed; his sharp little face was white as pastry, his eyelids swollen and red-rimmed.

Leah charged ahead, not wanting to see. She clumped and slithered through the bracken, waving a blouse of Lil's in one hand, and a pair of Lil's shorts in the other, and screaming 'We wish you a merry Christmas' at the top of her voice. At the pool, she changed behind a bush into Lil's things, then waded straight in, not looking while Jack tied Charlie to another tree. She splashed and yelled, throwing everything she had into the desperate business of enjoying herself. Her forced and high-pitched laughter bounced from rock to rock.

But the sun waned, the late afternoon grew cool. Leah climbed out of the water at last, and sat on a boulder – shivering in her wet clothes, and watching Jack who didn't seem to be feeling the cold at all. Behind her, Charlie crouched by his tree, silent and wretched. Leah couldn't see him, because she was very carefully looking the other way; but she could feel his misery; it came at her in waves across the grass.

And as she sat there, the brittle joyfulness she had built around herself finally cracked, and split open, giving a chilling glimpse of the darkness underneath. For a moment, she struggled to close the gap, but it was too wide and too deep. She was doing wrong, and she knew it. Staying here was wrong, and she couldn't run away from the truth of that any longer. 'Jack!' she called, in a troubled voice. 'Come here, I want to talk to you.'

'In a minute.'

'No, now. Come now!' She was trembling inside; if she didn't say it this minute, she might be too weak to say it at all.

'All right, what is it? You cold or something?'

'It's not just that. . . . It's I think we have to go home.' Her own voice seemed to be coming from somewhere outside herself.

'OK.'

Leah was amazed that he agreed so easily. ' . . . Shall we go now, then?' she said, faintly.

'Yeah – it's just about tea time anyway.'

'No, no, I don't mean the van. I mean our real home.'

'The van *is* our real home.'

'No it isn't, you *know* it isn't! Our real home is in London.'

'Don't be silly, Leah, that was a long time ago.' Jack's face was serenely happy, his eyes shining. 'This wilderness is much better than London. We live here now!'

11

Fantasies and realities

Jack was running his engine, and Leah was worrying herself sick. I don't know what has happened to Jack, she thought. I think he has gone in a dream world. I think he wants to stay here so much he has forgot the difference between real things and pretend things.

What is going to happen? There's enough food for two more days, perhaps, or three more days if we don't eat very much, but what is going to happen after that?

There were other things that bothered her, as well – things like not being able to wash properly, unless swimming in the stream counted for washing, and having to sleep in her clothes, and not having any proper privacy from the boys.

We ought to go home now, she thought. I'm ever so scared about everything, and I specially wish I could know what is going on in my house. My brothers might be all right or they might not. And my mum and dad might want me or they might not, but anyway I ought to go and find out.

And there's Charlie's mum, as well.

And Charlie should be in bed. He's got a horrible cold, and he's starting to make funny noises in his chest. And coughing again. He ought to be tucked up in bed with nice hot drinks. But Jack only thinks about his engine and his horse and his wilderness. He doesn't think about human people at all. I don't know what to say to Jack, to make him think about human people.

... Charlie wouldn't have anything to eat again. I think at dinner time he done it for spite, a bit, because he doesn't want me to rule him. He didn't want to give in to me when I told him to eat his dinner, but he ate the crisps after, because he was a little bit hungry really. That is all he had since breakfast, though. He wouldn't starve himself like this just for spite, would he? I think he is getting to be really ill, and we ought to take him home, but Jack won't even listen.

How can I make Jack see some sense? What can I say to him?

I think Jack is the unreasonablest person I ever met in my life.

... I can do one thing, though. I can make a proper bed for Charlie! I don't know how it works, but I suppose I can find out. You have to take the table out, and put something to fill in the space, and then spread the cushions over. I *think*. ...

Leah struggled to move the table, but awkwardly, and without success. 'Jack! Please help me!'

Jack went on running his engine.

'*Jack!* I want to ask you something.'

'I'm busy.'

'This is important.'

A disquieting thought struck Jack. Nothing to do with Charlie – to do with his engine. If he drove his engine too much it could run out of petrol, couldn't it! He must make sure to only do it sometimes. Now and again. For a treat.

Regretfully, he switched off. 'All right,' he said to Leah. 'What is this important thing?'

'We have to make a proper bed for Charlie.'

'*That's* not important.'

'It is. If Charlie doesn't have a proper bed he can get really sick, and have to have the doctor.'

Jack laughed. '*He's* not really sick. He's making out!'

'Look at him, Jack! He's just sitting there, and he looks terrible.'

Jack turned briefly in his seat, and quickly back again. 'He looks all right to me. You're exaggerating.'

'All right, I'm exaggerating. It won't do no harm to make him a bed, though.'

'OK, *you* make him a bed.'

'I can't. I'm trying to tell you. You have to help me find out how to do it.'

'. . . All right, I'll help you make the downstairs bed, but you have to do something back. You have to sleep down here with Charlie, and let me have the high-up bed all to myself.'

'That's not fair, though. I shall get all Charlie's germs.'

'Suit yourself.'

Leah scowled. '. . . All right, all right, I'll sleep down here with Charlie. *Now* will you help me?'

Jack climbed out of the driver's seat, with his most angelic smile. 'You have to take the table out.'

'I know. I tried.'

'You have to pull it like this. . . . Get Traitor out of the way first.'

Leah took Charlie's arm and pulled, quite gently. 'Come on, come and sit in the front while me and Jack make a bed for you.'

Charlie stiffened, and jerked away.

'Come on, there's a good boy.'

'You're too soft with him!' said Jack. He picked

up the string, which was still attached to Charlie's waist, and gave it a sharp tug.

'Ow!' Leave me!' Charlie began to cough, but Jack went on tugging at the string. There were tears of pain and wretchedness in Charlie's eyes, as Jack dragged him by the string, out of his seat and up to the front.

'You don't have to be so rough,' said Leah.

'It's his fault for making trouble,' said Jack. He got the table off with no difficulty. 'Now we fit it across. Like this, see?' The table slotted into place. 'Now put the cushions back.' Meekly, Leah replaced them. 'There!' said Jack. 'Now that's done, and I don't want to hear no more about Charlie for tonight – OK?'

'Come on, Charlie,' said Leah. 'You can have a nice lay down now, and tomorrow I think you will be better.'

But Charlie was restless in the night. He coughed, and wheezed, and moved about, trying to make himself comfortable. Leah sat up in bed and regarded him with deep concern.

They had been lying head to toe. Leah had decided they should sleep this way, to avoid sharing their germs, but now the night had come there was no sleep for either of them anyway. Knees drawn up, they sat facing one another – Charlie hunched over and wheezing, with his nose still running, and every now and again that disturbing little cough.

On the high-up bed, Jack shifted and grumbled. 'Can't you do something to shut him up?'

'Like what?' said Leah.

'I dunno. Something.'

'I'll just pop out to the chemist, shall I? And get him some cough mixture?'

'Oh, clever, clever!'

'We ought to take him home, Jack. We can't live in this wilderness without chemists and doctors.'

'Yes we can.'

'We *can't.*'

'We can. I seen on the telly you can, sort of, make medicines out of plants. Tomorrow I'll find some plants to make medicine for Charlie.'

'It won't work,' said Leah.

'It will. Trust me.'

Leah got up and turned on the light. 'What you doing now?' said Jack.

'I'm going to make a cup of tea for Charlie. I think that might help.'

'Well, hurry up. I want to get to sleep.'

'It's a lot worse for Charlie, you know,' said Leah.

Jack put his fingers in his ears and rolled over. He didn't like the feelings he was beginning to have. There was annoyance at being kept awake, but there was something else as well. Something was stirring, deep inside himself, that he didn't welcome at all. He didn't want to feel sorry for Charlie – why should he? Who had ever been sorry for *him*? No one! He pushed the uncomfortable feelings away, and thought about Treacle instead, and his garden, and the bathing pool down in the stream.

Jack drifted into sleep and delightful dreams; and Charlie went on wheezing, and coughing fitfully, through the night.

In the morning, he was still wheezing, but the cough had more or less stopped. 'See?' said Jack. 'He's better.'

'What about that funny noise he's making, in his chest?'

'That's nothing. That'll go away.'

'We'll see if he eats any breakfast,' said Leah.

She coaxed some bread and margarine into him, and he drank the tea she made, but wouldn't get out of bed. 'I want to go home,' he kept saying.

'Well, you can't,' said Jack, firmly. 'You can't go home because we live here now. I know you don't like it at the moment, but you'll get used to it, trust me! Leah's used to it already, ain't you, Leah? Anyway, nearly.'

'Getting used to here won't make Charlie better from his cold,' said Leah.

'I told you,' said Jack, 'I'm going to make some medicine for that.'

He jumped out of the van, and Leah looked anxiously once more at Charlie. 'Are you warm enough?' she asked him. Charlie hunched the blanket round his shoulders, but made no answer.

'You can have the duvet as well if you like, now Jack's not using it.'

No answer.

'I wish you would talk to me, Charlie. It's lonely trying to help you, when you won't speak.'

'I want to go home,' he muttered.

'I mean, like, say something else besides that. You said that enough times now. I don't think you have to say that again, because I got the idea now.'

But Charlie only turned his back, and blew his nose, and was silent once more. Leah sighed. She did the washing up, tidied the top bed, sighed again, and went to the cab door.

'Where you going?' said a small sad voice, behind her.

'Oh,' said Leah, pleased. 'You haven't forgot how to talk, after all!'

'Where you going, then?'
'Get some fresh air.'
'. . . Don't! Stay here.'
Leah came towards him, and sat on the edge of the bed. 'All right. . . . How you feeling now, then?'
'Horrible.' His voice was husky, and there was real fear in his eyes. Leah saw the fear, and her own anxiety deepened.
'What's the matter, Charlie?'
'You *know* what's the matter.'
'I know you've got a bad cold, but I think there's something else. I think there's something you haven't said.'
Charlie turned his back again. 'There isn't, then.'
'I think there's something special you're scared about.'
'No, there's not!'
Leah picked at the edge of the blanket. '. . . Actually, Charlie, if you want to know, there's something I'm specially scared about as well, so you're not the only one.'
No answer.
'If you tell me your secret, I'll tell you mine.'
Charlie coughed, and Leah waited for that to be over.
'. . . So?'
Charlie said nothing.
'All right, I'll say mine first. . . . The thing is, I'm scared to go home because I did something bad.' The words came out stiffly and with difficulty, but she was glad to be saying them really. It was a relief to be sharing her worries at last, and not bottling them up inside her. 'Do you want to know what I did?'

Charlie shrugged.

'All right, I'll tell you anyway. . . . I left my brothers all alone when I was meant to be minding them, and it was a really wicked thing that I'm really ashamed of now.'

'That's not a secret!' said Charlie.

'Yes it is.'

'It's not! You told about it before.'

'No, I never! I never told nobody.'

'You did! You said about it when we was being kidnapped. I remember. You shouted it out, here in the van.'

'Did I?' Only a few days, but so long ago she had quite forgotten. '. . . Anyway, that's the big thing that is worrying me. Now you tell me what's worrying you.'

'. . . I don't want to.'

'Have you got something to be ashamed of, as well?'

No answer.

'I suppose that means you have. . . . You can tell me, though, Charlie. I will understand.'

No answer.

'Charlie,' said Leah, 'do you believe I want to help you?'

'. . . Yes.'

'Do you believe I want to be your friend?'

'. . . I suppose so.'

'So tell me what's the matter.'

'You'll tell Jack, though.'

'I won't, I won't!'

'You will! You're always trying to make Jack be your friend, and push me out!'

'Is that what you think?' Leah was truly amazed. '*Charlie! I* don't want to make Jack be my friend! I don't even like Jack very much. . . . Well, I *do*. . . . You can't help it, can you, when he's being nice? But I never wanted to push you out, I never even thought of it.'

'Didn't you?'

'No, I didn't. . . . So now tell me your secret, and I promise I'll never tell Jack, not ever in the world.'

Charlie took a sharp breath.

'Well?'

'. . . *I've got asthma.*' Charlie's head hung low, the words came out in a shamefaced whisper.

Leah was puzzled; the revelation meant nothing to her. 'What's that?'

'There's something wrong with me.'

'Something you did?'

'No, not something I *did*, something I've got!'

'You mean, like a cough?'

'Yes, but it's worse than that. It's in my chest. It makes it so I can't breathe.'

'You can breathe! You're breathing now.'

'I know. But when it gets bad I can't breathe. If it gets very bad I have to go to hospital and have a thing over my face.'

'Is it going to be bad like that now, then?'

'I don't know,' said Charlie, and again there was the fear in his eyes. 'It's like it's starting to be.'

Leah stared at him, aghast. 'Why didn't you say that before? We must tell Jack, we must tell him now!'

'*No!*' Charlie's wheezing was suddenly faster and louder. His face was concentrated, as though breathing had become hard work.

'*Charlie,*' said Leah, 'you're silly! It ain't nothing to be ashamed of. It ain't like it's your fault.'

Charlie turned his head again. 'I don't want Jack to know.'

'But why?'

'I don't, that's all. I don't want anybody to know, really.'

'But *why*?'

There was silence before he muttered the words. 'I don't want people to think I'm different to other people, do I?'

'Oh . . . I see . . .' Leah thought she was beginning to, but she was greatly troubled. 'Suppose you have to go to hospital, though? What happens if you can't breathe, and you don't go to hospital for them to put that thing over your face?'

Silence.

'What happens, Charlie?'

'. . . I don't know.'

Leah was afraid to ask the question that was in her mind, but her thoughts were racing. What was to be done? She wished she had not given that promise about not telling Jack. Surely, if he knew, even Jack would see that it was important to get proper help! 'What do you think, then, Charlie? Do you think you *will* need to go to hospital?'

'I don't know. It was a long time ago when I went before—' Charlie stopped to take a noisy breath. 'It's not fair; it's not supposed to happen again! . . . I'm meant to be growing out of it, it's not supposed to happen! . . . My mum said that and the doctor said it as well. . . . It's not fair!'

'But you didn't grow out of it quite, yet, did you!'

'Nearly, nearly.'

'What about when you get out of breath, then? Like when you run, and climb up the hill?'

'I *don't!*'

'Yes you do, you know you do!'

Charlie hung his head again. '. . . All right, then, I do.'

'So I suppose that's because of the thing that's wrong with you.'

'. . . All right, then, it is.'

'You should have said!'

'I didn't want you to know, did I?'

'Don't you have any medicine to take? I mean proper medicine, from the doctor's!'

'. . . I have a sort of puffer thing,' he admitted. 'But I don't like people to see me using it.'

'Where is it now?'

'I left it in my school bag.'

'*Charlie!* You should have brung your puffer with you!'

'OK, you don't have to be so bossy about it!'

'I'm not bossy!'

'Yes, you are!'

Leah was silent. She hadn't known she was bossy; such a thing had never occurred to her. Perhaps, in the same way, Charlie didn't know he was horrid! Poor, horrid Charlie, with this unlucky thing he didn't want anybody to know about!

She got up, and began pacing backwards and forwards the short length of the van. She longed to be out in the sunshine, not stuffed up here in this caravan with Charlie's germs. But it seemed like Charlie didn't want to be left alone. Full of concern, Leah sat on the bed again. 'I wish the police would come,' said Charlie. 'In their helicopters, like they're supposed to!'

'Oh, *yes*, Charlie! Oh, yes, so do I wish that! . . . What about all that rubbish stuff on the van, though? Do you think that rubbish stuff will trick the police? Shall I pull it off?'

'How about we listen to the radio first?' said Charlie.

'Oh, yes, the radio, the radio! Let's turn on the radio, Charlie, and listen to the News! Let's see how the police are getting on with finding the van!' She had forgotten all about the radio, until this moment. How could she have forgotten the radio? Probably, she thought, because before, she hadn't *wanted* to remember it. 'How do you work this radio, Charlie? Show me which knobs to turn!'

Even that small movement made him short of breath. The children listened to the radio until the News came and then they listened to the News with desperately straining ears – but there was nothing about *Hideaway*, nothing at all. 'I think they have forgot about us,' said Leah, sadly.

Charlie crept back to bed. 'That's right,' said Leah. 'You keep nice and warm, and look after your a – a – what is it called?'

'Asthma,' said Charlie, turning his head to hide his flaming cheeks.

Leah looked out of the only window not obscured by dying greenery. 'Jack's coming back,' she announced, without enthusiasm. 'He's got all weeds in his hand.'

Charlie wheezed and wheezed.

'It's all right, Charlie,' said Jack, cheerfully, climbing into the van. 'You'll be all better soon, trust me!' He flicked back his uncombed hair, and smiled with unbrushed teeth. He looked scruffy; but his eyes were bright, his cheeks had lost their city pallor. The bruises on his arms were still dark, but the scratches were healing nicely. Jack pulled

Leah out of the way, and stood by the bed, radiating health and joy.

'What have you got there?' said Leah.

'Plants, of course, to make the medicine for Charlie.'

'How did you know the right ones to get, though?'

'Well, I don't,' Jack admitted. 'Not *exactly*. So I brought a bit of everything, to make sure.'

'It might be poisonous,' said Leah, suspiciously. 'How do you know you haven't got something poisonous in that lot?'

'Don't be silly, Leah, there's no poisonous things in a wilderness!'

'How do you know?'

'There's poisonous things in a jungle, but I never heard of poisonous things in a wilderness.'

'. . . Anyway, Charlie won't eat those weeds.'

'Did I say he had to eat them? I'm going to mash them up in some water, and make a drink out of them.'

'That won't work,' said Leah, 'you'll have to cook it, you'll have to boil it up.'

'All right, I'll boil it up,' said Jack. 'To make them mash up better.'

Jack found a saucepan, stuffed the assortment of leaves and flowers into it, and filled the pan with water. 'If you fill it too full it will boil over,' said Leah. 'Anyway, Charlie won't drink it.'

'Yes he will. You'll drink my medicine, won't you, Charlie? You want to get better, don't you? So you'll drink my medicine!'

'Don't, Charlie!' said Leah. 'It can be poisonous.'

The cooking mixture gave off a peculiar smell.

'That's the poison,' said Leah. 'The poison is making that pong.'

'No it's not,' said Jack. 'It's the goodness. Good medicine always smells funny.'

He mashed with gusto. 'There! I think it's done, now.' He poured the greenish liquid into a cup.

'Don't drink it, Charlie,' said Leah.

'Don't listen to her, Charlie,' said Jack. 'Come on, sit up properly, and have your medicine.'

'Jack!' Leah pleaded. 'Do you want to make him worse?'

Jack sat on the edge of the bed. He smiled his most winning smile at Charlie, and held out the cup. Charlie turned his head.

Jack grabbed a fistful of Charlie's hair, and tugged. Resisting with all his strength, Charlie began to cough. 'Stop it, Jack!' said Leah.

'It's for his own good,' said Jack; he tugged at the curls again. 'Turn round, and I'll stop!' Charlie's head came round. Jack waited for the coughing to finish, then put the cup against Charlie's lips. 'Come on, now, drink it!'

Charlie closed his lips. One hand went up to push the cup away, and the hot liquid spilled over Jack's hand, making him yell. Serve him right, Leah thought, but *I* ought to have been the one to do that! I ought to stand up to Jack more. . . . The trouble is, I'm so used to letting him get away with it.

Jack put the cup on the floor and sucked at his scalded hand. 'That was a very ungrateful thing to do . . . *Traitor!*'

'I told you he wouldn't drink it,' said Leah.

'He can't be ill, then. If he won't drink his medicine, that means he can't be really ill. So there's nothing to worry about, Leah, and I'm going to find my horse.' He pushed past Leah, and sprang lightly out of the van.

'Good!' Leah called after him. 'Go and find your horse. See if your horse will drink your rubbish medicine!'

Charlie was crying quietly; Leah put her arm round him. A daring idea was beginning to form in her mind. 'Charlie, now Jack is gone, shall me and you go home by ourself?'

Charlie did not answer.

'Shall we, Charlie?'

'. . . I don't think I can.' The words came hoarsely, unwillingly.

'How about we just *try*?'

'I can't!' He was panting now, his eyes full of fear, his breath coming in gasps as though the very thought of running away was making him worse.

'You mean you can't do the climbing? Because you'll get too out of breath?'

Charlie nodded.

Leah's heart began to hammer, and she felt the wetness in her palms. She swallowed a couple of times, and made herself say it. 'Supposing if I go on my own?'

'No!'

'You don't want me to go and find someone to help us?'

'Don't leave me with *him!*'

'All right, all right, I won't.' Leah was more than ready to agree. She sighed with relief that there was a good excuse for not going, but she was still desperately worried. 'Charlie, let me tell Jack. Let me explain to him about the hospital and everything.'

'*No!*'

'*Please*, Charlie! Please let me off of my promise!'

'No! He'll make fun of me!'

'He *can't*. Not about something like that! . . . Anyway, what does it matter if he does?'

Charlie turned his head.

'Charlie! Don't say you *still* want Jack to be your friend!'

'*No!*'

'So it doesn't matter if he laughs, so why not tell him? It can't do any harm. Most likely it will make him see sense! It's the best chance, Charlie!'

'*No!*' Charlie clutched at Leah, and begged. 'Don't! Don't! Don't tell him, you promised!'

He was upset again, and being upset was definitely making him worse. 'All right,' she soothed him. 'I won't tell if you don't want me to.'

'I'll be all right, I will! I wish I never told you nothing about it, now.'

'All right, Charlie. Don't you worry about anything.'

Leah cleared up the mess, throwing the mashed leaves outside, and tried to think. There was no clear way, no clear right or wrong. If she went for help, Charlie would be upset. If Charlie was upset, his asthma would get worse. On the other hand, if she didn't go for help, it might get worse anyway. Perhaps he would die – how could she know?

Her palms were clammy again. On balance, it looked like she ought to go. But it would be so frightening, doing it all by herself. And going against Jack. And suppose Jack caught her?

It's not just that I'm used to doing what he says, Leah thought. It's that he's stronger than me. I couldn't fight him. And I don't know what he would do to me, but look what he done to Charlie!

Leah looked at Charlie, with the string from his waist still trailing across the floor. Charlie had fallen against the cushions, sprawled under the blanket and half sitting up. He was breathing wheezily through his mouth, and he was asleep.

Perhaps the sleep would make him well. Leah would have liked to sleep herself; her eyes were sore from being awake much of the night, and her body felt heavy. She lay on the bed again, head to toe with Charlie, and tried to doze off.

Jack tramped through the bracken looking for his horse. He was serenely happy. Away from the van, he had slipped neatly out of his annoyance, and left it behind him, like an old skin. He had no use for annoyance and worries about people being ill. There was an exciting new idea that had just come to him, and he was on his way to make it happen.

He was going to ride his horse!

He just decided it, that was what he was going to do. He would put his arms round Treacle's neck, and the horse would stand quite still and let him pull himself up. The horse would be happy to have Jack on its back. They would gallop over the hills and . . . well, no, not *too* far over the hills! If they came to a road, or a house, or people having a picnic, then of course they would turn right back before anyone could see them. Treacle would soon get the idea of it. Treacle wouldn't want Jack to be caught, and taken back to London, any more than Jack did himself.

This morning, however, Treacle was nowhere to be found. Disappointed after half an hour of searching, Jack lay in the bracken and gazed upwards through half closed lids. Today there was a gentle breeze, and white puffs of cloud, not enough to obscure the sunshine, drifting lazily across the blue. The little clouds were lovely in the bright sky. How could he think of leaving this place? Well, he couldn't! He couldn't even think of it, and that was that.

He remembered that he needed seeds for his garden. This morning would be as good a time as any to go to the tumbledown house and look for them, he thought. Full of new purpose, Jack scrambled to his feet and began to climb.

The tumbledown house looked different in the sunshine, smaller than he remembered, and rather sad. Jack pushed open the rotting door and went inside. Now he was here, he was less sure that he was going to find what he was looking for. What had made him think there were going to be seeds in this place? There was a garden, though, and a garden has to have seeds to put in it! Jack didn't need many – just a packet or two left behind, that the people who used to live here didn't bother to take with them when they went.

He wondered where the seeds would be kept. Somewhere at the back of the house most likely, he thought. Out in the kitchen; or there might be a shed – he hadn't really explored, before. He found a room with a dirty old fireplace thing, stretching across most of one wall. There was ash spilling out of the fireplace thing, and a battered frying pan hanging from a hook, and a musty smell that was strong enough to make you feel you didn't want to breathe too deeply.

Jack supposed this was meant to be the kitchen,

and he didn't think much of it. He thought even less of the smaller room beyond, which had a filthy chipped sink in one corner, and a door with a latch on the opposite wall. Jack opened the door with the latch, and saw tiers of shelves, all covered with grit and bits of broken plaster.

And amongst the rubble sat several tins, and jars with what looked like food in them!

Jack's heart leapt with excitement. There was one of macaroni cheese, two of minced beef, and an assortment of soups. The tins looked very old. They were rusty, and topped with a thick layer of dust, but they didn't seem to be damaged in any way. They would be all right to eat, they would be fine! Jack examined the jars, and found bottled fruit and jam. The stuff in the jars looked all right too. His spirits soaring, he looked for a bag or something to put them in. In the cupboard under the stairs was a tatty old shopping basket – that would do!

The loaded basket was heavy. Regretfully, Jack took out two jars of bottled fruit and put them back on the shelf – and as he was doing that, his fingers touched something flat and knobbly that he hadn't noticed before.

It was a packet of dried peas.

At first, Jack wasn't going to bother with the peas. He was about to throw them down, when a brilliant idea struck him! Didn't Miss grow some peas in the classroom one time, or was it beans? Anyway, they were much the same thing, weren't they?

He had found some seeds for his garden, he had found some seeds, and he would go right back now, and plant them!

12

Bravely up the hill

Leah awoke from a short and fitful sleep. Her head was towards one downward slope of the van, her body sliding towards the other. On the high-up bed the slope had been away from the edge, and her head had been the other way round, which was more comfortable for sleeping.

At the other end of the bed, Charlie still slept, and wheezed. Carefully so as not to disturb him, Leah eased herself into a sitting position, and looked at his pinched little face. The dark circles under his eyes bit into the white cheeks, and even in sleep his face was strained.

She thought about what he had told her. How funny, to make a secret out of something like that. If she had that assma thing she would be quite proud of it, she thought. It would make her special; she would want everybody to know.

Was Charlie going to be all right, though? Here in this wilderness, with no doctors and no hospitals, would Charlie be all right?

Supposing – just supposing – she were to get up now, while he was sleeping, and run up the hill before Jack got back, and supposing there might be two nice people having a picnic up there, like before? Would she dare to do that? Would she dare to go for help, all by herself? Would she dare to decide it, when it might be the wrong thing?

Leah turned to the open window behind her,

and looked out. She couldn't see Jack, but of course he might be on the other side of the van. She tiptoed to the cab door and opened it. She peered round the little trees, but Jack was nowhere in sight. She stepped out of the van and went all round it, peering up, and down, and around.

With her heart banging, she started to climb the hill.

Leah was about three quarters of the way up when she heard a shout, coming thinly from a distance. *Jack.* She looked up in dismay, and saw him coming along the track. He was waving at her, and calling; and he was carrying something that looked heavy.

What should she do?

It was obviously too late to hide, but maybe she could run! She had a good start – if she ran really hard, she might get to the place where those people had their picnic, before Jack could catch up with her. Only please let them be there! Please let them be there! Leah turned, and ploughed blindly through the ferns.

She had forgotten about the bog! She didn't remember about the bog until she felt her foot sinking. In a desperate effort to find solid ground, she made a great stride over the bracken – and felt the other foot sinking too! With her legs widely scissored, Leah felt both feet being sucked down, down, down. She was trapped, and she was most likely going right under this time!

Leah screamed. 'Help me! Jack! Help me!'

He came up, swinging an old basket, and smiling his most radiant smile. 'Look what I found!'

'Help me, Jack, I'm going to drown!'

'No, you're not.'

'I am! Look, my legs have nearly disappeared!'

'You're exaggerating.'

'Help me, Jack, I can't get out!' She was terribly frightened. Wouldn't Jack take even this seriously?

Jack came nearer, but stepped back smartly when he felt his own feet slipping into the squelchy earth. He considered. 'I think you're supposed to lie down.'

'I can't.'

'Well, anyway, that's what you're supposed to do.'

'I can't. It's too awkward, my legs are too far apart.'

Jack put his basket on the ground, and lay full length himself. He wriggled forward. 'Give me your hand.'

'I can't. I can't reach you.'

He wriggled forward again, and grasped her leg, heaving and wrenching it out of the bog. 'Now lie down!'

Awkwardly, Leah toppled herself forward. 'Stretch out your arms!' Awkwardly, Leah stretched them. Jack grasped her hands and began to wriggle backwards, dragging her with him over the bracken.

Once they were both safe, he immediately lost interest in the adventure. He picked up the basket again, and held it out proudly. 'Look what I got!'

Still shaky from the fright, Leah brushed herself down. 'What is it?'

'Food! A load more food! And I couldn't even bring it all, I shall have to go back.'

'Oh.'

'Aren't you pleased? I got some seeds for my garden as well; I told you I would!'

'Oh.'

'What's the matter?'

Leah said nothing. Jack looked at her face more closely. 'What you doing up here, anyway?' he said, suddenly suspicious.

Leah turned her head. In her mind, she groped wildly for some excuse, but none presented itself.

'You're meant to be minding Charlie! Why ain't you minding Charlie?'

That, at least, was easy to answer. 'He doesn't need minding. He's too ill to run away.'

'You're exaggerating. You don't know his tricks. Come on – we best get back before he tries it again!'

Jack dropped the basket, and began to run down the hill. Uncertain what to do now, Leah followed him with her eyes for a moment, then turned and made for the track. In a wild panic, her heart banging against her ribs and the blood roaring in her ears, she scrambled up the grassy slope – grabbing at the turf with her hands as she went, to make herself climb quicker.

'What you think you're doing!'

He had noticed! Jack had noticed that she wasn't following! Leah reached the track and began to run her hardest. Jack caught her up with very little difficulty. He grabbed her by the arms, and his grip was like steel. 'What you think you're up to?'

The tears welled up in Leah's eyes. 'Let me go!'

'I know what's in your mind. I'm not stupid, you know.'

'I know you're not stupid.'

'Well, then. . . .'

'I know you're not stupid, Jack, but you don't

understand that Charlie has to have some proper help.'

'*Leah!*' Jack reproached her. 'You're supposed to be on *my* side.'

'It isn't a matter of whose side. It's a matter of who needs something.'

'Charlie doesn't need nothing.'

'He does, he does!' Leah began to struggle, putting all her strength into the effort. 'Let me go, let me go!'

'No, I won't! You're spoiling everything, Leah.' He began to frogmarch her down the hill. She resisted, digging her heels into the grass; but the thumping of Jack's knee against her back was painful, and so was the way he wrenched at her arms. 'All right,' she said. 'I'll walk.'

'You on my side again now, then?'

'Whatever you say,' said Leah, wearily.

'That's better,' said Jack. 'I was getting to be really disappointed in you!'

He pushed her into the van. Charlie sat up on the bed and gazed at Leah out of his strained, dark-circled eyes. 'Where were you? Where did you go?'

'It's all right, Charlie, I'm back now.'

'Where did you go, though?'

'I was trying to get help. . . . Don't be cross with me, Charlie, I was doing it for the best.'

Charlie was furious. 'I don't want you to! I said I don't want you to!'

'See, Leah?' said Jack. 'Charlie don't even *want* you to go!'

'You're sick, though, Charlie,' said Leah. 'You might have to go to the hospital.'

Charlie was even more furious. 'What stupid

thing are you saying, Leah?' He drew breath noisily. 'What you want to say . . . things about hospital for?'

Of course, of course, it was Charlie's secret and she wasn't supposed to tell! 'I didn't mean . . . I didn't exactly mean. . . .' Contrite, and confused, Leah blundered on. 'I just thought . . . you know . . . your cold might get worse, and . . . I just thought—'

'Well, you didn't think right . . . because I'm better now.' The wheezing was still there, though. He might be a little bit better, but not much, Leah thought.

'See?' said Jack. 'Charlie says he's better.'

'He's still making that nasty noise.'

'I'm fine,' said Charlie. 'Anyway, I will be in a minute.'

'Charlie's fine,' said Jack. 'How about some dinner, Leah?'

'I'm not hungry.'

'You can still make some dinner for me!'

'*I'm* hungry,' said Charlie, valiantly.

'See?' said Jack. 'Charlie's hungry.'

There was little choice of food now. Leah cooked the spaghetti, which she didn't much like anyway, and opened a tin of frankfurter sausages. With enjoyment and gusto, Jack shovelled spaghetti and sausages into his mouth, while Leah ate nothing, and Charlie chewed for two whole minutes on the same centimetre of frankfurter. 'He's not eating,' Leah pointed out. 'Look at him!'

'He's being slow, that's all, aren't you, Charlie?' said Jack.

'Yeah,' said Charlie, through the food in his mouth. 'I always eat slow.'

Leah was silent. After a minute, she said: 'In any case we have to leave here soon, because the cupboard's getting to be empty. You know that, don't you, Jack!'

'Leah, I told you! I found a load more food in the tumbledown house. *And* I found some seeds to plant!'

Leah sighed.

'Did you forget?'

'Oh, go on and plant your seeds! Go on and do it, I can't make you see any sense at all!' Leah began piling the pans and plates into the sink, and Jack watched her, thoughtfully.

'. . . I left my basket up the hill, actually.'

'Go and get it, then.'

'. . . Can I trust you, though?'

'What you mean?'

'You know!'

Leah shrugged.

'I shall have to watch you, won't I? All the time, I shall have to watch you!'

Leah shrugged again.

Jack considered. 'I don't like to have to say this, Leah, but I am going to warn you something. If you try to get out, if you just make one step outside the door, I'm going to tie you up. Not like Charlie, with a long string. I shall tie you up with your hands behind your back like when we were being kidnapped. And it will not be very nice for you, but it will be your fault, not mine, because you made me do it!'

Jack shut his problems into the van, and turned his back on them. There was a slight lingering unease in his mind, but that dissipated rapidly, floating away and away into the clear sunlit air. His feet were on springs as he climbed, with only the occasional backward glance, his thoughts fastened eagerly on the basket of hopes he had left at the top of the hill.

He picked it up, and was about to begin the descent when his eye caught a brief glimpse of something flashing, way across the valley. It was only the tiniest flash, and he only saw it for a moment, but the idea of something moving out there disquieted him. What was it? A car? Could there be a road over there? He didn't like the idea of that. . . . He probably imagined it, though. . . . That was it, he probably imagined it! He wouldn't give the matter another thought.

The patch of earth that was his garden, dug with such effort the day before, looked small and inadequate this afternoon. Never mind – there was all the time in the world to make it bigger, and meanwhile he had enough prepared for his peas. The peas would grow quickly, he was sure, whatever Leah said. They grew quickly enough for Miss in the classroom, anyway. And these peas would make other peas, and the other peas would make more peas. And he would find more things to grow. He didn't know what yet, but something would turn up.

Some ideas will come to me, Jack thought. Ideas always come when you need them. Well, anyway, they do to me. Most times. It's like there's a sea or something, all round, and the ideas are floating in the sea, millions of them, just ready to swim into someone's mind.

The ideas would swim into his mind, and he would make his garden bigger, and his life would open out the way it had started to do only better.

And he would never go back to the old life, never, never, *never.*

Jack poked the dried peas carefully, one by one, into the ground. The sun shone hot on the bare earth; already the top layer was crisp, and dry, Jack noticed. He decided that he had better water his seeds. Seeds couldn't grow without water, everyone knew that. He went back to the van. 'Where's the saucepans?'

'What you want a saucepan for?' Leah was sitting on the bed, gazing forlornly into space. Beside her, Charlie sat hunched against the cushions, his knees drawn up to his chest. They did not appear to be communicating with each other.

'I have to have some water. I have to have some water for my garden, and I have to have a saucepan for carrying it.' He found the largest one, and filled it to the brim. The water sloshed and slopped, as he carried it towards the door.

'You're wasting it,' said Leah.

Jack emptied his saucepan over the peas, and came back for more. 'Jack!' said Leah. 'That water doesn't come by magic, you know!'

'Be reasonable, Leah! My peas won't grow without water.'

Leah shrugged.

Jack returned to fill his saucepan for the third time. He thumped at the tap. 'What's the matter with this thing?'

'It's run out at last, what do you think?'

'All right, I'll use the drinking water.'

'Then we're going to go thirsty. . . . Anyway, there's not much left of that.'

'I'll fill it from the river.'

'Oh, *will* you?'

No, of course – he wouldn't. He couldn't leave *Jack's Shack* out of sight for so long. What a nuisance! Annoyed, Jack went back to his garden to review the situation.

It was only a minor hitch, of course, and one that would put itself right quite soon. Charlie would be perfectly well, by tomorrow probably, and Leah would see that Charlie was perfectly well, and then she would give up her silly ideas about going for help. She would settle down and be happy like *he* was. And Charlie would settle down, and be happy as well . . . And the water wasn't a problem, not really. It was a nuisance now they had to drag every drop up the hill, but they could take it in turns. . . . Actually, that could be Charlie's job. About time he made himself useful for something, instead of moaning all the time.

Meanwhile however, it was a bit of a drag, having to watch *Jack's Shack* to make sure silly Leah didn't sneak out again, and go running off to get the help that Charlie didn't need at all.

If only Treacle would come!

Jack's eyes swept around the sunlit slopes. There was a group of horses in the distance, and Treacle might be among them; it was too far away to tell. Jack willed the ponies to come nearer. There was a great ache of longing inside him – to feel those soft lips again, nibbling against his open palm; to touch that warm flank with his cheek; to have his heart flow over, like before.

If only he could be free to go and look. If only he didn't have to watch the van.

One solitary horse was moving in his direction. Jack peered eagerly, willing the horse to be Treacle. It wasn't. As the pony drew nearer, Jack's hopes faded, and disappointment took their place. This horse was bigger than Treacle, and brown all over. It had the same sort of eyes, though, and it looked friendly enough.

Cautiously, so as not to startle it, Jack sauntered towards the strange horse.

He felt in his pocket. Yes, the biscuits were still there. Cracked, and crumbling now, but a horse wouldn't mind that! Jack took a piece of biscuit from the packet, and held it out. The horse snorted, and tossed its head. He moved closer still, and the horse backed. Jack threw the biscuit on the ground.

With one eye on Jack, the horse sniffed at the biscuit. It crunched the biscuit between its teeth, and looked slyly for more. Jack took another piece from the packet, and held it out.

But the horse would come no nearer. Jack threw the second piece on the ground, and while the strange horse chomped on this also, Jack offered a third piece from his hand. 'Come on,' he begged. 'Come on, oh come on, *please.*'

At the sound of Jack's voice the horse snorted again, and glared suspiciously. Jack sighed, and threw the biscuit on the ground. The horse went for it, and while its head was down, Jack swiftly covered the distance between them. The horse tossed its head, and backed. 'Do you know something?' said Jack. 'You're silly! That's what you are, you're silly.' With confidence now, he put out his hand to touch the strange horse's nose.

And found himself flying through the air!

He landed in the bracken with a bump. The fall itself did little damage, but the pain from the place where the horse had kicked him brought tears to his eyes. He pulled down his trousers to inspect the injured knee, and saw a large bruise gathering round a bleeding grazed area.

The culprit still stood there, a few metres off, glaring malevolently. 'Go away!' Jack told it. The horse did not move. 'Go away, go *away*!' Jack took off his shoe and threw it. The horse snorted, and galloped off. Jack dragged himself painfully to his feet, and hobbled to retrieve the shoe.

The pain from his damaged knee was considerable. It's nothing, though, he told himself. It's nothing to make a fuss about; it'll be better in a minute.

Jack sat in the bracken and waited for his knee to be better. A bad knee is nothing, he told himself, meaning it; but his inner feelings were deeply hurt. He would have loved that horse almost as much as he loved Treacle, if it would have let him. Well, anyway, almost as much. He had offered kindness, and got only nastiness back.

Spiteful thing! Jack hoped something really bad would happen to it. He hoped it would get stuck in the bog, like Leah. He hoped it would sink into the bog, all four kicking legs, so it couldn't kick anybody else with them. And sink deeper and deeper, its body and everything, right up to its neck. And its sticking out neck could be jerking about all over the place, jerk, jerk, jerk, and looking really silly, so all the other horses laughed. And wet themselves with laughing. . . .

Jack lay back in the bracken, and thought how this was not altogether a good day, so far, but never mind because tomorrow would be much, much better.

* * *

Inside *Hideaway*, Leah watched Charlie getting worse. Now his wheezing could be heard from right the other end of the van. 'If Jack hadn't of caught me, you could of been in hospital by now,' she told him.

Charlie looked out of the window, and said nothing.

'Did you hear what I said?'

Charlie turned his head.

Leah lost patience. 'Do you know something, Charlie, I'm tired of talking to myself! I know you're angry with me, but you didn't ought to forget that I am your best friend in this wilderness, so there!'

'. . . I want a tissue,' Charlie muttered.

'*Please!*'

'OK, OK, *please*.'

'That's better,' said Leah, handing him one.

The tears rolled down Charlie's cheeks. 'It's hard . . . to breathe.'

'I know. I know, Charlie. I know it is.' Leah stuck her head through the push-out window – the one without the greenery – but she couldn't see Jack anywhere. Of course, though, of course, he would be on the *other* side, watching the door; watching to catch her trying to get out. She called into the wilderness: 'Jack, Jack, JACK!'

There was no reply; she hadn't really expected one. 'He will have to come back some time,' she told herself and Charlie. 'When he's hungry. He'll come back then, and I can have another try.'

Charlie gazed at her, with fear in his streaming eyes. 'I want my mum!'

Leah forgot to worry about Charlie's germs. She put her arm round him, and hugged him against her chest, and tried to comfort him. 'All right, Charlie, *I'll* be your mum! I'll do the best I can to be your mum!'

She desperately wanted her own mum, though – the mum who might not even want *her* any more. And in her mind it was Darren and Joel she was hugging – the brothers she could not even be sure were still there, safe and well at home.

Jack pulled himself to his feet and took one careful step through the bracken. The pain from his knee made him wince. He tried hopping, but progress that way was so slow he went back to limping again. A long step with his good leg, and a titchy one with the other. There! It wasn't so bad, he could manage perfectly well, it was nothing to make a fuss about, he just wouldn't do much more walking on it today, that's all.

He picked up his basket on the way, and carried it into the van. 'Do you want to see all these things I got now? Out of the tumbledown house?'

'No,' said Leah.

'What's the matter with you, Leah? You sound like you got the hump about something.'

'It's not what's the matter with me; it's what's the matter with Charlie.'

'There's nothing wrong with Charlie.'

'*Jack.* There *is!*'

'It's you! You're giving him the idea to be sorry for himself. You're cuddling him like he was a baby. You don't want to be a baby, do you, Charlie?' Charlie squirmed, and wriggled away from Leah's comforting arm. 'See?' said Jack. 'Charlie doesn't *want* to be a baby!'

'He's ill, though. He's really ill, we have to get him to a hospital.'

'Don't be silly.'

'I'm not being silly. It's you that's being silly. . . . All right, if you don't believe me, just listen to how he's breathing.'

'I can't hear nothing wrong.'

'You must have gone deaf, then.'

'Well, only a little bit wrong. He'll be all right by tomorrow.'

'He might have died by tomorrow.'

Jack laughed.

'I'm not joking, you know!'

Jack laughed again. 'You won't have died by tomorrow, will you, Charlie! You don't want to go to hospital, do you Charlie!'

Charlie was silent.

'See?' said Jack. 'That means he doesn't. . . . Come on, now, Leah – how about making our tea?'

'I can't.'

'Why not?'

'The gas is finished as well, I forgot to say. I tried to boil the kettle for the washing up, and there's no more gas.'

'Oh, *sugar*!' Jack limped to the kitchen area to check.

'What's wrong with your leg?'

'Nothing much.'

'Looks like you can't walk properly.'

'Yes, I can, then.' Jack shot Leah a meaningful glance. 'I can walk, *and* I can run if I have to!' He took one of the tins of minced beef out of his basket, and searched for the tin opener. Leah watched him, in silence.

Jack began eating the meat cold, with a spoon,

straight out of the tin. Charlie gave a little wheezing cough, and Jack limped to the doorway, carrying his supper with him. 'Where you going?' said Leah.

'Eat it outside.'

'What about Charlie then?'

'What *about* him?'

'*Jack*,' said Leah. 'Talking to you is like talking to somebody that's not really there.'

'Charlie,' said Leah, 'you have to let me tell Jack your secret.'

'*No!*'

'Charlie, you must! He won't listen, otherwise.'

'I don't want . . . him to know . . . *that!*'

Leah felt helpless, and all alone in her head. It was bad enough having to struggle with Jack's unreasonableness; it was monstrous having to struggle with Charlie's as well. It was a nightmare. Where was the sense in any of it?

A promise is a promise, though, she thought, and you can't break it. Never? Not even if it is for the person's own good? . . . I don't know, I don't know, I don't know what to do.

I seem to be going round in a ring, she thought. I'm going round and round in the same ring, and not getting any further on with this problem. I think the only thing to get out of the ring now, is if I break my promise.

But if I do that, I shall feel so guilty. It will be one more thing to feel guilty about, and I'm getting tired of all this feeling guilty. All the time I seem to be getting more things to feel guilty about, and I don't know what is going to be the end of it. . . .

Leah sighed, and went to the cab door. Not

daring to open it, she wound down the window and leaned through to call. 'Jack!'

He didn't answer at first, but he was not far away. She could see him only a few metres up the hill, sitting in the bracken, his thoughtful gaze on the van. She called again. 'Jack! I've got something to tell you!'

'No!' came Charlie's dismayed voice, from behind her.

'What?' said Jack.

Leah pressed on. She had started now, she would see it through. 'Come close, then, and let me tell you properly!' she called to Jack.

'I'm close enough now, what is it?'

'Come nearer, so I don't have to shout.'

'I'm near enough. This is as near as I'm going to come.'

It was quite dreadful, having to shout a private thing like that across a great space. With hot cheeks, Leah shouted: 'Charlie's got assma!'

There, she had done it. And she felt terrible, she felt like a traitor. Like Jack said Charlie was, only worse. She felt the sky must fall down, or the earth crack open and swallow her up to punish her for this new wickedness. Even though that wickedness seemed like the right thing to do.

Behind her, she heard Charlie's cry of protest. Jack shrugged – she could see his shrug from here. 'So? He's got asthma, what about it?'

'He has to go to hospital, and have a thing put over his face.'

'He doesn't *have* to!'

'What about if he dies?'

Jack laughed. 'You're exaggerating.'

'I'm not, I know I'm not. Why won't you even listen when I tell you something serious?'

'Because you're exaggerating. Asthma is nothing. I know plenty people with asthma; asthma isn't nothing to make a fuss about.'

'*Please*, Jack. *Please* let me go and get help. Let me out, and don't tie me up, Jack, *please!*'

Jack lay back in the ferns, and put his fingers in his ears, and gazed up at the sky.

13

A grave situation

Charlie was devastated. That was it, that was finally it! Jack would never want him for a friend again now. Until that moment, Charlie had not realised how much, deep inside himself, he still hoped. Horrible Leah! Horrible, horrible Leah, to tell his secret like that! And after she promised, as well!

'Charlie, don't look at me like that! Don't look at me like that, *please!*'

'You *told.*'

'I'm sorry, I'm sorry, I meant it for the best!'

'*You told Jack.*'

The tears gathered in Leah's eyes, and rolled down her cheeks. She brushed them away, and more took their place. 'You must understand, Charlie, that it is very hard for me to know the right thing to do.'

Charlie's chest heaved. 'I didn't want him to know!'

'I know you didn't.'

'So what did you do it for?'

'I'm not sure, now . . . It didn't do any good after all, did it? . . . Let's me and you be friends, though, Charlie. *Please* let's me and you be friends!'

'You promised, though.'

'I know. I didn't want to break my promise, but I just couldn't . . . I mean, I couldn't . . . like, I couldn't . . . Charlie, do you know your nose wants wiping?'

They sat without speaking. Charlie wheezed and strained, and quivered. At last, without looking at her, he put out his hand, feeling for Leah's. Full of gratitude at being forgiven, Leah took Charlie's hand and squeezed it tight. 'It's all right, Charlie, I'm here!'

Jack sat in the bracken, and thought about tomorrow. Tomorrow, he thought, he would solve the problem of the cooking. There was an easy way to get round that – he knew just what was to be done. He would make a fire, that's what, like in the Western films on telly. When they settled for the night, they made a fire to cook their supper on. Tomorrow he would make a fire, and Leah could do the cooking. Just like before. Better really, more fun!

Tomorrow was going to be good. He was really looking forward to tomorrow.

. . . All right, so Charlie had asthma, what of it? Jack knew plenty of people with asthma. Well anyway, he knew *some*. OK, he knew one. Besides Charlie. One time. But that person never had to go to hospital . . . Jack didn't *think* that person ever had to go to hospital, because of his asthma.

Anyway, Charlie would be all right, Leah was just exaggerating and looking on the bad side as usual.

Jack inched further up the hill. Because walking was painful, he did it on his bottom. Slowly and with discomfort, he took himself farther and farther from Charlie and his asthma. Anyway, he told himself, it's not my fault if Charlie's ill. It's not my fault; it's nothing to do with me, really.

The sun was low over the far slopes now, the evening chilly. Jack thought of going back to the van for George's jacket, but decided against it. He wasn't really cold, not really. If he wrapped his arms round his knees, like this, he wasn't cold at all. Hardly.

If only Treacle would come!

Jack's eyes scoured the moor hopefully, but there were no horses in sight at all, not even the nasty one that had kicked him that afternoon. He closed his eyes, and tried to make a picture of Treacle inside his head; but the picture was blurred, and wouldn't come clear. Jack tried to make the feeling come anyway, the lovely warm feeling he had before; but a funny sort of deadness had come inside him.

The wilderness had gone dead, too. Or, not dead, exactly, but dimmed down, and sad. All that happiness he felt around him before – where had it gone? It will come back tomorrow, Jack told himself, it *will*. Just wait till tomorrow, and everything will come right again, I just know it!

Charlie is going to be all right. Leah is just making a fuss.

Anyway, it's not my fault Charlie's ill.

It's nothing to do with me.

Anyway, I'm not going to give up my wilderness for Charlie. I don't even like him.

And my van, and my horse – I'm not going to give them up for Charlie.

I'm *not* going to give them up, I'm *not*.

It's all very well to hold Charlie's hand and tell him 'I'm here,' Leah thought. What's the use for me to be here if I can't do anything?

'I'm going to have one more try at Jack.' Gently, she uncurled Charlie's fingers with her free hand, and went to the cab door. She shouted at Jack, who was so far up the hill now, he was only just in sight. His head was turned, and he didn't even bother to turn it back when she called. What is he doing up there, Leah thought; is he going to stay up there all night?

. . . Night! It's coming to be night. And Charlie gets worse in the night. I have to do something about it, I have to! It's all up to me, and I don't like that, I don't – but who else is there?

Leah went back to stand by the bed. She looked at the open swing window, the one without the dying greenery, and there was the glimmer of an idea in her mind. She took a deep and shaky breath. 'Charlie, I want to try again. To find somebody to help us – I want to try again.'

Charlie clutched at her. 'No, don't! . . . Don't go!'

'Do you want to get worse, then? Do you want to—?'

'I don't want you to . . . leave me! . . . Anyway, you can't . . . Jack . . . won't let you!'

'There might be a way, though.' She took another deep breath and said it. 'Charlie, you don't want to die, do you!'

'No, no!' His eyes were terrified.

'Well then – you have to let me go!'

'It's . . . no good . . . Jack . . . will catch you and . . . tie you up!'

'I know he might. But we have to try. You have to be brave, Charlie.'

'I *am* brave,' said Charlie, with pitiful insistence.

'I know. You're very brave. You're very brave, Charlie.' Leah cast her mind wildly around for something brave that Charlie had done. 'You are very brave about your assma. To keep it a secret and everything. But now you have to be more braver still, and let me go.'

'... Do you think... I'm going to... die, Leah?'

'I don't know, but I think *you* think that, Charlie!'

'... I don't want it... to happen... all by myself!'

Leah gazed at the small heap on the bed, and her heart overflowed with pity. 'And I wouldn't want that neither, if it was me! I know how you feel, Charlie, because I wouldn't want that neither. But there is something else to think about, you know... I mean, what about your mum?'

Charlie's chest heaved.

'What about your mum – eh? Eh, Charlie? I think your mum is good to you. Your mum is good, and she will be sad and sorrowful all her life, won't she? If you... you know, if you... you *know!*'

Charlie's chest heaved again.

'So we have to take the chance. For your mum!'

'... *What* chance, though?'

'Well, what I thought was... you know Jack is up the hill!'

'Is he?'

'So if I climb out *this* window, he won't see me. I can hide behind the trees, and creep round, and get up the hill like you done that time... And Jack hurt his leg you know, so he can't run so fast now, whatever he says!'

'You can't... climb out... the window!'

'I can try. Come on, Charlie – for your mum? For your mum? Eh?'

The wheezing grew louder; the wheezing filled

the van with horrible sound. '. . . All right, then,' said Charlie, in a small voice.

Leah crouched on the bed, and pushed one leg through the window. She grabbed at the lower edge, and by painful inches managed to get the second leg through.

Now what?

The pushed-out window was in front of her, her forehead was against the frame above. Somehow, she must slide her plump body through the space – but how? The window was quite high off the ground, and she couldn't hang from her arms first because she was facing the wrong way. Too late, Leah saw that the thing to do would have been to climb out backwards. She tried to wriggle back to start all over again, and found that she couldn't. She couldn't twist herself, to get her legs back through the space.

The only possibility now would be to push on her hands, and lift her bottom, and jump – and she couldn't do it because she was too afraid. She would hurt herself. She would knock her head on the window, or break her leg on the ground. Because her face was above the window, Leah couldn't actually see the ground; but in her imagination there was a great yawning space below her feet, a huge space, a terrifying space. She couldn't jump into that space, she couldn't!

Half way in, and half way out of the swing window, Leah was stuck. She panicked, and her thoughts went into a useless spin.

'What's . . . the matter?' Behind her, Charlie was panicking too.

'I can't do it.'

'Jack's . . . going to . . . catch you!'

'I know, but I *can't do it!* She struggled feebly, then stopped. The world darkened and blurred around her. It was horrible – like the worst thing that happens in dreams; when you want to move, but you can't. When you try to lift your arms and your legs, but they won't go.

'Now . . . I won't even have . . . you . . . to hold my hand!' said Charlie, bitterly.

'I'm sorry, Charlie. I'm sorry, Charlie. I'm no good, am I? Oh, I'm *sorry!*'

Jack scrambled to his feet. 'All right!' he shouted at the wilderness. 'Don't blame me if you never see me again! Don't blame me, that's all!'

He began a limping run back to the van. He didn't see Leah until he was right inside; and then the sight of her solid form, half in and half out of the window, brought out all his scorn. 'You silly, stupid idiot, what you think you're doing!'

He grabbed her by the waist and pulled, taking her weight. 'Stop!' she protested. 'You're hurting me!'

'Serve you right!'

He pulled her into the van, and dropped her abruptly on to the bed, narrowly missing Charlie, who cowered in the corner. Once again, the tears rolled down Leah's cheeks. 'I suppose you're going to tie me up, now.'

'Who says I'm going to tie you up? Who says that?'

'I thought *you* did.'

'What you think I am, then? You think I'm George and Lil, or something? . . . Well, go on, if you're going!'

'Go where?'

'Up to the road to find a car, of course! That's what you want, isn't it? That's what you been nagging on about! . . . And don't look at me like that, I'm not a monster, you know, I'm a human person same as you! So go and find somebody to take Charlie to hospital. . . . And don't say it should be me instead of you, because I'm let off because of my leg!' There was a savage unhappiness in his eyes, but there was triumph there as well. 'See? I'm let off because of my leg, so I can have a last go of my engine. While you're up there looking for a car. So it's good luck, not bad luck that horse kicked me, after all!'

At first, Leah found, it wasn't so bad. The long summer twilight deepened so gradually, you hardly noticed the darkening light. All the same, she knew the night was coming, and she was frightened to be all alone. She climbed, with fluttering heart, and thought about Jack, and felt mean for thinking so many bad things about him. He had turned into a good person after all, hadn't he? Even though he did leave it a bit late.

Had he left it *too* late? Leah hurried her steps, forcing her heavy little body to go faster, faster, faster, till the blood drummed in her ears and the muscles of her legs were on fire. In her mind she heard Charlie's wheezing still. She hoped Jack was being kind, but anyway she thought Charlie might be too busy with his breathing now to notice. 'It won't be long, Charlie,' Leah told him in her head. 'It won't be long. I'll find somebody soon, and you'll be in hospital, and have that thing over your face, and your mum will come to see you in the hospital, I expect, and everything will be all right for you.'

Would everything be all right for *her*, though, she wondered? Because, of course, once Charlie was on his way to hospital, she and Jack would be on their way home. Fears about that homecoming crowded back, adding themselves to Leah's fears for Charlie and her fears of the coming dark. Suddenly her mouth was dry, and her head felt full, and tight. Swaying with dizziness, she stopped for a moment and swallowed rapidly, her hands clenching and unclenching as she fought to control herself.

I'm not supposed to think about myself now, she thought. I'm supposed to be thinking about Charlie. She reached the track, and turned towards the road – the road none of the children had seen, but which they all knew must be there.

Back in the van, Jack was already regretting his change of heart. 'There's nothing really wrong with you, is there!' he accused Charlie.

Slumped against the cushions, Charlie wheezed and wheezed. He did not answer Jack, but his eyes were frightened and pleading.

'You know Leah's gone, don't you!' said Jack, bitterly. 'You know she's gone to tell of us. You know it's all your fault. . . . *Traitor!*'

Charlie's tongue came out to wet his dry lips.

'There's nothing wrong with you! I don't believe there's anything wrong with you, really! You're putting it on for a trick!' Jack came closer and took Charlie by the shoulders. 'Come on, admit it!'

Charlie gave a weak little cough. 'I can't . . . breathe.'

'Yes you can, you're breathing. If you weren't breathing you'd be dead!'

'... It's getting harder ... Jack! ... It is!'

'I don't believe you! ... All right, you don't have to look at me like that!'

Jack half thought of going after Leah, to drag her back after all. But she had a good start on him now, and there was his hurt leg as well. His leg would slow him down. And anyway ... anyway, Charlie's breathing did sound a bit funny. Not *very* funny, not all *that* funny, but just a bit.

Jack limped to the driver's seat, and began to run his engine. For the very last time. And all because of Charlie, who wasn't much good for anything; who couldn't even stay well like other people; who had to spoil everything by getting sick, just when everything else was so wonderful.

And I never even rode my horse, Jack thought. I never rode my horse, I never even got to say goodbye to him!

And it's all Charlie's fault.

And I don't feel sorry for him a bit, why should I?

Of course, there were no picknickers beside the track. Although she had vaguely expected to find that nice couple from the other day, Leah realised now how unlikely that was. Not only had the sun gone; the colours had gone as well. All around were only varying shades of grey, and a few little rabbits, popping out of the bracken, scuttling this way and that on errands of their own.

Leah trudged stolidly along the track – on, and on, and on, trying not to think of how alone she was. The wilderness closed in on her. She was pushing her way, or so it seemed, through a sticky heaviness that slowed her steps, that tried to stop her altogether, even. And it was such a long way! Where was that road, where was it? Surely she should have reached it by now!

The track, which had been more or less level, was downhill now – sloping down, down, down towards . . . nowhere. The track was going nowhere, that was the explanation of it. A wicked witch had put a spell on the track, and magicked it, and turned it into a path with no ending. However far Leah went along this track she wouldn't get to anywhere. She could keep on walking like this for ever, going only further into nowhere.

For the third time that day, Leah began to panic. The bushes beside the path whispered to her to go back. Go back to *Hideaway*, they said, and safety! The whispers grew louder with every step she took, and it was hard not to listen to them, and obey.

But she kept on going, to find the road, because who else was there to do it?

Jack drove his engine with concentrated fury. He drove it like that, partly because it was his last chance, and partly because the noise drowned out the disturbing sounds Charlie was making.

But the noise of the engine couldn't drown out a persistent picture in Jack's mind. The picture hovered just behind his eyes, and the picture was of a small white face, full of fear. Jack couldn't get rid of it entirely, whatever he did; but for a long while, in his mind, he stamped on the picture, and went on stamping on it, trying to scuffle it out.

At last, grudgingly, he switched off the engine and listened. Charlie's breathing was coming in shorter gasps now, the sound of his wheezing filled the van. Jack got up, and limped to where Charlie sat, hunched over his drawn-up knees.

'You all right, then?'

Charlie's head shook from side to side.

'You want a drink of water or something?'

Charlie's head nodded.

Jack found the water can, and poured out half a cupful. There was barely another cupful left, he noticed. Charlie drank the water, his eyes frightened over the rim of the cup.

'It's all right, you know,' Jack said gruffly. 'Leah's gone to get someone, so it's going to be all right.'

Charlie said nothing.

The string from his waist still trailed its way across the floor. 'How about if I untie you, then?' Jack offered. 'You'll be all right if I untie your waist, I expect.' He fumbled with the knots. 'There! Now you can breathe more better.'

It didn't seem to make much difference. Resentful because Charlie was still making those awful noises, Jack went back to the driver's seat and switched on the radio. He found some pop music, and turned up the volume as high as it would go.

Leah had reached the road at last. She stood at the edge, her eyes travelling hopefully from right to left to right again, searching the dusk for the sight of car lights. Behind her, a high slope rose against the darkening sky. Across the road, the road fell away into yet another valley.

Now she was here, she was appalled at the thought of this next thing she had to do. To stop a strange car. Actually to stop a car with people she didn't know, in it. She might even have to get *into* that car. The very thing they told you at school, and at home, over and over not to do. Don't speak to strangers, they said, they can be bad people; and never, *ever*, get into their cars.

They never said that sometimes, sometimes you might have to.

If only a car would come, though! Before it got to be really dark. There was light in the sky still, but the puffy white clouds had turned into inky smudges, and a silvery crescent moon had appeared from somewhere.

Leah shivered. She had been in so much hurry to get away, before Jack changed his mind perhaps, that she had forgotten to look for a jumper. There was more breeze up here; she felt it against her arms and her legs and the thin cotton of her dress. She hugged her arms and waited for a car which didn't come, and didn't come, and didn't come.

Jack thought he might as well look back. Not that there was any point, but anyway, he might as well look. Charlie didn't appear to have moved. Jack turned off the radio and called, 'You all right, then?' across the van.

No answer.

Jack got up and limped to the back. Charlie looked up, still wheezing as noisily as ever. 'What's the matter, then?' It was a stupid thing to say, Jack wished he hadn't said it.

'... Can't breathe ... properly.'

'You want to go to hospital, then?'

'... Yes.'

'Will they make you well in the hospital, do you think?'

'... Yes.'

It had to be admitted that Charlie really was ill; he *wasn't* putting it on. I'm glad it's not me, Jack thought. It's like it's really hard work for him to breathe. Like he's suffocating. Lucky it's not me!

Anyway, Leah will be back soon.

Why doesn't Leah come, why is she taking so long?

'Do you want another drink of water?' said Jack – awkwardly, because he couldn't think of anything else.

Charlie nodded, and Jack gave him half a cupful more. He was thirsty himself, and was about to finish off the water in the can, when it occurred to him that perhaps he had better not.

Charlie might need it, he thought. Charlie needs it more than me, I suppose.

. . . I don't like seeing him like that actually. And I don't like hearing that breathing, neither. Anyway, lucky it's not me. . . .

I don't like seeing it happen to Charlie, though. Even if I don't like him. It's not nice to see a person ill like that.

All right, I *am* sorry for him. I can't help it, can I, with his breathing and everything?

And I wish Leah would hurry up, so they can get on with putting him in the hospital. It's too long waiting for Leah. It's too long for Charlie to wait. With his breathing and everything . . .

I wonder if there could be a quicker way . . . ?

He had an idea! He had a wonderful, wonderful idea, if only it would work! Excited, and eager now, Jack limped back to the driver's seat.

He switched on the engine. That bit was easy, it was the next bit that was going to be tricky. The next bit was, he had to get the van to move, and he had only the vaguest idea of how to do it.

Well, he knew one thing, didn't he? He knew what to do with the gear, to make an engine go in reverse. Lucky The Boss showed him that, because it would be no use trying to drive *Jack's Shack* forward – there were too many trees in the way. The problem was, though, he knew what to do with the gear lever, but he didn't know what else you were supposed to do.

The pedals on the floor, they were all for something – but what? Jack tried to remember what The Boss did with his feet, that night he let Jack help with the driving. But he couldn't remember because he hadn't been looking. Why didn't he think to look, that time? Why?

Perhaps it didn't matter too much about the pedals. Perhaps he could put the van in reverse without the pedals. Jack looked for the gear lever.

It was different from the one in the car. The one in the car was short and stubby, this one was long and thin. Never mind, it must work the same. Jack's heart raced as he tried to move the lever, the way The Boss had shown him.

He lifted it, he got it across – but try as he might, he could not push it forward. He struggled with all his strength, he jiggled it into different positions, but his best efforts would not make that lever go forward the way it was supposed to.

Why?

It must be because of the pedals. Now what *were* you supposed to do with the pedals?

There were three of them. Cautiously, Jack pushed at the one on the right, and that made the engine go faster, which was quite thrilling and he wished he found it out before, but it didn't solve the problem of the gear lever.

He tried the middle one, and that didn't seem to do anything at all.

The left one then, it must be the left one. Jack pushed it down. Now! Quivering, and with the blood singing in his ears, he tried again to push the gear lever forward . . .

Nothing.

He jiggled it. He jiggled, and pushed – and it *went.* The lever ground forward at last, and Jack shook with excitement as he waited for the van to move backwards.

Again, nothing. Puzzled, and disappointed, Jack sat still for a moment. Then he leaned back in his seat, and his foot came off the pedal.

The van gave a great jerk, and the engine cut out.

Well, at least he made something happen! Jack switched the engine on again, but again there was the jerk, and then silence. Now he couldn't even make the engine go. Why? Why?

It ran all right with the pedal down, he remembered. Jack pressed the pedal, and switched the engine on once more. Right. The engine was going again. Now what?

What about the right hand pedal, the one that made the engine go fast? Supposing he kept his foot on that, while he did the other things – might *that* make the van move? Jack braced himself to try it.

He was afraid. He was afraid because this might be the answer, and he almost didn't want it to be the answer because he was fully aware now what a terribly scary thing he was trying to do. He clenched his teeth, and moved his feet.

The van gave a violent judder, and the engine died once more. Jack waited a whole minute for his own shaking to stop.

He went back to Charlie, who didn't seem to have noticed the tremendous events taking place in the front. 'I tried to drive us to the hospital, but I couldn't quite manage it.'

No answer.

'I did try,' Jack persisted. 'I think it was a good idea. It *nearly* worked.'

Still no answer.

'Well, say it was a good idea, Charlie! It's not my fault it didn't work. Perhaps the engine went out of petrol.'

Charlie wheezed and wheezed, but said nothing.

'It's not my fault if it went out of petrol, you know. You can't blame me if I used up the petrol before. I didn't know we would need it for the hospital, did I? You couldn't expect me to know that!'

Charlie showed no interest in the matter of the petrol.

'I'm sorry about your asthma,' said Jack, desperate for a response. 'I'm sorry I didn't believe you before, as well. Next time I'll believe you, OK?' He leaned sideways on the bed so that he could look into Charlie's face, and smiled his most winning smile. 'Cheer up, Charlie, I'll believe you next time, OK?'

Charlie's eyes were blank. He was beyond caring about Jack, or Jack's apologies. He needed all his energies for himself, now.

* * *

Leah's heart leaped. A car, a car! She could see its lights way down the road. She hadn't come all this way for nothing after all, because here was a car! She crossed the road, to be on the right side for stopping the car, ready to wave her arms and shout.

The lights came nearer; Leah prepared to do the one thing she had been told never, never to do.

There was a stab of fresh unease. Surely there was something wrong with this car. It wasn't going straight, the way cars are supposed to, it was wobbling and swerving all over the place. There was laughing and singing coming out of it, as well. As it drew closer, Leah realised the car was full of drunk people.

What was worse, the drunk people had seen her! She hadn't waved her arms yet, but the drunk people must have seen her, because the brakes were screeching, and the car was stopping, and they were falling out on to the road – huge young men with rough, slurred voices! Dozens of them – well, anyway, at least four.

Leah turned, and fled into the bracken and the bushes.

She crashed down, down, tripping and stumbling in the almost-dark. And they were coming after her, they were. They would catch her, they would do terrible things to her! Frightened beyond reason, Leah flung herself under a prickly bush and lay there, still as death, trying to breathe without sound.

'Where's she got to?'

'Where's *who* got to?' That voice was *really* slurred.

'Little girl.'

'What little girl? You see a little girl, then, Ben?'

'Yeah, I did. I definitely saw a little girl.'

'You wanna cut down on the cider, you do!'

'Ha, ha, ha!'

'Where are you then, little girl?' Threshing footsteps, round and about.

'Come on out! Puss, puss, puss!' There was more laughing and whistling. Leah thought if they stopped making so much noise themselves they must surely hear her heart, it was drumming so loud.

'Come on, let's go!'

'Yeah, but – can't have little girls on the moor by themselves. In the dark. 'Snot right.'

'There wasn't no little girl! It's the cider, you daft pillock!'

'*I* saw a little girl, though.'

'You're another one can't hold your cider!'

'*Who* can't hold their cider?'

'*You* can't hold your cider!' More raucous laughter and threshing footsteps.

'Come on, we're missing the party!'

'Little girl on the moor by herself, though. 'Snot right!'

'Puss, puss, puss! Come on out, then, nice puss!'

The shouting, and the laughing, and the rough, drunk voices receded, but Leah went on lying under her bush, too terrified to move.

14

Crisis

Jack stood by the bed, watching helplessly while Charlie struggled to breathe. Was he getting worse? It was hard to tell. 'You all right, then? You all right?'

Charlie shook his head.

Jack bit his lip. 'What's happened to that Leah? What's happened to her? I dunno – I think she must have fell down a rabbit hole, or something!'

'. . . Hospital!' Charlie wheezed, without looking up. 'I have to go to . . . hospital!'

'Well that's up to Leah, innit?' Seething with frustration Jack thumped the sink top with his fist. 'What's the matter with her? What's the matter with her, taking so long? She can't be trying properly, she should have found somebody by now!'

Charlie raised his head for a moment. 'Help . . . me!' His eyes beseeched, his nose ran unchecked.

'Well, I want to, don't I? I want to, what do you think? But the thing is, you see, I don't know how!'

Three days of hiding. Three days of doing everything to prevent being found. But if you *wanted* to be found, how could you set about telling people you were here?

Shout? Jack hobbled into the darkness outside the van and cupped his hands around his mouth. 'Is anybody there? Is anybody there?'

Useless, of course! Jack heard how thinly his

voice pierced the night air, travelling for such a little way in all that boundless space.

Was there some other way of attracting attention?

Something people could see, how about that?

What people, though?

. . . Well, there was that road he thought he saw, for instance. Perhaps it really was a road, after all! Yes, yes, now he came to think of it, it most likely *was* a road. . . . Or there could be other roads he didn't know about . . . or somebody out for a walk.

Jack limped back into the van, and turned on all the interior lights, and the headlights as well. He went outside to view the results, and was not much encouraged. The headlights shone only into the trees – the others were poor and dim. The mess over some of the windows was not helping, of course. Jack pulled that off, but the effect was not much better.

Something brighter!

A fire, how about that?

Of course, a fire, a fire! He was going to make a fire for the cooking anyway, wasn't he, so lucky that idea was all ready for him to think of now. Only this fire must be not by the van, so low in the valley, but up the hill, where it could be seen from a really long way away. So as not to miss any chances.

Somebody out there would see it, there must be somebody! A really good idea like this couldn't get wasted, could it?

So what was there to burn?

The ferns, probably, the ferns would do! Full of hope and excited anticipation, Jack found the matches, the ones Leah used to light the cooker. Lucky the box was still more than half full! He turned the headlights off to save the battery then climbed painfully to a spot rather more than half-way between the van and the top of the hill. Was this high enough? He went higher to make sure. Blundering about in the dark, he dragged at the ferns, and piled them into a small heap – in the middle of the grassy patch, of course; he wouldn't want to set light to the whole hillside.

The first match went out in the breeze. Jack positioned himself with his back to the slight wind, and lit another match, cupping the flame with his hand. He held the flame against his pile of bracken, and watched that go out also. He tried a third time, and a fourth, and still the ferns would not burn.

They must be not dry enough. He need not have worried about setting the hillside alight, these ferns wouldn't burn at all!

What about the ones on *Jack's Shack*, though? They had been in the sun for two days nearly, and some of those he pulled off just now had been quite shrivelled, and papery to the touch. Surely, *surely*, those would burn!

As fast as he could, Jack hopped back to the van, and squatted on the ground with a few of the dried ferns in his hand. He would try them out here first, he thought, just to make sure he wasn't wasting his time.

Hopefully, he struck a match and held it under one curling frond. The frond smouldered and smoked; but as soon as the match went out, the smouldering died away. Jack tried again. . . . No good, no good, what a swindle! What was the use of these good ideas coming to him, when they wouldn't even work?

All right, all right – the ferns wouldn't burn, so what *would* burn? What would make a proper blaze?

. . . Paper would burn, and wood, and cardboard. *Cardboard.* There was cardboard in the van – all those empty packets screwed up and stuffed in the waste bag. From the mashed potato and corn flakes, for instance. And paper from the biscuits, and things like that.

Confident again, Jack climbed into the van. 'It's all right, Charlie,' he announced with shining eyes. 'It's all right. I found the way to help!' Scrabbling to collect the empty packets, and empty a few more for good measure, he kept up a constant stream of reassurances, which didn't seem to be interesting Charlie very much, but never mind.

Jack was just going to start back up the hillside when yet another idea struck him. George and Lil's clothes, they would burn! Jack pulled a pillow from the high-up bed, ripped off the pillow case, and began stuffing it with Lil's underwear. There were shoes in the tall cupboard as well. They might burn – Jack tossed them in. And George's jacket, and a pair of George's trousers, and two pairs of George's shorts. The rest of the clothes were in the lockers under Charlie's bed, but anyway, Jack had as much as he could carry now. 'It's all right, Charlie,' he said again from the doorway. 'Don't you worry; it's going to be all right now!'

Up the hillside again, painfully, dragging his load.

Because he thought of them first, Jack started with the packets. He made a pile, unscrewing them a bit to make the pile bigger, and they flared up immediately. Jack fed his fire with more packets, then with Lil's knickers; then – careful not to smother the flames because he was getting the idea now – with George's things. (George's huge shoes didn't seem to want to burn, but they made useful pokers.) As George's jacket went up in an orange blaze, Jack sprang away from the heat, and excitedly watched the smoke billowing up and out, in glowing puffs, into the night sky.

Now they'll come, he thought, now they'll come! And he hurried back to the van for more fuel.

'Move!' he told Charlie. 'You have to move, I have to get the rest of George and Lil's clothes out of the lockers!'

Charlie wheezed and wheezed, and didn't seem to hear.

'*Move*, Charlie!' Jack seized him by the armpits and lifted him on to the floor. Charlie sat in a limp heap, while Jack delved into the lockers. 'You OK?' said Jack.

Charlie shook his head. His nose still streamed, over his mouth and chin, and dribbling down his neck.

Jack reassembled the bed, and lifted Charlie to sit on the edge, draping the blanket round his shoulders. 'It's all right, you know, Charlie,' he said. 'I'm making a fire up the hill, and somebody's sure to see it.' He gathered his bundle. 'Did you understand what I'm saying, Charlie? I'm making a fire to make people come!'

Charlie understood. He said, 'Make them come . . . quick.'

'Well, that's what I'm doing,' said Jack, eagerly. 'That's what I'm doing, Charlie, trust me.'

But outside the caravan, looking up the hill, Jack saw his fire was nearly out. By the time he reached it, it would *be* out. He would have to start all over again!

. . . All right, all right, he had to start again, what about it?

More paper to get the new fire going? . . . George's maps and things, Jack knew where they were! . . . And more thick stuff to burn? There needed to be a load of stuff, a whole pile of stuff, he realised that now! The pile must be all ready before he lit any of it, so the new fire wouldn't go out while he was getting more fuel.

Where was he going to find enough stuff to make a fire like that?

Actually, someone had seen the first fire.

On the other side of the valley, a far distant road carved its path over and around the slopes. Travelling along this road by car you could get, for a minute or two, a glimpse of Jack's hill. Very few cars used that road. Hardly any cars used it at night.

But that evening Terry and Michelle, who were in love with each other, were going for a nice long drive on the moor – and had specially chosen this lonely road, so they could be alone with each other. 'Oh look!' said Michelle. 'Something's burning!'

'It's me,' said Terry. 'Burning for *you*.'

Michelle giggled. 'Not burning in the car, silly – over there! Right over there!'

'Where?' said Terry, turning his head.

'Can't see it now,' said Michelle. 'It's gone out of sight.'

'Probably nothing important,' said Terry.

A moment later, for both the occupants of the

car, Jack's fire was as forgotten as though it had never been.

The fuel he needed was all around him! All around Jack he realised now, were things that would burn: the big mattress, the part of Charlie's bed he wasn't using, the quilt, the pillows, the undersheet on the high-up bed. It would hurt to do it, of course; it would be like burning part of himself.

Can't think about that now though, he thought.

I suppose . . .

No, that's right, that's right, can't think about that sort of thing now!

Jack dragged everything out of the van. It looked like a good big pile, and he was pleased with the pile, but annoyed by the small voice in his head which kept saying 'not the mattress'. And he wasn't going to take any notice of this rubbish voice, why should he? Only then he remembered what they said on the telly, about the stuff inside people's sofas and things, that if it caught fire it could make poisonous smoke that could kill you.

Perhaps it was the same stuff inside the mattress.

And he didn't want to be breathing any poisonous smoke, thank you very much! He didn't want to die!

Frustrated, and angry with the mattresses for being poisonous perhaps, Jack climbed back into the van for a knife. He found a pair of scissors, which was better, and began ripping the covers off the mattresses. The pile looked sadly reduced when he had finished – not big enough now, he needed more! Jack climbed back into the van, and winced and swallowed as he tore the covers from the front seats, and ripped the carpet and the lino from the floor.

How about that, then?

'You take care now, Charlie!' Jack called. With difficulty, he began to drag the first instalment of his load up the hill.

Stiff with cold now, Leah lay under her bush. She did not think she would ever have the courage to come out of it. Not for herself, not for Charlie, not for anyone. At any rate – not till it got light again.

Jack peered into the darkness, across the valley, but there was nothing to suggest a road there now, and anyway he had forgotten just where to look.

It was a splendid fire, though! The flames leaped into the sky almost as though they were alive. Almost as though they knew the desperately important job they were meant to do. Now somebody *must* come! It was totally, absolutely impossible, that Jack should make this wonderful fire, and no one come to investigate it!

Steve, Russ and Danny were driving along with a truckload of sheep which didn't belong to them. Steve, Russ and Danny were old hands at sheep-stealing, and so far they hadn't got caught.

'Good night's work, eh?' Steve's voice was hard, with no bad conscience in it at all for the dishonest thing they were doing.

'Yeah, right!' said Danny.

'Hey, look!' said Russ. 'That fire over there. Somebody else doing a good night's work, I reckon.'

'Yeah, right!' said Danny, who was a bit slow,

and only pretending to understand what Russ was talking about.

'Not the best place to choose though, Danny, wouldn't you say?' Steve took considerable pleasure in catching Danny out. He was always looking for ways of making Danny feel how stupid he was.

'Yeah, right,' said Danny.

'Tell us where *you'd* choose then, Danny,' Steve invited him.

'I dunno. Somewhere else?'

'Brilliant!' said Steve.

'He means lower down a valley,' Russ explained, taking pity on Danny. 'Out of sight, see. . . . Most likely some sucker's motor getting finished off. Nick the motor, see. Strip for parts. Burn what's left – no fingerprints. Neat!'

'Good luck to 'em anyway,' said Russ.

'Yeah, good luck!' said Steve. 'Sharing the world's wealth round a bit, that's what I like to see!'

Leah curled up under her bush, and sobbed with cold, and guilt, and fear. I'm meant to be finding someone for Charlie, she thought. It's my job – there isn't anybody else! But I can't, I can't, *I can't*. It's too hard for me; I can't do it!

And I know it's the night. And I know Charlie will be getting worse. And I know he needs to go to hospital and have that thing put over his face. If he doesn't have that thing put over his face he may die. I know he may die, but I still can't go back to that road again, I can't! I'm scared of the dark, and I'm scared of the bad people out there, and I'm scared about going home too, only that seems such a long way away I can't seem to feel it's real.

Anyhow, it seems the whole world is full of nothing except things to be scared about. And I just want to lie here, that's all I want to do.

Only I didn't ought to, because who else is there to help Charlie?

It will be my fault if he dies, won't it!

I can't help it, though, I can't help it. They didn't ought to make me do such hard things!

It's not my fault I'm too scared. I did *try*.

. . . Shall I just try again, though . . . ?

. . . Once more, shall I just try . . . ?

Trembling inside, Leah straightened her legs, and rolled from under her bush. She staggered to her feet, and began to climb the steep slope, picking her way through the bushes. The blackness of night had finally settled. Some light still lingered in the sky, and there was the little moon, and a few pale stars. But the shadows were deep and bewildering, full of strange shapes that might be horrors really – how could you know?

She reached the road, and because it was too cold to stand, waiting for the car which just might come, she began to walk. Swinging her arms across her chest, and stamping her feet, Leah walked by the side of the road, all by herself in the shadowy night.

And suddenly, she realised she wasn't afraid any more! Something had come round her, like a blanket, shutting all the fear outside. The wilderness was no longer threatening; it was looking after her – or at any rate, that's what it felt like. It even seemed to be talking to her, not out loud, but in comforting thoughts coming into her mind. It's all right, Leah, the wilderness seemed to say; just keep on going, and you'll be all right. You're quite safe, nothing's going to hurt you, but just you think about Charlie, and stay on this road for him!

It was a wonder that no one had come yet. It was really surprising they were taking so long. A good fire like this, Jack reasoned, you'd think they'd be here by now!

PC Strickland and PC Webber had been called out to investigate a burglary at a lonely cottage on the Moor. They had finished inspecting the mess the burglars had left, and questioning the distressed owners, and now they were going back to the police station in their panda car. 'Stop a minute!' said PC Webber. 'Over there, look!'

'Oh, ah!' said PC Strickland. 'Another of those jokers!'

'Looks like it.'

'Probably scarpered by now,' said PC Strickland. 'Half way to Plymouth or Exeter by now, most likely!'

'We could get lucky, though – what do you say?'

'Best go and see what's going on, anyhow!'

The police car turned, and began racing back the way it had come. At a junction, the car turned again and raced down another road – down, down, down and up again, rounding a bend and levelling out. 'Hey!' said PC Webber. 'Stop! *Stop*!'

'All right,' said PC Strickland. 'I've seen it.'

'What do you know! All on her tod!'

The small figure in the road was waving frantically. 'Dirty work?' PC Strickland wondered. 'Another poor kid attacked?'

'We'll soon find out. Doesn't seem to be hurt anyway; that's one good thing!'

The panda car braked, and PC Webber jumped out. 'All right love, all right. We're here, what's the trouble?'

At the sight of the reassuring uniform, Leah lost what was left of the calm which had so recently enveloped her, and burst into hysterical tears. 'Help me, help me!'

'All right, all right, that's what we're here for.' The policeman took off his jacket, and put it round Leah's shoulders. 'You must be freezing. Come on, let's sit in the car, and you can tell us all about it.'

Inside the car, Leah sobbed and shivered. 'He's going to die. I think he's going to die!'

'Who's going to die?'

'Charlie. He's got assma.'

'*Oh!* . . . Where is he, then? Tell us where he is.'

'In a – c-camper van—'

'Just a minute,' PC Strickland interrupted. 'Did you say *Charlie*?'

'Yes.'

'*Charlie with asthma*?'

'Yes.'

'What's your name, then?'

'Leah.'

'I thought it might be! Good God – the police all over the country have been looking for you! . . . Which way, then? This way?'

'I'll show you, I'll show you, only hurry!'

'Ambulance?' said PC Webber.

'I reckon.' PC Strickland lifted the radio.

'He needs to go to hospital,' Leah sobbed.

'I know, I know.'

'He has to have a thing put over his face.'

'Don't worry. They'll have a thing in the ambulance.'

'He can't breathe, he can't breathe, he can't *breathe!*'

'Hush!' said PC Strickland, firmly. 'Not so much noise back there! I'm trying to make an important call!'

The fire was not quite so bright.

Why don't the people *come?* Jack thought. Where *are* they?

I think I shall have to find something else to burn on my fire, otherwise it might go out again like before.

I know, I know, what about those branches we planted behind the van! I didn't try them yet, I forgot about them!

Limping and stumbling, and guided in the dark by the glow from *Hideaway*'s windows, Jack ploughed down the hillside once again.

Should he go in the van first? He was distinctly reluctant to do that, he found. He was reluctant to have to look at poor sick Charlie, and reluctant to have to look at *Jack's Shack*, all spoiled now with its soft bits ripped away. I suppose I better though, he thought. I suppose I better go and see about Charlie for a minute. Just make sure he hasn't got any worse!

Jack braced himself, calling out as he climbed through the doorway. 'You all right, then?'

No answer.

Charlie still sat on the edge of the bed, where Jack had left him. He was leaning forward, and his breath was coming in desperate, urgent gasps.

'You all right, then?' said Jack again. He knew it

was a stupid question, but he couldn't seem to stop himself. 'You can just say no, if you like,' he added.

Charlie said nothing.

Why doesn't he answer? Jack thought. He could shake his head or something, couldn't he? That's not much trouble for him to do, is it?

. . . He looks different than before, though. He sounds different, too. . . . I'm frightened – he's not going to die, is he? 'Come on, Charlie,' Jack encouraged him. 'Don't die! Don't you go and die, now!'

Charlie was definitely worse. He was really fighting for breath now. I can't stand this, Jack thought. I can't stand seeing a person this way, it's too dreadful!

The blanket had slipped into a heap, on what was left of the bed. Distraught, Jack picked up the blanket, and wrapped it round Charlie's shoulders to keep him warm. And Charlie made no sign that he had felt the blanket, or was aware of Jack standing in front of him, or aware of anything at all except his own all-important need to keep breathing.

Why don't they come? Why don't the people come, to see my fire?

My fire!

My fire, I have to get the branches for my fire!

I have to keep my fire going, because the people could still come, they *could!*

. . . Hang about, though, I know something better than the branches. Ha, ha! I know something will burn for certain sure! And lucky I thought of it, because it's a *hundred* times better idea than the branches!

Jack turned from the bed, and dived into the

little cupboard where the tools were kept. He found the hammer, and with the claw end began hitting the cupboard door, savagely, trying with all his power to smash it up for firewood.

There was the noise of blows and splintering wood. The van was split through and through with shattering sound – and still Charlie made no sign that he had heard any of it . . .

In fact, he was *not* hearing any of it. He had gone into a place, deep inside himself, where sights and sounds from the outside world could not reach. In that place was only struggle. The struggle filled his heart and his mind; there was no room for anything else, even fear.

Inside Charlie's chest there was a sort of strangling, and the struggle was against the strangling. The struggle was to force the air, somehow, *through* the strangling. In, out; in, out; in, out. It was getting harder. In, out; in, out; *in*. . . . It was getting harder, he was tired. His strength was getting all used up. In, out; in, out; in out. . . . He was *so* tired. . . . In, out . . . in, out . . . he couldn't keep it up much longer, he couldn't. . . . In, out . . . in . . . out. . . . Not much longer. He was just too tired. . . .

Charlie felt himself very near to something very safe and happy. He wasn't afraid at all. It would be easy to stop trying; in a way he wanted to.

The thing was, though, his mum would miss him.

What would his mum do without him? She wouldn't have anybody to live for, would she, and she would be sad and sorrowful all her life!

Charlie struggled hard again, willing the extra strength to come from somewhere. In, out; in, out;

in, out! He could do it, he *could*. He would do it, he *would*.

Not for himself, for his mum.

And a few centimetres away, the tears rolled down Jack's cheeks, as he smashed up the thing he loved for Charlie, whom he didn't even like.

He had just started lugging the wreckage up the hill when the police arrived. He was so upset that he went on doing it, even when PC Strickland passed him, carrying Charlie bundled in his blanket – up towards the police car which would speed to meet the ambulance, already speeding on its way.

It was PC Webber who put a strong arm round Jack's shoulder, then gently prised the burden from Jack's arms, and said in his warm West Country voice, 'It's all right, son! You've done your bit, it's our turn now!'

15

Some pieces of school work

The most exciting adventure of my life
by Leah

The most exciting adventure of my life was when I went to Alton Towers. With my mum and dad and my two little brothers. We went to Alton Towers. For a selesbrashon. Because I got home safe from when I was kidnapped. All the police in the country were looking for us. But they never found us. and my mum thout she woud never see me again. So we had a selebrashon for it. at Alton Towers.

And my mum says its her fault I got kidnapped. Because I got too much resposibulness. At home. and I was amazed when my mum said that. and I dident really agree with her. But anyway my mum has got a difrent job now so she can come home early. so I wont have so much responsibulness. In the fewcher.

I have got a kind mum. and I have got a kind dad. and I dident know my mum and dad were so kind. And I wish everybody had a kind mum and dad like me.

It was exiting at Alton Towers. We went on all the rides. We went on the big dipper. And the big weel. And the water splash. and the gost train. And. . . .

(Clearly, this was a day that Leah would never forget.)

A brave act
by Charlie

One day I saved my best frends life.

my best frend is called jack he is in the secondary scool now.

One day I saved jacks life I saved jacks life from a wild hors the hors had big teeth and the hors attact jack with its big teeth and it kict him as well but i jumpt out of the bushes and i shouted and made the hors go away and jack said you are my only frend Charlie and i said what about Lea and jack said lea is alrite but you are the best. the end.

PS it dident relly hapen

The most exciting adventure of my life
by Jack

The most exiting adventure of my life was when I got kidnapped by a gang. It was a rubbish gang acshully. they went to a nother country I think and I hope they got shiprecked and have to live on a dessert island for the rest of there life. The police asked me a lot of questions about the gang for there investigations but bad luck they never found them yet.

Anyway the gang took me in a van called Jacks Shack and they tied me up and that is why I hope they get shiprecked because it is crewel to tie people up.

I never tied anybody up only a littel bit.

Anyway I escaped from being tied up only they cauhgt me again and they left me in the van in the midel of a wildernes. I forgot to say that Leah and Charlie was kidnapped as well. Leah was quite

useful but Charlie got on my nervs he was always winjing.
The wildernes was fantastik wen I got use to it.
The wildernes was great I had a horse called Treacle and I road on his back nearly and I had a garden and I went swimming and I was extremely happy.
When Charlie got ill the others dident know what to do but trust me I knew what to do I sent Leah to look for help and I made a fire to make pepul come. Afterwards everybody said that was very clever. and lucky I had that good idea because otherwise Charlie would have died.
I was on the telly as well but I never saw myself on the telly because my mum forgot to make a video of it.
Anyway it dosent matter about the video I dont care about the video What I care about is the wildernes and Jacks Shack and Treacle.
Acshully I had to give them up in the end but it dosent matter becaus I kept them in my head. the colors and the happyness and evrything its all inside my head and I think it will be inside my head for ever and ever and ever and ever.
Its lucky I could keep it in my head because Im saving up to go back to the wildernes but I only got 3 pounds 26p up to now. So I expect it will be a long time to wait.
The end.